Davidia and GRANDMA'S MEMORIES

Ken Spargo

Published in Australia by Sid Harta Publishers Pty Ltd,
ABN: 46 119 415 842

23 Stirling Crescent, Glen Waverley, Victoria 3150 Australia
Telephone: +61 3 9560 9920, Facsimile: +61 3 9545 1742
E-mail: author@sidharta.com.au

First published in Australia 2019
This edition published 2019
Copyright © Ken Spargo 2019
Cover design, typesetting: WorkingType (www.workingtype.com.au)

Spargo, Ken
Davidia and Grandma's Memories
ISBN: 978-1-925230-66-6
pp254

ABOUT THE AUTHOR

Ken lives in Melbourne, Australia.

His first venture into writing began on a sewerage farm whilst engaged in an aquaculture project in 2002. On a boring Friday afternoon, Ken's imagination got the better of him and he decided to fill in his time by writing a nonsense short story  called *The Frog Who Hopped on One Leg*. Within a year he had written a series of short stories and a year later began his first novel *Stumped*.

Imagination provides an endless supply of ideas used to create and craft into his crime and fantasy fiction novels, his preferred genres.

Ken loves to travel; with many places he has visited providing inspiration for his novels. He has travelled extensively throughout Europe, Asia and other parts of the world and lived and worked in Austria, Europe, New Zealand and Papua New Guinea. Caravanning locally is of great interest also.

Ken's primary occupation is as an accountant currently running his own business.

Sport has been a major influence in Ken's life. His two crime fiction novels have both been influenced by his involvement with sport (cricket and golf).

Ken's inspiration for writing the Davidia series of novels has been his daughter, Sophie. He has assisted in raising two children.

His novels have been written with a sense of humour, giving

him a refreshing feeling and allowing him to relax from the seriousness of life.

'We all need escapism at times.'

*To all the grandmothers for the wealth of memories provided
and continue to be provided to the younger generation,
and long may they always be remembered.*

CONTENTS

'It's not true, is it? Aren't they just rumours? I find it difficult to believe that about your grandma,' said Davidia, intrigued by what Slirander had said.

'My parents should know. They've known her a long time,' replied Slirander.

'Would she really tell them that? I know it's hard to keep a secret, but that I find hard to believe.'

'I think it's true. My parents wouldn't reveal exactly what the details were but they eluded to lots of hearsay and what they believe to be fact.'

'How will we know if what has been said has any truth to it?'

'We could delve into grandma's memories, which are stored outside in a special place. If we could access them, then perhaps we might learn whether there is any truth to that comment.'

The girls were discussing an unbelievable comment made by Slirander's parents about her grandma and what she had achieved in her early life. Slirander hadn't seen any evidence about the secret life of grandma.

The stored memories may disclose some historical aspects to grandma's life that will transform the girl's "Age" thesis they were preparing for school.

*　　*　　*

'Get down if you don't want your head blown off. This trench is worse than a sewer,' said an authoritarian female wearing a blue scarf.

What memory was this? The girls had been transformed into a dangerous playing field during World War Two. They had been inadvertently put at serious risk with the prospect of never returning from that memory.

Life as a sewer-rat was most unpleasant. Constant danger, personal risk and muddy filth all combined for a terrifying experience.

'You will be safe over there in that cave.'

It was almost a fatal strategy.

What was that secret spoken of but never revealed?

Would the future provide an unexpected answer?

Grandma had the nickname of The Blue Rat, why?

*   *   *

The Shadow was quicker than a ferret in a pugilist free-for-all against the worst assortment of male boxers. Competition against the meanest men alive was ripe for someone to be smashed. A lithe, smaller-than-average sized male, lined up against the hulks for body building and bad attitude development. It was style and agility against brute force. Conversation was interspersed with a few expletives and grunts. The crowd were maniacally male dominated, baying for a bashing of someone.

Davidia wondered where in the hell she was.

Where was grandma?

Who really was the Shadow?

It was another memory shrouded in mystery.

What else did grandma's memories involve?

Long forgotten secrets may finally be revealed.

What were they?

The school curriculum for the Year 10 students listed as part of their program a series of themes from which each student was able to select their thesis for study. It was an extensive and comprehensive list, which allowed all students from that year to develop an area of interest. It had an appeal to all students, so it was thought that the group would handle the requirement with ease. Miss Green was the class teacher responsible to oversee the relevant student's work.

Each student could select one theme exclusively; however, a spat erupted between two students insisting on the one theme, that of "age". Sometimes it was allowed that two students could work together on a project. Davidia and Slirander had selected the "age" theme together as a respectful project for Slirander's grandmother. The other student was the belligerent class bully who often off-sided both girls because she thought that she could and wanted to retain "premier rat" status amongst fellow classmates. She always took aim at Davidia, thinking she was an easy target. It was a case of brains versus brawn; however, Davidia was no shrinking violet. The other student had tried many times to upset Davidia, but she had a skin thicker than a tortoise shell.

'I see teacher's favourite has brown-nosed her way into the good books again. I wanted that theme,' she said sarcastically, as she raised an offensive finger at her. This action was played out in the schoolyard.

'You might think you look sixteen, but remember, a mirror will tell you otherwise. I hope you have one wide enough,' replied Davidia.

She wasn't impressed by rudeness, but had no qualms about dishing out offensive dialogue to rebut any comments directed at her. Unfortunately, it was a forced issue if you wanted to appear strong and not wilt under offensive dialogue. There were schoolyard standards to maintain – strength against aggression.

'Those wrinkles that you have are real. There's a whole tribe of them on your face partying all the time.'

'I haven't got time to play childish games. When you grow up, you'll realise the futility of trying to squash others. Friends are more important than bad-mouthing others. I've got the "age" theme, so suck it up.' Davidia walked away.

The other student had no answer. She puffed up like a puffer fish and stuttered to her friends. How dare she be spoken to like that. Give a kick and receive a kick. It was a verbal see-saw. There were no real winners. Age is a relevant thing when individual actions represent it.

*   *   *

'Mum, can I stay with Slirander this weekend? School has given us a thesis on age and we need to work together on the project. Slirander wants to base it on her grandmother and we need to go through some old documents as research.'

'That sounds a nice thing to do. Don't stay up late.'

'It's okay, mum, I'm old enough to make my own decisions. I'll be fine.'

'As long as it's okay with Slirander's parents, it's fine by me.'

'It's all good.'

The weekend came soon enough. Research into a person's past may reveal forgotten truths or unexpected surprises. What would the girls discover?

Davidia arrived at Slirander's home and knocked on the

front door. Rolet, Slirander's mum, opened the door. This was Davidia's first glimpse at an element of age which she hadn't previously considered; however, the thesis began to bring things into focus, age focus.

'Hello, Rolet,' said Davidia.

'Welcome to our home,' said Rolet, with a warm expression. 'Come inside.'

Davidia hesitated for a moment. She studied Rolet's face. It had its fair share of wrinkle and laughter lines which decorated it. Her smile moved them around. Davidia had never really noticed them before. She accepted Rolet as she was. The new thesis may alter that structure of understanding of what age means to every walk of life to everyone who has it. All living creatures have an element of it depending on their stage in their life cycle.

'Is Slirander home?'

'She's waiting for you. I hear you have some interesting research to do for school.'

'It's nothing really. Just a thesis on age. That's all.'

'Don't take anything for granted. It isn't a warning, but her grandmother is quite a unique individual. There are things about her that even I don't understand and she is my mother. There was always a feeling of mystery about her when I was young. Well, enjoy finding out your facts. If you discover anything new, kindly let me know.'

Davidia was suddenly puzzled as to why Rolet would warn her, if she was. A simple rummage through some old books and photographs shouldn't carry any difficulties. How hard could that be? At home, all the old photographic albums contained photographs and history of her family. They were just an ordinary record of an ordinary family. She wondered whether she had been fed a thought virus which could now permeate anything she looked at in relation to Slirander's grandmother.

It was an unwelcome mental visitor whom she hoped wouldn't distort her research in an objective manner.

'Hi, Davidia,' called out Slirander.

'Hi, Slirander,' replied Davidia, as she alighted the stairway.

The two friends greeted each other warmly. Their eyes met and Davidia's set suddenly scanned Slirander's face. She noticed that her facial skin was far less wrinkled than her mum's. It was also far smoother. She turned around and fronted the usual beautiful mirror and studied her own face. It had remnants of laughter lines and the potential growth for wrinkles. A few light creases had already formed. So that's what age does to you, even at an early stage in life, she thought. Was this age thesis going to cause age stress for someone so young?

'Slirander, are you ageing?' Davidia asked, considerately.

'I suppose so. I'm no longer six or below double-digit figures, so I suppose I am,' Slirander replied.

'I never thought that I was ageing. I thought that I was growing up instead. I never thought of that as ageing.'

'From the day we are born we age. It's also called growing up. There is a transition to the day we cease ageing and that's when we pass away.'

'That's rather morbid.'

'Life is a circle. We just happen to be on different parts of it as we live. We are on the early section.'

'So, as good-looking as I am, I'm ageing?'

'Such is the circle of life.'

'I need something to cheer me up. Let's rummage through your grandmother's things. Where are they kept?'

Davidia was keen to refocus and learn about Slirander's grandmother. She expected some fun in looking through old documents, photographs and decaying papers. What gold moment would she discover?

'Dad has a special place for historical documents of the family. They aren't kept indoors,' said Slirander.

'Don't you have an attic? Most places do and that's where old stuff is stored,' said Davidia, disappointed that they couldn't rummage in an old cobweb-filled attic, alive with musty smells and a dust coating over ancient furniture.

A new experience was about to unfold by fiddling through somebody else's things, old or otherwise. Whatever expectation was imagined, reality was usually stranger than fiction. A thought can often be a mirage on the mind that never materialises.

'There's an outside storage place. It's been years since anyone, even my parents, have visited it. I'm not sure that anyone has. No one has had any reason to go there until now. The trigger of a thesis and especially on age has churned up my interest. My grandmother had more age than any of us. Isn't it exciting delving into the past?'

Slirander was quite pleased to be visiting the records of her grandmother. It would rekindle fond memories of her. When she was a small girl, the two of them would sit in the darkened bedroom and grandmother would regale her with imaginative stories of gloom and dastardly deeds by mysterious forces of the cosmos and from the middle of the earth. Lots of laughter and moans and groans could be heard behind closed doors. She always ended with a hug and kiss and calming words of kindness. This visit might be a special journey and who better than to share it with except her very special good friend, Davidia.

'Where is this outside storage space? Your backyard doesn't have any out-buildings to store anything. I can't see them. They do exist, don't they?'

Davidia searched the backyard. It was a building blank; however, from a side hill there was a protruding waste pipe, or it looked like that, with a very small diameter that a rat would have difficulty traversing. The girls walked toward it. The backyard suddenly had the chill of snow. The ground became soggy and it was a bright, sunny day. The trees began to behave like an adoring audience of a popstar, waving their canopies to and fro. Davidia felt a strangeness that didn't exist at her home. Was this normal backyard behaviour at Slirander's house?

'It's not too far now,' said Slirander, noticing the expression of concern arise on Davidia's face. Did it age her?

'I've been walking for five minutes, yet I've covered only five metres. Is there an underneath backward grass escalator that I can't feel that is impeding my progress? My intuition tells me that this is no normal backyard. This is exhausting.'

Slirander didn't answer. She kept plodding forward. After another five minutes of hard slog they had made it to the protruding water pipe. They stood there for a moment or two recovering their breath.

'This is it,' said Slirander.

'This is what?' questioned Davidia.

All she could see was a small water pipe; however, she noticed that no waste water drips escaped from it. It was a dry pipe. Most pipes had seepage of water, slime and gunk hanging on its end directing water to the ground, pooling in a splodgy pond. There was none of that present.

'This is the storage space where the historical information on the family is kept. It's been a long time since anyone was last here.'

'Pull the other one. I'm not blind or stupid. That is one skinny waste pipe stuck in the ground, albeit on a hillside. Stop joshing me. Where is this storage space? There's nothing here.' Davidia was becoming frustrated. She couldn't see any storage space.

'This will take a minute while I remember what to do.'

'What? Say a chant, do a rain dance or cast a spell. Take your pick. Have you noticed that we have actually walked through a paddock, yet we are still near your home? My maths isn't that bad that I can't judge distance and time and my calculations don't equate to where we are. What has happened?'

'This is an exceptionally unusual landscape and sometimes I don't understand it myself. All I know is that we are here now.'

Slirander was short on explanation. There was no need to expand simple into difficult or disbelieving.

'Did your grandmother live out here somewhere, maybe in that pipe?' asked Davidia, lashing out with obtuse language. Little did she realise that comment had an element of truth in it.

'Be patient. I have to concentrate and remember the secret coded access sequence.'

'What? Touch a blade of grass, kick a clod of dirt, eat a tree leaf or pee on the pipe. Take your pick. I'm fresh out of suggestions.'

Davidia slumped to the ground thumping her delicate rump on the soggy grass matting. She felt exasperated.

Here were two above-average intelligent schoolgirls standing in what was a backyard paddock confronting a protruding water pipe and conversing with it. The definition of insanity wasn't evident, but was verging on a visit.

'That's it,' said Slirander. 'It was the bum sit that did it.'

'You mean wiping one's arse on the grass is a clue to you remembering a secret access code. Do you need another clue? I could kick myself instead.'

That was also a supposedly funny remark, but it also had a ring of truth in it. Davidia unknowingly was good at guessing without being aware that her comments had some relevance. Suddenly, Slirander began to perform a highland reel with high leg kicking, leg flicking, jumping, twirling and ending up in a heap on the grass after the final bow. It was purely a show demonstration which had nothing to do with any code; however, it was performed to ensure that anyone present believed it to be and it had to be replicated perfectly if the code was to work. Davidia was stunned at the athleticism of her friend. There wasn't any way she was prepared to repeat that performance. Slirander smiled with appreciation at having remembered that dance.

'Was that it?' asked Davidia. 'I assume that we are closer to your grandmother's past.'

'Not long now.'

Slirander walked to the water pipe and knelt before it, acknowledging an inanimate object as one pays reverence to a sacrifice on an altar. She nodded her head and said, 'Granny, Nanny, it's Slirry- poo to meet you.' She waited a moment and put her hand into the water pipe.

'Don't be stupid. I wouldn't do it,' yelled Davidia. 'You have no idea of what might infest that pipe.'

Slirander ignored her. Was there a rabbit or snake in there? Normally it's dangerous to place hands down holes in the countryside. All sorts of nasties could reside in there. Davidia watched cautiously in case her friend had a hand amputation. Suddenly, Slirander had retrieved her whole hand. It was pure relief for Davidia. Slirander took hold of the water pipe with both hands and gave it a twist. It turned. A rush of wind emanated from it, gently brushing Slirander's hair. She moved her head as if her mother was brushing it in preparation for school. A familiarity encircled her. She nodded.

The water pipe enlarged to their height. There was no light. The darkness was uninviting. Davidia shuddered with uncertainty, or was it fear?

'It is safe to enter,' said Slirander. 'Follow me.'

She entered without hesitation. Davidia didn't want to be stranded, so she quickly followed. It was astonishing walking in the dark unafraid, which wasn't an expected feeling. The water pipe closed behind them as they moved forward. Davidia turned around and all she could see was a diminishing light source until there was none.

'Where are we?'

'In grandmother's special place.'

'It's a room.'

'It is. It's well below the surface for protection from the outside world. Grandmother spent a lot of time down here with her various projects that the family aren't fully aware of. I don't know much of her history either. She was an unusual character. We need to tread carefully with what we might discover.'

*   *   *

'Miss Green,' said Davidia, 'can this thesis on age be about anyone we know or is it about age in general?'

'It is a study that affects everyone alive and whoever you select to base an individual study on, it will have an attachment to them. The importance is appreciating and respecting it from the date of birth to the date of death and how fortunate we all are to be able to enjoy it. This is a general comment only. Many opinions may differ, depending at what stage of age the living subject is and who comments on it. Do your best.'

'Are you old?' Davidia asked.

'In relation to you, I might be; however, in relation to my parents, I'm young. Age can mean different things to different people at various stages in their lives.'

'Does that mean that Principal Jones is ancient in relation to you?'

'He is older, but I'm closer to your age than him. I'm in my late twenties. He's in his late forties. You are only a decade my junior; but you notice how you have interpreted age to have a somewhat different meaning based on the number of years we represent? You could be old to a ten-year-old, but you would consider yourself young. It isn't an easy topic to master, but consider it a challenge when preparing your work. There is no correct answer. It has an extreme range of variables. I'm looking forward to the results of your opinions and please treat your thesis with respect.'

'Slirander and I are working on this together. We are studying her grandmother as a special person and hopefully learn from her time and what it meant to her. It's quite exciting to study someone else's history.'

'Enjoy the experience. It may teach you both an understanding about the meaning of age. Class dismissed.'

The Year 10 students trudged off campus full of studious thoughts about their varying topics. No one knew what result would emanate from whatever research was carried out.

Were Slirander and Davidia in for a surprise?

2 GRANDMA'S SPECIAL SPACE

The room known as grandmother's space was once again filled with life. Davidia and Slirander made it live. There were no magic mists or mysterious noises to send shackles of fear up their spine as they absorbed the emotion of the moment.

'No one has been here since she passed,' said Slirander. 'All her belongings are as she would have left them. Even mum and dad haven't been in here. I don't know what to expect, except tread carefully. I'm not sure what will happen by sifting through her life's items.'

'Is that supposed to make me feel better? It's like mental scaring without the protagonist. I'm sure that whatever happens, it will be fine. Your grandmother only loved her family, didn't she? There weren't any mysteries, were there?'

Slirander shrugged her shoulders.

The girls were standing in a room which was completely enclosed with no outdoor lighting. One wall consisted of solid rock squares which seemed impenetrable. Another wall was made of baked mud undulated with hand impressions as the decoration. The third wall was solid slate which shone reflectively. When touched, it sent a freeze chill along the hands and arms, almost freezing them rigid. The fourth wall was made of hessian, which fluttered without a breeze. The closer the girls walked toward it, they never got any closer. The room didn't increase in size either.

How could they see in the dark? There was no natural light or manufactured light to assist. The girls thought that it was impossible to see without night-vision goggles. Had they developed night eyes of the animals of the jungle who hunt during the night?

'How come we can see in the dark?' asked Davidia. 'There's no light, yet I feel I can see.'

'It's a special mental skill that you absorbed as you walked along the pipe. Your imagination has sight, but you think it's the eyes that give you vision. It's an illusion.'

'You're telling me that I can see with my mind and not my eyes.'

'Only in here. It doesn't exist elsewhere. Embrace it. It's a rare event and privilege to be given this gift, for however long.'

Davidia took a moment to accept the explanation. It challenged her accepted knowledge about sight. She scanned the room. There was not one lousy piece of old furniture, chest or trunk that would creak by opening and conjure up the thought of rising dead bodies. She was deflated.

'There's nothing in here. It's an empty space. Didn't your grandmother keep anything at all? My attic at home is full of old stuff. Perhaps we should go there instead?'

'Give it a chance. I just have to locate the handles to each of these walls. They are camouflaged so well it's terribly difficult to find them. Start looking.'

Now that made sense. Secret door handles. She could accept that. Davidia faced the hand impression wall and ran her hand over the undulations. Each handprint was far larger than hers. No protruding fingers stuck out to break or twist as a handle. She had almost covered the complete surface without one bloody hint. She felt tired and leant against the wall when her right hand slotted into a handprint as a perfect fit. Suddenly, the wall began clapping in silence. Each handprint was as busy as a pianist's dancing pair over the keyboards playing a lively polka.

'This wall is clapping madly. This is insane. What is happening?'

Davidia was uncertain of what to do next. She had never encountered a living wall before or one that gave her, so she thought, accolades. She took a bow, but no one was throwing flowers.

'Fantastic. You found the handle. It wasn't that difficult after all. Hard to find, isn't it? Grandmother made a puzzle of the locations in case anyone was here uninvited. It doesn't work for everyone. I'm not sure how an intruder would be treated? Expelled probably. It worked for you because she feels you as a close friend.'

'Do you know where the other handles are to the other three walls?'

'Not really. They also have to be found like this one.'

'When do I stop waving?'

'Remove your hand.'

'I can't pull it out. It's stuck.'

Slirander gave assistance. They both tried to remove it. It didn't move. A teardrop was about to emerge when Davidia, in her haste in the "unseeable dark" to remove her hand, tripped over her own feet whilst seeking another position from which to exert extraction pressure. She had disappeared. All that remained was a sole hand still firmly adhered to the handprint, except now it was the back of her hand. The wall had given way for her to pass through.

'Slirander, where are you? I've fallen through the wall, but my hand is still attached. I want it back.' The friends were separated.

'Hold on.'

Slirander went to remove Davidia's hand when she too fell through the waving hands wall and joined Davidia on the other side, "hands free".

'What is this place?'

'It's obviously one of grandmother's special places. I've never been here before.'

Davidia scanned the room like a submarine periscope, hoping to discover an item to sink or at least see. The result was an all-clear, flat horizon.

'This is just another room with not a jot of old furniture, or library shelves of books, or any strewn documents over the floor to retrieve and sift through as a forensic detective seeking clues – to what: a murder, clues for a ransom or dirt upon which to nail someone? How are we to do any research without any old evidence to trawl through? I don't mind getting my hands dirty, but there is no dirt either. This is one unusual room. It feels like we are clay-shooting targets without an explanation as to how we get shot.'

'It does make me wonder also. Search the room. Surely there's an exit button somewhere.'

Slirander was as lost as Davidia for any explanation.

Once again, they sought something; however, the ceiling in this room was just above head height and dangling downwards was a few straggly tree-roots of the non-edible variety. They annoyed Davidia as she brushed past them. Her skin was irritated by their constant tickling. Fed up with their persistent touching, she yanked a few of them as hard as possible. At first, a few dirt particles fell down, then gradually the ceiling fell into the room leaving an exposed square hole. The girls were shocked at almost being buried alive; however, the dirt only covered the floor. They raised their heads like ferrets from a burrow and discovered another landscape quite unknown to them. The hole from which they emerged disappeared as soon as they were clear of it. A grass covering had grown over the top and would act as an animal trap if anything walked across it. This was the only escape route available. It was essential that they could relocate it later, otherwise it would be perpetuity in whatever land.

'Where in the hell are we?' said Davidia out loud. 'There

are no documents here. I'm not sure that I'm enjoying your grandmother's "old" documents. What is this? A weird landscape of oddities, baubles and walking bushes. That's what they look like to me.'

'It's certainly an eye-opener. Grandmother always had a purpose. Sometimes it wasn't easily understood. I think that she wanted us to find this place.'

'That's obvious. We're here. Where's our hole gone? It's disappeared too. Maybe we will meet the same fate? We could be stranded in nowhere land.'

The landscape that they saw spread out before them was as foreign as growing hair on the soles of their feet. They were some distance away from what they perceived to be a mixture of a mobile stubbly-growth forest and stationary woodpiles made from tree branches.

This was the land of the Pollitons. The land of the "aged".

Their homes were a work in progress, constantly evolving with changes to the inhabitant's age. They lived mostly in old, wooden dwellings with the rear wall made of solid rock. That element of the construction never altered. The timber used was from the aged forest and cut by hand. The Pollitons had the ability to hand-make everything with hand waves, hand jerks, hand slicing and imitating a chain saw. It was a magical quality inherited when a certain age was reached, which was acquired in the third decade of their existence. They ran their hands over the trunks of trees and cut them into beams for roof supports. The walls were a mixture of leaves stretched by hand and used as wall tiles. The roof was formed by long strips of bark and sealed with saliva as roof mortar. The final structure looked like it was decaying from its initial construction. It had built-in rot and obsolescence.

In the front of each home lay a pile of different coloured rounded balls imitating a collection of rainbow sheep pellets.

They were used as decorations and an al fresco food source. Different colours and sizes meant different meal times and, of course, product. It was a marble-alley scape.

'Those moving objects appear to be individual bushes going from one place to another, then camouflaging into those stationary structures. I've never seen the flora of a forest walk anywhere before. I wonder what they are,' said Davidia.

Trees, bushes, shrubs or any plant life rooted to the soil stayed in the one site and grew from there. Davidia had never known a shrub that walked. Had one of her mental thoughts been infected with uncommon sense? She wasn't sure if her eyesight needed an optometrist visit. Her senses were on high alert.

'It is weird,' said Slirander. 'As a child I once dressed up for the kindergarten pageant as a tree shrub in the story of *The Ogre was a Child*. I played a tree as it went by devouring all the swamp animals. I was about four years old and froze when it breathed on me. I thought that I was going to be eaten. That fearful thought has stayed with me all these years. Watch out for any Ogres. There could be some lurking here.'

Slirander sounded unsure if there were; and if there were, she didn't want to meet them. Childish fears are sometimes impossible to dispense with. Time is a good healing factor, but it doesn't necessarily wipe out clean the long-ago memories.

'Nonsense, there's no such thing as Ogres. It's only in stories. Besides, there's no swamp here.'

Davidia had no idea if that was true, but sounding confident was meant to stiffen Slirander's backbone about her fears. Davidia had her own set, but they hadn't been mentioned yet.

'Should we approach them?' asked Davidia.

Presently, their existence was unknown. Should it stay that way? If so, there is no purpose being where they are. Slirander took the bit between her teeth and suggested that she alone should approach the inhabitants first. That way, if anything bad befell her, Davidia could escape by jumping in the grass-covered hole that they had emerged from and escape safely. That went down like a lead balloon. Davidia had no intention of abandoning her friend. If disaster struck, it hurt less if shared.

'You go and meet them,' said Davidia. 'I'll watch from a close surveillance position. If you need any help wave like those wall hands.'

Slirander took a worry breath and strode forward. She was a young, formidable girl when her confidence was up. At present it wasn't well-fed. She made her way toward the village of foliage. It only took three steps. How odd is that? Suddenly, she stopped. The homes were only one metre tall. Stranger still, the inhabitants were slightly smaller. There was no rush to greet her. In fact, nothing greeted her. She stood like a maypole in the middle of the fairground with no one to play with. This was ridiculous. She thought that in all her adventures and at school, she had never been this badly ignored. Her face turned red in anger. Her confidence was now being well-fed. Even that new guy at school who tried to ignore her failed because once he could see the capabilities of her mind, he succumbed by paying her some real attention. Her anatomy was only back-up if required. Males certainly knew how to connect with a female in the modern world? No woman likes to be ignored and Slirander was no exception. If the attention is unwanted, then that is a different scenario.

'Is anyone home?' she yelled at the top of her voice, expecting a flurry of responses or at least sets of peering eyes from each hut, if that's what they called them.

A lone shrub emerged nearby shaking its leaves. It dawdled toward her leaving a trail of detritus behind. Was it a mobile compost heap? It certainly didn't engender any hugging feelings. It had a slow crawl walking action on short legs which lacked strength. The arms and legs moved in perpetual slow motion. The hands were gnarled tree knot bulges with skinny twig protrusions for fingers. Only the eyes had a youthful look. The two mouths it had were a complete surprise. One was used for food, the other for drink and it could perform both actions simultaneously. Its whole body was enshrouded in a body cape of age, draped recklessly over it as a burden borne by all. The height of these inhabitants was usually one metre, which was actually fifty per-cent of their height growth capacity. There was a reason they never grew taller and it wasn't the water. It took quite a few minutes for the parties to meet and stare at each other. Slirander had to lower her gaze due to their height difference.

'Can you speak?' asked Slirander.

It took a few moments for a response.

'Yes,' it said slowly.

Age, in a Polliton's early years, inhibited fast speaking so each response was a measured effort of word usage. Patience was required at all times for any discussion. It often took fifteen minutes to eke out a few sentences. Slirander didn't have the patience of a Saint.

'Where exactly am I?' she asked.

A further delay was imminent when the response was being researched. She paid strict attention to which mouth it spoke with in case she ignored the wrong one. She noted it spoke simultaneously like twins conversing together as if they knew what each other was about to say.

'In a memory.'

'Who's memory? Have I been invited? What am I doing here?'

Slirander wondered what the hell she and Davidia had landed in. Memories can be forgotten with older age and the mind forgets what's filed in it. When that occurs, the memory ceases to exist. Did that mean she and Davidia would cease to exist also?

'An old lady called Grandma. I think that's what she's called. I remember that much.'

'What exactly are you?'

'I'm a Polliton. I live in the past, but try to grow into the future. You are so tall. We all want to be tall but cannot exceed the allotted life metre because of what we are.'

'Why can't you grow any taller? You look like a bush. Do you lack water? What do you do?'

'We are memory holders, so when we reach a certain age, we can absorb memories of others. Our families live in the minds of things like your grandma's and probably you. We are growth inhibited because the memories need to be shared amongst us all and there are so many that we cannot absorb what we need to grow taller. We stagnate at half our potential. If we had the capacity to absorb far more memories, then we would become tall. So many memories are recalled. We have an "in" and "out" tray for them. If memories weren't used at all, we'd be giants. If we were taller, then we'd have longer memories and if recalled as a tall memory means that whoever's memory it is, has lived to an older age just like us.'

That seemed to be a plausible explanation.

'So, what am I?'

'One of grandma's memories.'

'If that's correct, then what am I doing in here? My grandma has passed.'

'Her memory might have gone, but yours is alive and well. She's in your mind and because of that you have met us.'

'This is confusing. You're telling me that I'm in a memory of my grandma's, even though she no longer exists. That's not possible.'

Slirander turned towards Davidia and waved her to come down. She sprinted like the athlete she would become and was breathless with the short sprint.

'Who's the bush?' said Davidia, thinking what a great fire it would make on a beach weekend cooking fresh fish and staring into the deep azure eyes of her latest date, with her body smothered in olive oil for the perfect tan. This was one of her memories.

'This is … ,' started Slirander. 'What is your name, or do you have a label or botanic term?'

'My identification is Pole due to the smooth, cylindrical shape of my Grey Ghost Gum legs. Are you identified as anything? That other thing that has arrived is not of your family memory. She's an imposter.'

'We are called girls and our names are Slirander and Davidia and I invited her here. She's now part of my memories so you will have to lump it.'

'Does this place have a name?' asked Davidia. 'What map is it on?'

'This place is called Pollital, the home of the Pollitons and the keepers of memories. We live in the memories of others.'

Davidia thought carefully for a moment.

'What about my memories? Do you know any?'

'We are in Slirander's grandma's memories only. Yours are held elsewhere by other relatives of ours. You have only accessed grandma's set. Any memory you discover here is only from grandma.'

'We are doing a school thesis on age and what better place than to start with a few of grandma's memories. There must be loads here. Show us a couple.'

'It isn't that simple. Each recall of a memory must be earned and there is no prospect of knowing which one of us has any particular memory of any particular period. Something has to provoke a recall, but be careful of what you receive. You may not like it. Not every memory is a sugar-coated, lovely sweet. Some are mysterious, unpleasant, fun, sad and so on. I'm becoming tired. This communication is draining. I must return home.'

Pole turned around and ambled homeward. His tree coverings looked wilted and exhausted after speaking with the girls. Davidia walked after Pole.

'Now we're here, where do we go for a memory?'

Pole sighed and a few leaves fluttered to the ground.

They were on their own.

3 Now What?

Pole disappeared into his well-camouflaged hutsal. The girls were now alone wondering what they had encountered. Being inside someone's memories had them both unsettled.

'What if we discover something unpleasant about grandma that the family don't know about? She may have privately disposed of property that no one knew she had. Could she have been an assassin, undercover operative, call girl, had flings, or maybe she isn't my real grandma?'

Slirander's mind was having a field day of new thoughts and suspicions. Were any of them true?

'Don't worry, Slirander, families often keep secrets from the others to "protect" them. Isn't it exciting to be inside another person's memories? I wonder what we'll find.'

Davidia was upbeat about the adventure ahead. Her vision of a top-quality thesis had her mentally accepting the accolades of her peers. It would be so enthralling.

'Exactly, how do we locate one; a memory? There isn't a handwritten list that I can see. They aren't dangling from any trees and there's no one about to ask. Where would they be? They must be somewhere otherwise we could be in someone else's memories.'

'I haven't seen any either. They wouldn't hang around in gangs, would they? Would they be filed in something? Why not ask Pole and see if we can elicit a memory response from him. He must know many because he said he was a keeper of them.'

The girls approached Pole's hutsal. On the way Davidia picked up one of the coloured balls that littered the ground outside it. There seemed to be a never-ending supply of them lying loosely around in no particular formation. It was a rubbish ball park. The colour selected was red, the brightest and also a personality match for her. It was very light, soft to the touch like satin and rotated very slowly when attempting to play with it. Other than that, it had no identifiable marks, so a random selection had been made. It was also the largest of the colours. The girls had to bend over and kneel on their knees to knock. The door slowly opened. Pole got a shock to see them and aghast that they had handled a red ball, let alone any ball.

'What are you doing with that?' he said, pointing a shimmering arm at the red ball.

'It was lying on the ground so I picked it up,' said Davidia. 'Your front yard needs a good clean-up with all those rubbish balls creating an eyesore?'

'You must carefully place it back where you took it from.'

'And if I don't?'

'The explanation will be evident. I cannot help you. Your friend might understand better. Those coloured balls have an important purpose. They provide our food source.'

Pole had only stated half their purpose. He declined to advise that each coloured ball contained one of grandma's memories and each one was stored when he ate one of them. It was a large pile as grandma had lived to an old age and there were so many memories to consume. It was pot luck which one was eaten and stored. It was an impossibility to know what each memory was; however, the different colours represented the quality of each memory. Red, as a colour, had a fierce reputation as feisty, dangerous and the strongest of memories. It had an uncertain element.

'Do you want to eat this one?' said Davidia, as she proffered it to Pole.

He politely refused.

'I can only consume the selection that I personally make. That memory in your hand may never be known now as it has been handled by a non-recognisable memory consumption authority. It is now damaged goods. Regardless, you must still place it back from exactly where you picked it up.'

There was a polite firmness in his voice. The girls' knees began to hurt. They stood up. In doing so, Davidia accidentally pricked the red ball on an overhanging twig from Pole's hutsal roof. A red mist suddenly swirled around them blanketing any vision.

*   *   *

'Scrub those floors till they shine like a mirror,' yelled someone giving orders. 'Miss any dirty spots and it's no rations tonight. I'll be back later to inspect your work. Stop gawking and get on with it. This is a place of discipline and you girls need to learn lots of it if you are to survive in the real world.'

'Who does that old bat think she is? What a tough bitch. The next time she berates me for doing nothing wrong, I'll crumple her bonnet.'

Davidia hadn't yet twigged that she was one of the floor scrubbers. She was on her knees in a long, grey dress that dragged along the floor wondering what she was supposed to be doing. Around her there were another few girls all sloshing sudsy water with a hand-held, hair-scrubbing brush attacking a perfectly well-made floor as if trying to remove its upper surface. Faces were littered with exhausted looks and a tinge of sadness. She had never performed a menial physical job of this difficulty before. Her hands still retained a fresh quality about them. They were soft, almost wrinkle-free and her palms were soft as eiderdown. Why was she on four knees imitating a well-loved pet?

Her floor-sloshing companion didn't look like Slirander at all. It was another young lady with fine features with a ferocious attitude that would make any mouse squeak in fright. She gazed at her for but a moment.

'What are you staring at?'

'I was hoping that you were my friend, Slirander. She seems to have been misplaced.'

'Well, I'm not. Scrub that patch thoroughly otherwise there's no evening rations for you.'

'Rations! Who eats rations?'

'We all do.'

'What is this place?'

'An institution for the insane. To be here, one has to have an element of it.'

The look of shock on Davidia's face showed her naivety. The other girl smiled. It was meant as light banter. Where in the hell was she and who was she with?

'Is it a boarding school? I've never visited one before.'

'You aren't visiting it. You are living here. This drab clothing is the uniform.'

'Really? I must be dreaming.'

'Stop talking. Get on with the scrubbing. Make yourself useful.'

'My name is Davidia,' she said with confidence, assuming a positive response.

'Nobody cares what your name is. Bitch, stupid, cow, idiot and imbecile, are all used here, so you can be none, one, or all of them. It's your choice on how you behave.'

'What's your name? I suppose you are called something pleasant from time to time.'

'It's Michelle, but keep it to yourself.'

Davidia thought carefully. Now, didn't she read, or had Slirander mentioned the name of her grandma. Could this

Michelle be her? After all, she was in one of grandma's dreams, but where did Slirander disappear to?

'Do you know if a girl called Slirander is boarding here too?'

'There's none to my knowledge. Scrub that floor and don't waste time with the questions. It's "get the job done", or be punished. I've warned you. This place is the pits. We're caged like prisoners. One day I'll leave here without warning.'

Before that avenue of thought could be explored, the head female made a surprise visit. She had a bonnet stretched tightly over her head covering what was assumed a head full of lice; either that, or it was rumoured that she was bald. Her drab, long dress was navy-grey and swirled as she walked, inspecting the cleanliness of the floor. Her face was etched with wrinkles, small furrows and nodules, probably from poor skin maintenance or bad genetics. She was tougher than a steel spike. In one hand she held a whip with a deadly unwritten message and the other hand pointed ahead of her at patches on the floor that hadn't been cleaned to her satisfaction. The fact is that was impossible because she loved meting out pain and suffering. The floor could never be clean enough. Her childhood was blamed for it, but that was only an excuse. A sadist can exist in any form and she was a full-blown representative. Occasionally, she cracked the whip into her hand to scare the girls under her charge shitless and enforce compliance. Michelle was not compliant most of the time. She believed education was more than being brutalised into submission like trained animals. Her day would come.

'You, the Dav girl. You've missed that patch completely. Do it again,' commanded the overseer.

Davidia was also a non-compliant individual and when she believed she was correct she'd say so.

'Excuse me ma'am. I've cleaned that space perfectly. There isn't one speck of dust left. Run your hand over it and see for yourself.'

'You insolent bitch.'

Suddenly, a whip lashed Davidia across her back with such force she fell backwards onto the floor and kicked the dirty suds-filled bucket over the overseer's feet. The shock of being belted didn't appeal to Davidia. She didn't scream in pain like a wimp, but held in the hurt. Her eyes were riveted on the overseer. The visual gesture was most unladylike. She scrambled to her feet as best she could. She was as tall as the overseer and somewhat sprightlier.

'You will never do that to me again,' said Davidia, feeling as if someone was scratching her back with a pair of scissors.

She stood immobile. The other girls thought that she was stupid standing up to the overseer as she did, except Michelle, who thought that here was a girl after her own heart. A few tears of pain began the downward trickle. Michelle rushed over to assist her to stay upright. Work had halted. It was late in the day. The overseer didn't flinch openly at Davidia's defiance, but had her marked for trouble. She felt it was time.

'That's it for the day. Return to your dormitories.'

The overseer glanced at Davidia and also Michelle with hatred for assisting the brazenness of a hussy threatening her. We'll see who threatens whom, she thought. Her authority had never really been opposed before. It wasn't a happy feeling. Someone will pay.

Michelle assisted Davidia to the dormitory, careful not to touch her back, which by now would be stinging painfully. Red welts grew where the whip had struck her pearl-like, delicate skin. Those red blemishes across her back would be a permanent reminder, until they healed, that obstinacy and standing up for one's point of view had a price to pay, in her current environment.

'Sit here,' said Michelle.

The dormitory bed was a wire-sprung construction, close to the floor, which sagged badly in the middle. One slept in a banana shape. Bad posture and back pain were consequences of such "luxury" sleeping accommodation. The mattress was as solid as soft cement, obviously laid with no planning. Lumps abounded where the inner filling had compacted, ensuring a comfortable night's sleep was another fairy story. The solitary grey blanket was the only warmth provider. It felt like sandpaper to the touch. Sleeping with another girl in a bed purely for warmth was banned. There were twenty girls to a dormitory, each with a managing attendant. Lights out at 8 pm, no chatter and the overnight toilet event was a large unstable bucket at the end of each room. One had to have good balance to properly perform this nightly task. Privacy was almost non-existent; however, the girls made do in what they considered was a hostile environment. Everyone wanted to leave, but where to and how?

Davidia was now experiencing the full pain of being whipped. She shed a private tear. She was still only a girl. Her resilience arose within from that one incidence of being mistreated. That would never happen at home.

'Ouch, that hurts,' said Davidia, whimpering.

Michelle peeled back her dress. The welts had arrived. Fortunately, no skin was broken.

'It doesn't look too bad. The skin's intact. It will hurt for a day or two, but will fully heal.'

'Are all the girls treated like that? I don't like it. If I was a boxer, I'd … '

'Whilst here, you must obey the rules whether you agree with them or not, otherwise it's more punishment.'

'Why are we all here?'

'This is the home for abandoned girls. Most have been thrown out of home for being too troublesome. Many have lived on the street and ended up here. Be careful what you say or do and to whom. No need to be knifed for telling a joke.'

'What about you? What caused you to be here?'

'I think you should rest a while. I'll get some cold water for your back.'

Michelle went to the bathroom to fetch a dish of cold water and a cloth to bathe Davidia's back. The overseer had slipped in to observe the new arrival. Her opinion of her wasn't pleasant. She stepped out from behind the door and confronted Michelle. She forcibly thrust her whip under her chin with Michelle now viewing the ceiling.

'That new Dav bitch had better watch her p's and q's whilst here or otherwise I'll ride her like a pony. Don't you misbehave either? You know better than anyone the consequences of disobedience. You do understand, don't you?'

The overseer allowed herself a self-satisfied chuckle. She made Michelle's skin crawl. Michelle knew that she was one A-grade bitch. For the time being she acted humbly to avoid prosecution for her behaviour.

'Yes, ma'am.'

'What are you doing in here?'

'Fetching a cloth and a dish of cold water for Davidia's newly installed wounds.'

'Get out. There is no water for her. She can suffer for her arrogance. She's been warned.'

Michelle had no alternative but to return empty-handed; however, she was determined that Davidia would receive some treatment, meagre as it might be.

'My back hurts,' whined Davidia. She couldn't lie down and had to sit in bed with her back bare to avoid rubbing it against anything. 'Where's the water?'

'The overseer has denied it to you. Wait until dark and I'll sneak down and get it.'

'What if you get caught?'

'I have to be caught first. Try and rest. Darkness has a bad habit of seeping into one's mind. Don't let it rule your thoughts, regardless of how badly you want to use it.'

Michelle waited until it was almost pitch-black. She alighted from her bed and crept carefully toward the bathroom. Not a sound could be heard, it was so deathly quiet. She expertly avoided the unstable bucket, made it to the bathroom and used a torn-off strip from her hemline to soak in soothing water. She returned quickly to Davidia, pressed the cold cloth on her back, momentarily soothing her pain, and then hid the cloth under her bed. The night wore on with its monotonous meaning. Davidia didn't sleep well. Her mind filtered the word "revenge" in an unending array of possibilities.

At 6 am the alarm sounded. It was loud enough to snap a sharp splinter. The girls scrambled like pit-lane staff trying to reach the main food hall first. The best seats gave the better food source. They all sat at a large table with a spoon and bowl each to eat the slop that masqueraded as nutritious food. It definitely wasn't located as nutritious food in any good food guide. Davidia walked slowly. Michelle walked with her. An open space was made available. As Davidia went to sit down, a larger girl with a weatherboard face and train tracks for eyebrows, deliberately bumped her backwards and took her seat. Michelle quickly supported her and directed her to sit elsewhere.

'Who is that bitch?'

'She's a patsy for the overseer. She is her trained piece of shit who bullies others. No one is game enough to stand up to her.'

'Does she have balls? Those ugly pills she takes certainly work a treat.' Davidia's humour was on a re-visit.

'Just remember, we all have a back story and assumptions are often misdirected. I'm not sure of her case, but I've heard that she is from a broken family. Let's eat. I'm not starving, but the crap they serve here is one grade above sewerage, with a slightly improved taste. Many of us have had to eat both. Not all punishment is by whip. If you don't eat this muck, then it's a long wait until dinner.'

Davidia attempted a mouthful. She recoiled violently and some of it landed on the larger girl a few seats away. A huge form arose, side-swiping her food bowl over the floor. Her face glared with such intensity and menace. All Davidia could do was wait for the confrontation. It was on its way even without an invitation.

'What you do dat for? My dress is dirty. You clean.'

Her words were pie-filling to an uneducated audience.

'I'm sorry,' apologised Davidia, 'the taste took me by surprise. I see you spilled yours. Would you like to share mine?'

Her protagonist stopped her advance. She had to think about what was said. Nobody had ever said those share words to her before. She didn't feel any animosity from Davidia, which also surprised her. She was so used to fighting, bullying, bossing and standing over the girls, but this one somehow felt different.

'Thanks.'

A large pair of hands snatched the bowl and returned to her seat. There were no extra bruises to be worn today as a badge of dishonour.

'I think she needs a friend,' said Davidia.

'She stabbed her last victim. Be careful.'

'There is good in all of us. It just has to be located.'

'What do we do during the day? I haven't seen a swimming pool, gymnasium, sauna or outdoor parkland to enjoy. I suppose they are all on the other side of that tall fence. Is it electrified?'

'Calm down. Take it easy. Too many questions make others suspicious. The fence isn't electrified, but no one has been known to survive the fall on the other side. Quiet, the overseer is observing us. Sit quietly. It's better to go unnoticed and blend in.'

The overseer ambled past Davidia and scraped a hand over her smarting back. The red welts reacted like a bucking rodeo horse in pain. Her body tensed, screaming, 'Let me at her'. A tear tried to wash her face, but she was having none of it. She sat as immobile as possible without giving the overseer any sense of victory. A moment passed. The overseer walked on, silently swinging her whip, eyeing who might make its acquaintance next. There was relief all round when she exited the breakfast room.

'Doesn't anyone stand up to her?'

'It's not wise. The law is on her side and, besides, this is the last resort hotel of life for many here. If you misbehave, then prison is a real option. Many girls would not survive that visit, so technically we are "free" prisoners.'

'I'm not staying here. This place is terrible. My friend Slirander would know what to do.'

'She's not here. You have to decide your fate. Whatever you do, be careful.'

Davidia wondered if what she was experiencing was real or a figment of her active imagination. One moment she was standing with Slirander, then next she's employed doing hard labour for an insane institution. Her mind was made up to escape somehow. Someone had to be the first to succeed. That day there were no educational lessons. It was morning labour with a half-day break. Davidia intended to enjoy her restricted liberties. In the afternoon, feeling exhausted – it was the same every day – she sat quietly minding her own business because if you didn't someone else would, when Michelle unexpectedly turned up quite agitated. She sat down. The seat began to undulate. Someone wasn't well.

'What's up with you?' asked Davidia. She hoped Michelle wasn't having a fit of some sort.

'I've just come from the overseer's office. In her wisdom, my stay has been extended another five years, with no explanation given. That's it. No more Mrs Nice Girl. I intend to escape tonight. There is no other choice for me. That bitch! That bloody bitch … ' Michelle's voice trailed off into a softening verbal mist.

'Why tell me? Won't I be implicated?'

'Not at all. You're coming with me.'

'Are you insane? You did say this was an insane institution and you want to live up to its name. It's pure madness, isn't it?'

'I feel I can trust you. Walk with me.'

Everyone knew that Davidia had received a "good advice" whipping, so as she ambled around the grounds, nodding sneers, fake coughs and sniggering giggles were audible. Mostly she was ignored. Normally that would incense her, but not today. At school she was always worth a second look. She was too young to date the teachers, but she knew she was noticed.

'Where are we going?'

'Around the grounds. Take notice of everything. The gates, doors, walls, shrubs, windows and room locations. Have you noticed that our dormitory is not far from the main gate and office? I intend to steal the gate keys and leave like a shadow.'

Davidia wasn't sure of the strategic brilliance of the simple plan. Perhaps its simplicity was the audacity of trying to achieve it. Who would think it would work because it was so obvious? The overseer kept the keys around her waist at all times, even in bed.

'How do we get out of here without raising the alarm?'

'The plan is to wait until the overseer is asleep and dummy up two bodies sleeping in our beds. We steal the keys from her, tie her up to her bed and dress in her clothing and walk out the front gate as twin arseholes. Everyone will think she has a twin sister. The dark will be our friend.'

'Won't we be noticed? There are so many girls here and I'm sure someone will warn the overseer, just to curry favour. I'm uncertain about it all.'

'I'd rather try than rot in this hell hole. Wouldn't you?'

'I do miss my manicures, wearing new clothes on a budget and eating real food. Do they have a McDonalds here?'

'Is that a toy?'

'Never mind.'

That evening the plan was set. Around midnight the girls quietly awoke, undressed and shoved their awfully-designed and drab-coloured dress under the bed blanket in the shape of a sleeping person. In the dark the silhouette tricked the eyes. All present if a visual roll call was made. They crept carefully along the floor avoiding any creaking floorboards. The door attendant had fallen asleep. Being overweight, sedentary and grazing in a good paddock ensured their escape wasn't barred. The snoring sounds were like the sounds of the oboe of an orchestra. Suddenly, her chair creaked. The girls froze. They waited. All resettled.

'So far so good,' said Michelle. 'Now to the overseer's quarters. My heart's thumping with adrenalin and excitement. Isn't this exhilarating?'

Michelle was hyperventilating.

'Let's keep moving.'

Davidia was more in the fear factor area with her emotions. Prison; it was the prison word that kept her alert, her sore back kept reminding her that punishment wasn't far away, if caught.

The overseer was flat as a board lying on her back on her bed. Even her natural undulations were as flat as … The bed had a softer mattress and a colourful, crocheted bed quilt, the envy of all. Her head sunk so deeply into the pillow, the indent turned the two outside sections into giant earmuffs. She seemed to be at peace, but was her mind really relaxed? Nobody knew. Michelle signalled to Davidia by hand to grab the whip, which would be used to tie her to the bed. The trick was to subdue her without her screaming some fear of abduction or abuse, which would thwart their plan. Michelle had to supply the answer, quickly. In her youth she had been a talented sprinter with long jump potential, but had really fancied herself as a martial arts exponent. Suddenly, the overseer knee-jerked awake and was surprised to see two silhouetted figures around her bed. Were they the death demons to take her away for her bad attributes? It was a shock to realise that she was surrounded. Couldn't one at least be a male so she could then admit to others that she once had a man in her room. Normally her relationships were a desert, dry and arid. Michelle, with the reflexes of a fox, straight-armed her jaw. The overseer gurgled an incoherent sound as she fell back onto the bed. Davidia quickly tied her up. She thought about giving her a whipping stroke as retribution, but violence wasn't supposed to be part of her personality. Michelle gagged her and unhitched the keys. Success. All they had to do was walk out the front door. Suddenly, a huge shadow emerged in front of them. It was that bully girl the overseer used as a threatening weapon. Her frame was frightening. One word and it was over. Tension grew like fungi. There was no food to share tonight.

'What dat you do?' she asked.

Davidia wasn't used to lying, so she told her straight that they were escaping. Michelle pulled up short. The girl thought for a moment.

'Can I come with you?'

Davidia and Michelle couldn't believe their ears.

'Yes, you are most welcome.'

All she needed was a friend.

Michelle placed the key in the huge lock, twisted it and the gate creaked as three desperate women urged their bodies to push. The dubious education behind those gates was over forever. The girls stepped forward to freedom.

*   *   *

'What have you been doing?' asked Slirander, agitated like a stressed pony with a poised hoof ready to kick.

'Where have you been should be more like it,' replied Davidia.

Had Slirander abandoned her whilst she was wasted doing menial chores in an educational home?

'One minute you were standing next to me and then you disappeared. A red mist swirled around me and I couldn't see or hear you. Where did you go?'

'Was your grandmother called Michelle? I think I met her.'

'Yes, she was. What do you mean, met her?'

'After that red mist, I ended up scrubbing floors with a Michelle, about our age. She was nice and tough. She pole-axed the overseer where she lived with the best right cross and left that dreadful home. Did you know she was a servant in a home for abandoned women?'

'No. I wonder why I wasn't there with you.'

'It's probably because you didn't exist in those times. She was your grandmother.'

That sounded reasonable with a certain amount of clear thinking. There was no point following that thought now that it had been explained.

'What next?'

4 Memories

'We're still stuck here outside the Pole house,' said Slirander. 'He was none too pleased about destroying that red ball even though it was accidental. I have a strange feeling about being in someone's memories as if we shouldn't be here. We need to be careful about what we do here. I hope we don't change them or become encased in one ourselves from which there is no escape. Do you remember how we got here? My recollection is already failing.'

'You aren't suffering from early Alzheimer's. You're just being stupid. Don't try to scare me. What's the purpose of standing here? Is that miniature tree going to explain this memory system or do we have to find out ourselves?'

Davidia once again dropped to her knees. She wasn't learning a habit to worship another religion. She was trying to make contact with Pole. He must have many memories that he could share with Davidia and Slirander, but would that be directly after he had eaten one memory, or many?

'I wonder if we'll be invited in for dinner,' said Davidia, waiting patiently for the front door to open as she lightly tapped.

There was no answer. She tapped again. Still, there was no response.

'Maybe they are out gathering other memories and ignoring grandma's because we spoilt one.'

Davidia stood tall. There were no life movements anywhere. The village of Pollital was a group of shrubbery-small dwellings covered in tree debris. Each house was surrounded by coloured balls of different sizes exactly like the one that Davidia had destroyed. The homes stood like a candle in a kid's ball pen usually found at fun parks. They had been warned not to touch any of them. The girls wondered what to do next. There didn't seem to be any old trunks to sort through to look for remnants of grandma's life.

'There's no action here,' said Davidia. 'I'm bored.'

'Wait a few minutes and enjoy the silence. I sense a movement nearby,' replied Slirander.

Something was happening. but it was ever so excruciatingly slow. In the modern world everyone made out that they were time-poor. Here, it was reality that there was plenty of time to enjoy if one was prepared to slow down. Nearby, a pile of the coloured balls began to gently move bouncing off each other. They didn't elevate very high, but had a gentleness of movement. They watched for a few moments more. A treed figure was hurriedly, in Polliton time, moving around. Could it be lost? Was it planning tonight's ball menu or playing a childish game of ball nose-pushing? It soon became clear. The girls approached the athletes? They daren't get too close in case they damaged any memories. Suddenly, a clutch of balls adhered to both of them like cling-wrap. A sea of balloons surrounded each of them. They froze. There were no fearful feelings. They both looked like clowns ready to make balloon figures at a carnival.

'What's happened? We didn't do anything,' Davidia called out.

'Stand still. There's an obvious explanation. We have to be told what it is. Where's Pole?'

Slirander felt intimidated by grandma's memories hanging onto her and she didn't know what was in any of them.

'Don't you two look amazing? I've never seen that before. What to do? What to do? I've never seen that before. What to do? What to do?' said Pole as he ambled out from amongst the coloured balls. Both his mouths smiled. Was it a good memory that had just registered in his recall section?

'Now what?' said Davidia, sensing that this wasn't kosher.

The memory balls had misbehaved. They soon became known as the Hanging Balls of Pollital. The girls were immobilised with the strangest of feelings. Their bodies stiffened quite unexpectedly. Pole ambled off to his hutsal and from behind it dragged out a wooden seat. Soon, a sea of wooden seats had been arranged around the girls in a circle. The villagers had arrived. The girls represented a stand-up meal for the Pollitons. It was a first in their history. No more will they have to scurry around at ground level chasing the round items to consume a ball. Often it was difficult to capture one. At the slightest touch they would move. Now, they had two human trees to detach a captured ball from. It didn't matter at all what their appearance was like. They could now select self-serve style from a fresh memory object-holder. The balls had covered the girls completely. It was almost impossible to identify them with their new artistic dress. They weren't happy when they learnt that they couldn't leave that spot until every ball had been consumed. It was a disaster. That meant there was no way that they could complete grandma's thesis or worse still never return to complete it.

'We're seriously stuck now. I have no intention to being a fast food server or a fresh memory kitchen. We need to escape. Life's too short to stand around as a Pole. Any bright ideas? I'm glad our peers at school can't see us. What a mess.'

'It is unusual to be holding and being surrounded by memories of grandma. I feel quite comfortable knowing that she is all around me. As a small child I don't think I've felt this close to her as I do now.'

Slirander was feeding her emotional self, but not by eating a ball.

'It may be dangerous for us to stay here. What happens if we fall over or drop a memory? If that occurs, could we accidentally change your grandma's memory and how would that affect you, as a descendant? I don't want the responsibility.'

'Pole should be able to explain its meaning.'

'Excuse me, Pole, what is the meaning of this, us standing covered in coloured balls?'

'Unfortunately, the great memory mind of Pollital has selected you to ease our burden of ground- scrounging for the balls. Your height was noticed and it was felt that you could ease our food-gathering techniques by elevating the balls to stationary status and hence easier to collect. Collecting and retaining memories is an arduous task very few enjoy; however, being stationary and at height, meant the problem was solved. Note that we are slow eaters. You should be with us a while.'

'We can't stay here. We don't live here. We need to return to school and complete our "age" thesis. Our friends will be frantic if we don't return. What good are we for your memory consumption?'

'Life has its ups and downs. Yours is a down at present. There is nothing to be done until all balls have been consumed and did I not tell you that once a ball is removed, it's immediately replaced? We can eat forever. Height certainly has an advantage for us even though we personally don't possess it. I'll take that small blue one for a snack.'

Pole gently tugged at the blue ball. It popped as it escaped. Suddenly, another ball replaced that spot. It seemed as if a magical force was sending the balls at the girls. They adhered easily to them. Did their perfume attract them? Was it their body heat or the fact that there had never been a taller structure in Pollital before? It was a mystery.

Davidia was incensed. She wasn't a food statue for anyone. Instead of spitting her anger genes around, a more sensible approach had to be thought of. There wasn't one good idea she had at the moment, so she decided to bide her time, observe her captors gorging themselves on memories hoping some of them would make them sick, and work out an escape strategy. Slirander was enshrouded with her good feeling vibes. Davidia felt that she wouldn't be too helpful in the short term. They were now pillars of the community against their wills and didn't need a council election to achieve it.

*   *   *

'Have you met any other memories before?' said a green ball to a yellow ball.

'We aren't supposed to meet each other. Each of us has a separate and unique identity that we are always individually recalled. How is it that we can communicate from within our rounded structures? You are my first discussional memory. I wonder if it's catching. We might not want to know what another is carrying,' replied a yellow ball.

'I notice that we are at height and that warmth emanates from the structure that we are attached to. Maybe it's allowing us to react in this manner. This is my first opportunity ever to contact another memory. It normally isn't possible.'

'Stop the crap. I've got a rotten memory. The nice one got stolen. I've had to live with the nasty ramifications of what a divorce can lead to. There's a whole family of us clustered together in miniature form. It's a continual breeding ground for unpleasantness. Try to engage with any of ours, and it's the last thing you want to be; someone's memory. Have a listen and see who survives it the best.'

The green and yellow ball listened for a short while. That memory set was nasty, vicious, rude and offensive – to actually think of that many ways to screw a person. At least they harboured two pleasant ones.

'Are these all grandma's memories?' said Davidia. 'There seems to be an awful lot of them if they are.'

Pole was listening.

'No. You have been attracted by a mixture of memories, so there is no way of you telling whose are whose. I only eat your grandma's memories so you can follow them. That is the only way you will know.'

'That last affair was a ripper. You know that both parties were caught in a swimming pool together, having both cheated on their respective partners. This group around me all arrived together as a collective. Now we can share each of them first-hand with the others. The cheated parties were aware of the goings on and secreted themselves behind the pool shed. Needless to say, a splash was heard. A dash was made for the clothing and the house was locked. The closed system security cameras captured the whole wet episode. The tape made was dispensed to the local newspaper with the caption "Beluga Whales sighted in Pool". That created sets of more humorous memories for the general public. Thanks for sharing.'

'I can't express my distress at the memory I hold,' said a bright pink ball. 'One evening a person had bad thoughts about stealing the neighbour's kid's bike to teach him a lesson. He'd been a footpath terror, threatening to run into small children and skidding in front of others believing an accident was about to happen. One evening, the bike disappeared. The neighbour didn't steal it. The kid deliberately hid it and blamed them. Another set of compatible memories covers those thoughts. I'm glad I'm not in those. The kid's parents used unsavoury threats and armed themselves with a weapon. Suffice to say someone got hurt and it wasn't the neighbour. My fellow thoughts can explain it better. It certainly is one way to be drained of colour.' The pink ball began to fade.

*   *   *

Time didn't seem to have a measuring stick in Pollital. It came and went like living in Forever Land. Davidia was thinking her way out of an impossible situation. What could a person, stiff as a board, achieve by being permanently immobilised? She wondered how she would survive and who was going to feed her. There was no way she could consume a memory. She was a talented individual, but even she baulked at memory consumption. How long could she last? Surely, she had to wither over time. Her magical friend was in emotive land trying to connect to a grandma memory, but there were none attached to her body that were able to pass on to her. It seemed that their early demise as young girls was instigated, but was it? Davidia noted the tentativeness of some Pollitons in their approach to plucking a memory from her.

She could still speak, see, breath and sense. She tried to shake her body with one of her on-trend dance moves. It reacted like a coffin — zilch. Next, a jump was attempted. Once again it felt like she was encased in a non-shootable, lead-bullet casing – zilch. What if she hummed out loud? Surely her rendition of a pop song would be appreciated; after all, at school people fought over her voice to have her on their musical debating team. Alas, it wasn't a singing part though.

'Slirander,' she whispered. 'I'm going to hum the school anthem for them and see its affect. What do you think? They wouldn't appreciate or know Beyonce?'

'Better you bore them than me. I never did like it much; besides, I have more important things to hug.'

That was most unlike Slirander to cough up a meaningless sentence. The memories are suffocating her rationale. A cape of bulgy balls was a great theme costume, but not to wear for life. Davidia began softly. Her throat was in excellent working order. She didn't need to exercise her larynx. There were no me, me, me, fay, fay, fay or lah te dohs. The Pollitons stopped whatever it was they were doing, eating, shuffling, crawling or matters of a private nature as they listened to a vocal intruder. Both mouths were agape. What do they do with it, the noise? It gradually grew louder as Davidia struggled with her breathing at high-note pitch. The atmosphere had been invaded. None of the Pollitons could recall such an insidious sound. It had no vowels or structural form. It hurt their delicate eardrums. After all, keeping memories was a delicate task. Never before had they encountered an open sound memory that had escaped from its encased ball. All memories were delivered exactly alike in those coloured balls. This was almost turned into a calamity. The Pollitons had no escape from the humming diva.

'Who is making that terrible din?' said Pole, slowly turning around to Davidia, the source of the problem. He then realised that the performing Pole clown was causing the issue. 'Please stop. You may destroy many memories,' he pleaded.

All memory consumption had stopped. With the delay now in place, it would take ages to catch up again. Davidia stopped; however, a moment before she did, she felt all the clinging memories start to detach. The vibrations were shaking them loose.

'I'll stop if you can release us from our stiff structure and get rid of all these balls. I enjoy movement just like everybody else. If not, I'll continue on. I might break into words, or I might shout, scream and say unpleasant things to match many of those whispering memories. Many of those memories are downright wicked. I'm glad you don't harbour any of mine. What's it to be?'

'I can't release you,' said Pole. 'It's not allowed. Only the great memory mind of Pollital has that power.'

'Well, where is it? It can't be afraid of a demure girl, can it? I'm as soft as a marshmallow.'

'It exists near those slightly taller hutsals. It was able to gain height with earlier better-quality memories before modern-day memories swamped us with impure thoughts that stunted our growth. The bad outweighed the good, but slowly the good worm is wriggling free once again.'

Pole smiled, or it looked like it. Two open mouths can give a false impression that it's a smile.

'Go get it. I can't be expected to be polite all day.'

Pole baulked at the request. Davidia sensed his reluctance. Once again, she hummed the school anthem. Her parents would be proud that she knew it at all, let alone in harmony. The sound shook Pollital to the brink of collapse. It wasn't that bad. The memory world was a delicate organ to operate and sensitivity abounded. Davidia felt a wind gush – it wasn't one of her own – that ran up her legs around her growing upper body and over her head. All the coloured balls had dropped their bundles by detaching for safety and had gently floated to the ground. It was an "M&M'S" display without the crunch. Surprisingly she was free. Her movements had returned. Once again, she was a fully functioning, feisty sixteen-year-old girl ready to best the world. Slirander had also lost her set of clingers, but had tried to keep a few. Had her mind been infiltrated with inappropriate collective thoughts that she wanted to retain what she thought was grandma's memories? A descendant wasn't able to be involved in that way. Disappointment is often hard to accept especially when emotion is the basis of it.

'Slirander, leave them alone. You know what happened last time. I disappeared and no one was too happy.'

'I suppose I'll find a proper grandma memory somewhere here.'

As the girls were discussing their "new found" freedom, a

grey striped cloud of balls approached. There was no sequence of a leader. They continuously rotated as a swirl. A thin mist encased it all as a salad dressing does a salad. It was a silent symphony of mobile art. Suddenly, a brazen, stupid or brave ball escaped from the group. It was hard to tell what game was being played. It zoomed closer, observing the girls as closely as preparing someone for a firing squad. It was totally cylindrical. It had no gap for a speaking organ or any organ of any type. It definitely wasn't human. The girls observed it. Davidia put out a hand, fingers tightly together to avoid any damage or offensive gestures, and attempted to touch it. That was a mistake. A nasty flash of light zapped her hand as if she had been tazered. A nasty memory whizzed along her arm, one which she dared not repeat in case it offended the reader. Each hair on her arm became a small blonde spike. It now imitated a distant albino relative. Davidia fell backwards spitting chips. She normally did backward somersaults at sport and not in front of the public.

'The bastard. I was only being pleasant. What did that to me? Show yourself. I'm not going to eat you. I daresay, I could go for a burger right now, just the same.'

The silence was deafening. The grey swirl continued to swirl. The girls watched like eagles preparing to latch onto their prey. After being tazered, Davidia wished she had huge talons to grip the offender and inflict an equalising dose of excruciating pain. Pain was part of normal life, but not usually expected at that intensity. Suddenly, the grey swirl hovered. Two long tentacles much like two supple tree branches emerged. Where's the bloody chain-saw when you need it, thought Davidia. They moved effortlessly near her and Slirander. Was it a taste arm much like snakes flicking out their tongues to "smell" the air? Was it a talking funnel for communication, or something more sinister; a grappling pincer to draw in whatever it intended to be caught?

Davidia had also noted that Pole was about to chomp on a grandma memory, but it was stuck on his lip because when the swirl had arrived, all Polliton movements ceased as if a photograph had been snapped.

It was stalemate as the girl group stared down the swirl. Tension was the new emotion of the day. One tree tentacle snatched the memory ball from Pole and it disappeared into the grey mist. The other tree tentacle lingered like a lost spaghetti strand before it latched onto Davidia's wrist and absorbed her into the grey. Slirander had been deliberately ignored. She wasn't happy.

'I was grandma's favourite. Davidia isn't even her granddaughter and she gets to share the memory. What are you staring at, you stunted shrub? What am I supposed to do now?'

'There is nothing you can do except wait and hope that your friend returns with the contents of that memory ball. I don't remember what colour it was,' said Pole. He knew that Davidia would not return with the intact memory. Had he underestimated Slirander's feisty friend? 'Here, use this seat. I have a lot of eating to do. Too much time has been wasted already.'

'Where has she gone?'

'Into an unknown place. The great memory mind deletes any opposition to our constant memory consumption. I'm afraid your friend might become a past memory of yours.'

'Can she escape from wherever she has gone?'

'That is an unknown. Every memory has the possibility of recall and in doing so can, in some people's minds, recreate that memory as real.'

'Is it possible for me to follow? That swirl is still there. It appears agitated.'

'Wouldn't you, if you swallowed something as large as your friend? You are banned. Please wait.'

Slirander recalled her family background of long ago and remembered their ability to transform into different matter when under extreme danger. This was that moment. Whatever occurred, the girls had to both return to Pollital as it was their escape route back into the real world. Was Pole in the real world as well, but in a different one? Memories and reality are such complex subjects. Slirander was determined to follow her friend. If they were to cease, then be it together. Such loyalty was a benchmark of her family history. She needed to recite an ancient word arrangement that in the modern world is known as a poem.

Stuff is solid, stuff is soft, stuff is strong, stuff is weak,
Stuff is transparent, stuff is small, stuff is thin, stuff is tall,
Stuff can change, stuff can mist, stuff this thought and particles exist,
Stuff can travel the speed of light, stuff is able to turn to flight,
Stuff is a burden not borne alone, send this girl to stuff the clone,
Stuff the journey and return to home, stuffed.

A strange silence permeated the air. A change was about to take place. No one was ready for it or would understand it, except Slirander. Pole had both mouths open in surprise. His eating would have to be deferred whilst he mentally dined this time. Slirander began to disappear and develop into a blue mist equally as agitated a swirl as the grey one.

'Where are you going?' Pole asked in astonishment.

First a memory was rudely snatched away and now a pleasant girl was leaving them in a most unusual manner. Nothing had ever melted in Pollital before. These intruders into his life of memory consumption grated rather badly. It meant delays in consumption for any loose memories that to date had been ignored. It was important that all memories had the right to retention and as quickly as possible after formation, otherwise they could be forgotten.

Slirander was now a swirling mass of blue, which was the colour of the snatched memory ball. A wind howled, not in pain, but in its natural actions, as the mass of blue did a figure-eight loop and then whoosh, it fled into the grey mist in hot pursuit of Davidia and one of grandma's memories. There was no predicting the outcome or where she was headed. Inside the grey mass, visibility was nil. Only at the end of the journey would the reveal take place and whatever that was, it had to be.

Pole never received an answer to his question. It would have to wait. He may never receive that answer. Pollital gradually resumed normality as the memory munchers once again consumed the round ball trash of coloured memories. Anyone for dessert?

Where was Davidia and now where was Slirander?

What was their Pollital fate?

Had the thesis on grandma overtaken their lives to the point of cessation?

Where were they?

'Keep quiet. Don't even whisper. This trench is worse than a sewer. Tread carefully. It could be booby-trapped. Follow my hand signals only. Keep silent.'

It was nearing dusk as a weary group of females trudged slowly and carefully, as if in a Cirque-de-Soleil routine, traversing enemy lines. Amongst the dozen or so groups were a few mercenaries, a few rough-house women having witnessed the travesty of war, and a leader affectionately known as The Blue Rat. The name was bestowed upon her after a fracas inside a barn with the inhabitants fighting for their lives. The last moments of the enemy's existence was the sight of a swirling blue scarf tightly drawn around the face of an angel, an angel of death. The last words uttered in disgust by an unfortunate, was 'blau rat'. The name stuck as did most of their dishevelled and filthy clothing in a brutal non-ending physical contest – war.

The leader was a young woman in her mid-twenties with a steely resolve and battle-hardened strategies. The Blue Rat was a secret undercover operative with the task of saving fallen airmen and soldiers, transporting them back to safety in impossible terrain and past those who were spies for the enemy. To trust unequivocally was to live a short war. A knife often replaced a hand signal as it sadly silenced a noise.

Tonight, was a particularly important mission. Amongst their group were two airmen who held secrets of an invasion plan and to have this extracted from them would mean further danger. The farmhouse they passed at a distance had been passed many times before; however, tonight it felt different. The lights that normally escaped from the small windows into the darkness were themselves held captive by closed shutters. The Blue Rat couldn't see any foreign movement. A hush came over the group as they stopped and settled, with heaving nervous breaths revealing their anxiety. The signal to stay and drop was drawn on by previous farming experiences when orders needed to be obeyed.

'Wait here,' The Blue Rat whispered. 'I'll check it out.'

She withdrew her blood-stained knife and stalked the barn and farmhouse like the lord of the jungle. Her petite buttocks bobbed up and down as she covered each mound of dirt successfully. Stealth and silence were requisites for survival. The landscape seemed to be perpetually wet. Mud clung to everything. It was a sod-soaked clod epidemic. As she neared the barn, discovery meant termination, torture and other rather unpleasant holiday fun times. A muffled noise alerted her. Lack of sound clarity had her imagination on a swinging ball. Was it a radio tuned into a clandestine radio station sprouting like earache, expressing propaganda support and, dare one say, public lies to the masses? Was it an over-amorous pair of possums not yet captured and eaten in support of the war effort? The Blue Rat climbed up a drainpipe which hadn't yet been destroyed, rotted or damaged. It held its strength for the lightweight "night rodent". She was a stealth machine. An open top hatch allowed entry. Even the dry straw that normally shrunk, scrunched and crackled underfoot presented no sound issues tonight. It was as if an unknown force had lifted her over it. She peered over the edge and sighted the problem she was to face. Nothing had prepared her for the encounter.

A young girl sat tied to a chair, mouth taped, feet lashed with thin rope and a flashy blue scarf sat around her neck. She was struggling to free herself. Her situation wasn't friendly. Someone had kept her there away from the farmhouse for purposes not yet imagined. The Blue Rat was aware of the danger of being personally exposed. Her senses told her it wasn't an immediate threat in a military sense. Had she created an unforgivable misdemeanour, or was she to be a conquest for foreign soldiers and kept for that purpose? The real reason would not be discovered because she was to be released. At personal risk to herself, The Blue Rat quickly climbed down a ladder and ran toward the young girl. Her eyes swelled to small dessert plates of fear. Was this maniacal bitch with the knife going to stab her or at least attempt to reduce her beautiful locks without a pair of proper scissors? The Blue Rat signalled to Davidia to stay silent. That would be some forlorn hope after her situation. A hand signal went to her lips in a 'shush' sound. The Blue Rat deftly cut the rope and removed the tape over Davidia's mouth.

'There are some crazy bastards up at that farmhouse with strange accents. I didn't understand a bloody word they said. Have you come to hurt me too?' said Davidia, reeling from being interned.

She hadn't grasped the fear of her situation at all after having recently arrived from Pollital chasing grandma's memory. She didn't recall having worn a blue scarf before either. She wasn't complaining about that. It was so pretty.

'Who are you?' said The Blue Rat.

Davidia was still shaken with fear.

'David, Dav, no, no, it's Davanda. Shit, I can't even remember my own name.'

'Quiet, we must leave immediately.'

'Why should I? I've a good mind to kick arse at that farmhouse. They've trussed me up like livestock and I'd like to repay the compliment.'

'Now, I said, now.'

Outside the barn, those strange accents flowed louder

and louder. The farmhouse guests were seeking party-time. Fortunately, they left their real weaponry behind and only brought with them their muscle weaponry in the hope of firing off a few pellets.

'If you want to live, get behind that bale now.'

The Blue Rat dragged Davidia by the hair with her other hand over her mouth. She slapped her face for good measure to shut up the chatty chick in case she exposed their position. The barn door opened. In walked two soldiers from a foreign-speaking army. Mains had been eaten at the farmhouse and dessert was to be barn-shared. No sooner had they neared the vacant chair when they were set upon by a vicious, fire-breathing dragon far taller than either of them. The Blue Rat had silently slid behind them and her agile form was far too quick. Not another word was said. Two male forms lay prostrate on the barn floor. Blood soaked into the loose straw as a gurgling noise broke the silence.

'What happened to them?' said a dazed Davidia.

She hadn't seen the gymnastic performance and the whirling Dervish knife dance.

'I gave them a bloody nose for their insolence and bad manners.'

The truth remained hidden to Davidia.

'I'd like to kick them in their meatballs. This is Italy, isn't it?'

'We're in France. We must go now. You aren't safe here. Come.'

Davidia wasn't used to being bossed about. At home it would never happen. There would be discussion, pouting, a few tears and a hug with a parent before comfort was provided by her fluffy doona and the computer world of her bedroom. Had anything changed? A volley of bullets whizzed perilously close, shattering the barn walls with splinters performing like trapeze artists. Bullets ricocheted around them.

'What the ... ?' said Davidia in exclamation.

'Stay and you are dead.'

The Blue Rat disappeared out the rear of the barn relying on the advantage of darkness and the ability to circle around the property unseen. Davidia didn't see the sense of inviting everyone to church for her funeral, so she quickly followed suit. She did her best to be invisible. Any bullet would ruin her outfit besides causing serious pain. Being in a memory was fraught with danger if it had to be lived out. Not every memory had a successful ending. The trail they followed was soon devoid of any trackers. They circled around the farm to connect with the group. It had stayed immobile and well-hidden. Everyone was accounted for. Now, they had one more.

'Nice scarf. I haven't seen anything like that for a few years.'

'Why not? I buy them all the time. Pretty, isn't it?' Davidia doubted that it was hers.

'Are you serious? Do you know where you are?'

'No. It's a girl's night out, isn't it? It looks like fun, all this hiding and getting dirty. At home it's usually a night-time possum hunt with torches and a few drinks at the finish.'

'This girl isn't real. Listen, you are in a war zone in France where the likelihood of not being alive in two days hence is a reality.'

'Are you sure? That lady gave those two men back in the barn a bloody nose each. Someone tried to scare us with a gun or two. I thought it was like a game.'

'It's to the death. This isn't a game. Living depends on each other.'

The Blue Rat put up a silencer with her hand and waved it across her throat as a warning to cut all chatter. Unnecessary chat could reveal their location. Davidia was taken to one side by The Blue Rat.

'Listen, I don't know where you came from or what you are doing here, but your ignorance of the country's situation is astounding. This is real life. People die all the time. We are at war. This group is to be taken safely to another town for safety and they rely on people like me and a few of my followers to do their job. If you can't hack the difficulty of the job, once we get to safety you go too. We can't afford anyone who doesn't put in. We don't trust those who don't. Now, who are you and what are you doing here? You seem lost and out of your depth. That scarf of yours has to be dirty. Take it off and scuff it.'

'My name is Davidia and I am … on holiday from the London War Office having been transferred here recently. I was captured by those awful speaking army men. You'd think they'd speak English. I was on my way to Lyon.'

Davidia had whitewashed the truth. She realised that as she spoke, the others listened intently. She didn't want to appear incompetent or not doing her bit. Her astuteness had summed up the situation correctly. Shit, she was in a war zone. She wondered whether Slirander knew about her grandma and war activity. She assumed The Blue Rat was grandma. If she was in the Second World War, there was danger everywhere. This might not be a memory she wished to experience.

She attempted to take off her blue scarf. She struggled to undo it. It didn't want to go.

'You obstinate piece of material. Get off me.'

The scarf was rubbed in the filthy, muddy water and given a rinse. Its colour faded quickly. There wasn't any time for drying it on a line, so she once again wrapped it around her neck. It smelt and stuck tightly.

'You do that again and I'll strangle you.'

Was that a voice she had actually heard, or was her mind playing tricks on her? It did sound like Slirander, but had she imagined it needing a friend in a tight situation? She rearranged her scarf loosely in case those words rang true. War is a mind game where fear permeates the inhabitants daily and influences behaviour in non-standard ways.

'It's time to move.'

The group hadn't washed for days. Davidia wasn't used to unmasked body odours. They followed The Blue Rat like zombies, zig-zagging, keeping low and furtively glancing everywhere expecting an ambush at every moment. It was all about survival. As the night wore on, the night sounds of sloshing mud through the muddy trenches were replaced by firm footing under tree lines. There was no rest. The occasional frog that hadn't made it to the dinner table croaked without enthusiasm. The night lacked any cheerful sounds. In the distance, the dull thud of what was perceived to be cracker sounds grew louder and more frequent. They were entering a combat zone. It was unavoidable. Safety was on the other side. Confrontation or discovery was to be avoided at all costs.

The Blue Rat was herself a foreigner in a foreign land assisting the war effort. She had been visiting London when the war erupted. She couldn't see how an office desk would be a constructive worthwhile war companion, so she opted for a fresh outdoor activity. Little did she know that her basic French learnt at school would lead her to dangerous exploits across the Channel. Duty overrode her emotions. She was now on the radar of the enemy as a wanted fugitive. During her tenure, she had exhibited the cunning of her nickname many times. The opposition army were her pest exterminators, if only they could capture her. It was noted also, that each member of her group wore a blue scarf, even though the colour had faded and it was saturated with dirt. This gave a minimum of protection if the group was located and time to escape. Which one was she?

'When do we eat? I'm very hungry. I haven't seen any shops anywhere,' said Davidia. Her comfort zone had been left behind.

'There is nothing. Keep quiet. By morning we may locate some bread. Food is impossible to find when the army devours it all. We live on meagre scraps and often after someone else has had a go first.'

'You mean you actually eat someone's waste food. There are diseases amongst those.'

'It's called survival.'

The night wore on. It was a hard slog. They didn't see any other inhabitants, living or dead. Legs ached and bodies were exhausted, but the urge to survive was greater than any pain. The dawn gradually crept up like a daylight assassin revealing the human lumps trying to remain hidden. A startled snail – even the snails move quickly sometimes in France – didn't move when it was trodden on. Creatures of all denominations suffered. They were now at the edge of a field where a lone cow was tethered in the centre. It grazed in a circle. This was a trap for any would-be thief. A minefield had been placed outside of the grazing distance, but with the access path obscured. Kaboom! It was avoided. The smell of fresh bread tweaked their nostrils. It drew a crowd. Some were discreetly hidden, especially for the passing Blue Rat crowd.

Davidia was wilting under the exhausting exercise of overnight trekking. Even her local gymnasium workout couldn't match her overnight effort. She began to wonder if The Blue Rat was actually grandma. She had to know.

Sudddenly, a mortar bomb exploded nearby. Those who had never soiled their pants before in fright now had a few more exponents of the involuntary task. The group hit the deck. They hadn't been sighted. Davidia took a mouthful of grass like a cow relishing in its deliciousness and spat it out. She was no milking machine. Besides, she didn't have multiple stomachs, multiple thoughts, yes, and not a nice one amongst them.

'Are we under attack? I'm too young to die. My wardrobe would be adrift without me. Grandma, save me.' A frightened young girl almost disclosed their position.

'Shut up. We must stay hidden otherwise your future will become history. Those army columns are the enemy.'

Davidia hadn't noticed that during the night, other members of the group were armed to the teeth. All carried knives and other death-delivering accessories. Self-preservation was more important than conflict. The group rested. The Blue Rat slunk off for her rendezvous with the bread maker. It wasn't for emotional purposes, but for a simple feed of bread to sustain them on the last leg of their journey. She withdrew her pet knife called Lex, named after her friend who had been killed some years earlier. Revenge is often said to be a meal best served cold. It wasn't revenge she sought, but she was determined not to meet that same fate. The blade didn't glint anymore. The dried blood stains hid a perfectly beautiful steel object formally used as a kitchen utensil. Its serrated blade spoke often before she did. She didn't know if ever the proper use for that knife would be reintroduced into her life again. If it was, peace would have been a reality.

Davidia sat down as obedient as she could be. She slumped to the ground as a heavily weighted object, emotionally and physically drained. Her clothes were a mess. Not an ironed crease in sight. Her dress had ripped sections. Dirt covered her feet as if she was a Papua-New Guinean mud-man. Welts and scratches acted as leg decorations. Her face had gained a dry, tough-skin feeling without her nightly exfoliation process on her porcelain skin. Imagine any blemish on that at home and all hell would break loose. Now she felt a respect toward others not previously experienced. Did Slirander know any of this? There was also a real chance she wouldn't live through this memory. It was so real.

Davidia's scarf began to wriggle. There's not a snake in it, is there, she thought. Was it larva from a disgruntled bug that had lost its habitat, or maybe it's a rodent searching for new digs and both were opportunities to eat "fresh"? Alas, it was only a few dried dirt particles that had made her skin itchy. She unfolded the scarf. The fabric had a strange feeling, in a good way though. It filed through her hands. She felt the dirty patches and the dried and clean patch sections as it softly landed at her feet in the shape of an S. There wasn't any complaint from it this time as it lay on the ground. Davidia imagined that she saw a mirage, or could it have been a smile or just another scrape of soil? Was her friend following her? It certainly felt like it. She knelt down on one end of the scarf. It gave a kick.

'Is that you Slirander?' she asked.

'What's with the talking to the scarf? Given it a name, have you?' said another group member.

'The stress is showing,' said another. 'Leave her to sort out her imaginary friend. We all seem to have at least one. Such is war.'

'This is grandma's memory. You shouldn't be here, if that's you in there. Now, I'll have to protect my scarf as well as me. I think The Blue Rat is her. Breakfast will be served shortly.'

Bread rations weren't her ideal breakfast food. What about …?

'Scatter. A snoopy group of army privates are heading this way. There are four of them scanning the perimeter.'

The group hid amongst the tall grass as best they could. If a bullet had intent and accuracy, the tall grass was no defence; however, the surprise of ambush gave them the advantage. Tension flew upwards like a bird ascending to heaven. No one wanted to join it on that flight. A foreign language translated that the strangers were searching for a rodent of some sort. All knew what that meant. The group withdrew their knives, dumped their guns and dressed down to nothing more than what an underwear model wore. Even in their dirty, dishevelled and bad aromatic state, the women easily passed as some of the most beautiful formations a human could construct. A deadly spider, no matter how beautiful, is still just that, deadly. Davidia was shielded by a dense mass of grass. She was half-hidden in a swampy section with poor visibility. She wasn't attacking anyone, but had employed her hide-and-seek strategy. No one had ever successfully found her. She waited like a wallflower at a dance. Thank God she wasn't approached. If so, that meant a memory of grandma's history might be altered.

The sounds of slosh, splash, hiss and thump were heard. There were no verbals. What had happened? Had the soldiers fallen down a cave, sink hole or drowned? A few minutes later, a group of underwear-clad women emerged from the tall grass, some stained with red marks over both their clothing and skin. Their knives had also been redecorated with Davidia's favourite colour. It was a solemn moment.

'We pray for their souls,' said one, as she crossed her chest in a religious manner.

'Where did the soldiers go?' asked an innocent Davidia.

War was foreign to her. She was a memory visitor and not a participant in a conflict.

'They have gone and won't cause any more trouble.'

No other explanation was needed as the group dressed, sheathed their weapons and readied for the return of The Blue Rat. Breakfast hadn't been eaten yet. The members didn't discuss the demise of the soldiers. They felt Davidia was innocent and the less she knew the better. War gave sense to understanding situations.

'All clear,' said The Blue Rat, returning laden with two fresh bread rolls.

They were dispersed quickly. Ravenous mouths ripped at the yeast-filled product with the ferocity of a man-eating animal.

Any loose fingers at that moment would become part of the meal. Some bodies winced in agony at the roughage being swallowed and others gratefully relaxed with swelling stomachs. That was it. Davidia was grateful. It relieved some of her angst. She was thinking when was it a good time to ask The Blue Rat her real name? Would there ever be an ideal time? She decided that now was the right moment with a stomach partially full of food, she may elicit a good response.

'Excuse me, Blue Rat,' said a cautious Davidia, 'does anyone use their real names in your group?'

'What does it matter? How have you assumed that is my title? Anyone of us can be that individual as evidenced by us all wearing a blue scarf. Maybe we are all blue rats and are also known by other names. That lady is called Knife, no guesses why. That mess is Stunt. Be careful what you ask for. That wiry ensemble is String. She ties a mean necklace and that animal is Shithead. No guesses what she approaches in combat. Forget the others. They all have code names as well. It's been so long since we have used our real names. It seems an offence to utter them.'

'I've told you mine and I don't have any code name.'

'If you became part of the group you would. You seem too soft to fit in.'

'I've never hurt anyone before.'

'Once, neither did we. Look at us now and what we've turned into. War is a life-changing situation and not always for the good. It creates too much pain, loss and suffering. Why are you here, anyway? You haven't disclosed anything about yourself. Are you a cadet newspaper reporter wanting to experience the real war? Can you handle a knife or a gun?'

'I'm not into violence. I've been sent here on a private mission for a friend of mine. It's called a thesis.'

Her blue scarf began to tighten. Slirander was feeling left out.

'I've heard of the name, Greek, isn't it?'

Davidia wasn't sure how to proceed, so she made the blunt approach.

'Is your name Michelle?'

The Blue Rat gave off no recognition. Her group was listening. A real name could be a death sentence if known. Better to be an unknown nobody than a known somebody. Under extreme interrogation that truth may come to light, but whilst in the field as little information as possible is revealed.

'Let's go. We must keep moving. Be alert. The risk increases once we pass this field.'

The group moved on leaving behind remnants of bread-roll crumbs for the fortunate insects that still existed as well as a foursome, having done the last tango were now another war memory lying amongst flattened grasses which harboured them as enemies. Daylight was not their friend. They crept along a river bed to a well-used cave. The entrance was hidden by fallen, shrapnel-blasted trees and shattered rocks. It was believed that there wasn't any further tactical advantage of the river. It was now ignored; however, it was a safe refuge for some. That day the group sat bored and disinterested. Conversation was often alien as each member had their own thoughts to deal with. Davidia was still curious. Her question about a real name hadn't been answered. She tried again. This time she was out of earshot of the others.

'Excuse me, Michelle,' said Davidia, tentatively.

She wasn't sure of the response this time, or whether had she used the appropriately worded approach.

The Blue Rat turned around crimson-faced with anger. Her facial veins were erupting like strands of worms all over her face. Davidia sat quietly. She didn't feel threatened, but Michelle was showing threatening behaviour toward her. One hand ran its fingers down her knife sheath and Davidia sensed that the hilt was about to be gripped. A dark moment passed.

'Are you an idiot or do you possess a death wish? Do not persist with name integrity. It could lead to your end.'

Davidia was persistent, if nothing else.

'I won't tell anyone. Nobody knows I'm here except my friend, Slirander.'

Once again at the mention of her name, the blue scarf became agitated. Davidia didn't know what that meant.

'I know you won't tell anyone because I will not confirm or deny it. You don't understand safety in times of war. I doubt that you worked for any war office. Your skills lie. Stay out of my way. Once we reach our destination, you are gone. I have far more important work to do than waste time over a name label.'

Davidia sensed that was an end to it. Would The Blue Rat admit to being grandma? Even if she didn't, the fact that she was in one of grandma's memories answers that question. Secrecy had to be maintained.

Suddenly, the droning sound of a fighter plane split the airwaves. It sounded as if it was directly overhead. Boom! A bomb landed at the front of the cave. Rocks and debris exploded in all directions. Everyone hit the dirt cursing at having been located. Someone had leaked their whereabouts. The plane did another run. Boom! More blasts. Davidia was petrified. She slunk further into the depths of the cave without any torchlight or natural light. There was nothing anyone could do except ride it out and hope for the best. There was nowhere to run. The group waited patiently.

Davidia had almost gone too far into the cave and hadn't noticed that some parts of the rock roof had been dislodged, hanging tenuously to their almost-former home. Then the strangest thing happened. Her blue scarf unravelled itself from around her neck and lay flat on the cave floor. It wasn't long before a visage appeared which was that of Slirander. It smiled. Davidia smiled too. A moment later, the blue scarf formed into a large blue shroud that completely enveloped Davidia. She was now a caterpillar in a blue cocoon, unable to move or say anything. This was nuts. She struggled hard. Then it erupted. Another bomb had exploded and shattered the cave's entrance. She was being entombed. Slirander held her tight. She acted as a small blue Zeppelin as she floated out toward the cave entrance. The group were covered in dust and debris, but were still intact. They watched the floating slug pass by. Davidia got so close to The Blue Rat she was able to mime the word 'Michelle'. There was no verbal response, but the eyes said it all. Yes.

That was the last Davidia saw of grandma as an undercover operative. The next moment of awareness was back in Pollital sitting amongst the many coloured balls once again with Slirander by her side.

'How did we manage to escape and return here?'

'The blue scarf. It was the blue scarf.'

That was all Slirander was prepared to say; however, they were safe once again and able to continue on the memory journey of grandma and perhaps compile their thesis.

Davidia didn't have any war wounds, just a fresh set of memories.

6 The Shadow

The two girls pondered their next move whilst the coloured balls bounced aimlessly around them ignoring their presence. The idea of discovering grandma's memories had led them, or at least Davidia, into dangerous past activities. Would the next effort subject her to further or worse dangers?

'This is no fun park,' said Davidia. 'These coloured balls can certainly dish up surprises. I really wonder whether we should explore any more of them. I don't want to push my luck. We should leave here. Sometimes peering into people's past isn't always such a good idea. We might learn something that we shouldn't. Relating that knowledge to other relatives might be devastating for them. I don't want to be the bearer of bad news.'

'What actually happened back there?' asked Slirander. 'When I was the blue scarf, I was only aware of being around your neck as a security blanket. It was for your protection only. I didn't participate in the actual memory story.'

Before Davidia could respond, Pole dawdled over to them. It seemed that he was a deciduous Pole as his treed covering began to shed. That had never happened before. A mysterious virus had impregnated his body. It was called "Young Girls". In his world, memories were never tampered with under any circumstances because once created they are there forever. It was impossible to alter them; however, with the arrival of Slirander and Davidia, the unending planned storage of memories had been disturbed; in fact, twice now. They hadn't actually been altered, but now they were shared by someone who should not have had access to them. They belonged to others who actually had that experience. The stress and anxiety began to show. Other memory inhabitants were also on edge. The town of Pollital was in turmoil. Their structure was being unpleasantly nudged. Unhappy memories started to increase amongst the Pollitons when they shouldn't have had any of their own. Their purpose was to save other's memories. There was to be no barbeque of thoughts in Pollital. A memory council was called. The girls noted a long stream of shuffling treed inhabitants shedding excellent compost material as they shuffled toward the main Pollital structure, a huge round rainbow coloured ball. The girls were prohibited from entry.

'Pole, what's happening? Where are all the memory keepers going?' asked Davidia. 'Is it a conference of some sort?'

Slirander felt the emotional aspect of the general feeling of the Pollitons. She was a very sensitive girl in empathy with her emotions. A small tremor of nervousness filtered through her body signalling to her to be on her guard. Something unpleasant would soon head their way.

'I don't like the feeling I'm experiencing being here at the moment. I think we have outstayed our welcome. We should depart quickly and find our way back to that hole in the field we had entered by.'

'They don't scare me. They're so small. What harm could they do to us?'

Davidia wasn't scared of confrontation. Sometimes, it was a challenge to be different.

'We could be kept captive in grandma's memories forever. Imagine how that would go down with the family. They'd never know what happened to us. We couldn't go on and create other wonderful memories for others to enjoy. What a loss that would be.' Slirander was a common-sense person when she really thought about it.

'We came here to discover grandma's memories and I want to know more before we leave.' Stubborn Davidia had arrived. She had changed her mind.

They watched the procession of Pollitons merge into the horizon. Pole had hung back on purpose. The girls didn't know it, but he was protecting them from bad memories. A few of the agitated Pollitons began throwing memory balls at them and none of them were from grandma. He deftly deflected those floating time bombs because if one exploded and revealed that memory, the girls were cactus, the variety was immaterial. They would enter an unknown person's memory and only disaster waited there. They would become non-retrievable. The air by now was full of bouncing balls floating to find someone to memory-eat them. A large build-up occurred. Whilst the Pollitons were heading toward the meeting, no memories were being consumed and the supply of them was endlessly multiplying. Pole was toying with a last-minute effort to consume one of grandma's memories, when he inexplicably handed it to Slirander. She felt his emotional trepidation. What was grandma doing in this one? Should it be revealed? Pole slowly turned and trudged after the others, shoulders sagging.

'What's his problem?' said Davidia. 'He needs a good watering.'

'He's concerned over the meeting. I get the feeling we won't enjoy the outcome.'

'Oh well, we'll wait and see. What's in that ball you have? It's black and white. That's really the first one I've seen like that. Let me feel it?'

'I don't think that you should.'

'You can be selfish. Let me touch it,' she yelled.

Pollital shook in fright. Once a headache merges with a memory, confusion reigns. Yelling wasn't an allowed sound.

No sooner had Davidia touched it when her hands disappeared.

She quickly retrieved them in fright and found both of them visibly missing. Something began to tug at her. Her body felt the fearful touch of ash-laden fire embers stretching into an embracing blanket without any niceties. She had become one huge, fire-blackened rash. Slirander tried to control the erratic behaviour of the memory ball, but it had a memory of its own. Davidia hadn't observed memory-ball protocol by not touching it. Only Slirander had that privilege and now Davidia had ruined it for her. The ball given to Slirander was to be for her only to experience a private memory of grandma's. Now with girlfriend interference, its true meaning had become distorted. The girls had no idea where this would lead them. Davidia had been transported as the black rash and Slirander followed shortly thereafter as a staff rod. The pair weren't playing Halloween dress-ups; however, that's exactly what they appeared to be. The sky went dark and into a void they flew. In that space, neither would recall that moment as a personal memory.

*

'Are you her bodyguard?' questioned a person with bulldog facial features.

Its nose was bent sideways with fresh air inhalation and exhalation possible from one nostril passage only. If not for the gentleness of the eyes, this person could be a natural Halloween participant.

'I'm not anyone's bodyguard,' replied Davidia.

'Well then, why are you dressed like the billboard behind you and standing outside the Black Hole boxing rooms?'

'I was just walking past. I'm on my way to Halloween School for a training session in scare tactics.'

'Follow me.'

'But I'm not allowed in there. I might scare too many patrons. Besides I'm too y… ,' Davidia trailed off.

Davidia had landed outside a famous boxing centre where only the toughest and meanest of two-legged pugilists squared off with often an injury ending the bout. It was purely a male dominated sport. Women were thought to be too weak and soppy without the physical or mental streak to combat male bravado, rhetoric and physical attributes. They were usually banned entrance, but on occasion, the night was thrown open to all-comers. Tonight was that night. Davidia was ushered into the stadium where she was amazed at the sight of brutish thuggery amongst those training with punch balls, punch bags and punching sparring partners like they had a personal vendetta against them. Sweat dripped onto bouncing floors. Faces grimaced with pain. Ropes were stretched to their elastic capacity keeping opponents within the boxing ring and managers with acerbic abusive tongues ladling instructions, 'kill, hit, jab, stick him', while running around like annoying insects. The thick smell of liniment and repulsive body odours twisted into the atmosphere. Even the change rooms held their own "fresh air" perils. Women were prohibited from these areas. It was all macho, macho man territory. If any female was located in this particular area – thank goodness cameras were also banned unless by an official photographer – they were unceremoniously evicted with a barrage of foul-tempered language. This was a male only domain. Women were seen as doe-eyed sheep under male dominance. That was an opinion Davidia and Slirander didn't share and apparently neither did another feisty young female who had a life statement to make.

'What exactly is this place?' questioned Davidia.

'All the blokes know this place. What about you?'

Davidia had to think quickly. She lowered her voice a decibel or two to a deep timbre sound.

'I'm new in town and heard of this place. It has quite a pedigree. This is my first visit.'

'No worries, mate.'

Davidia's theme costume hid the reality that she was female and a banned person. She would have to be careful how she moved around to avoid being discovered. There was a risk that she would be taken into the male change rooms where many boxers were naked and for her perhaps some embarrassment. Under no circumstances was she to remove any of her outfit. If discovered, the result might be a beating, mistreatment or even worse. She wondered why was she in such a seedy establishment where the law was too often scared to enter. Assaults were a regular pastime and many patrons wore the mantel of a grated suntan from time in prison. Spittoons were a waste of usefully-placed equipment. The floor and someone else's clothing wore that badge. Davidia carefully considered her position. How does she survive being undiscovered? More importantly, if she was here now, what has this place got to do with grandma? Was she a part-owner and smoked Cuban cigars? Had she once been kicked out of the place for smuggling herself in to watch a bout? Was she a member of the law enforcement brigade that had kicked butt and often? It was a minefield of thoughts.

'Excuse me, mate, can I sit in the stand for a moment?'

'Sure. Don't wander around where you aren't supposed to.'

The usher disappeared. He was once a well-known boxer and now managed the establishment. A worker scurried by as if a bunch of flies were attacking his backside by the way he was flicking his hands behind him.

'Excuse me,' she said, assertively.

The fleeing staffer stopped dead. His face showed fear. What was bothering him? He almost wet his pants spying Davidia. Whoa insanity, the grim reaper is after me.

'What?'

'When is the next bout?'

'Tonight, at six o'clock.'

'Who's on the card?'

'Brawlers, thugs and muggers. Some can box, but most can fight. The most dangerous are the street fighters. I'm sure they hate the world. They can be so cruel and vicious.'

'Is tonight open to anyone?'

'Yes. It's an annual bash-a-thon. It's the last individual standing after all bouts. Last year's event was won by Bugger All, a stage name. I'm glad it's not me in there.'

'Are all competitors male?'

'No female with a sane gene would enter. She'd be minced within seconds.'

'Have there been any odd or new entries this year?'

'A couple of strange ones, but most are regulars or well-known. It's odd that one of the new competitors is wearing a full body suit. He calls himself The Shadow. It's a mystery competitor that no one has heard of. Tickets are a sell-out.'

'Am I able to watch the bouts? I'm new to town. My parents think this will be good for my education.'

The staffer thought for a moment.

'It's fifteen minutes to start time. The crowds will be here at any moment. I'll hide you in the utility cupboard until show time. You can stand with me then.'

Davidia had somehow connected with a complete stranger. Maybe the Slirander staff rod had influenced the staffer. The darkness in the cupboard created a darker feeling, further enhancing apprehension about the Black Hole boxing rooms. A small keyhole that had lost the struggle to remain a security holder now provided a rounded view. From the outside it was doubtful if anyone spotted the roving eye.

The facility was filling quickly with customers, officials, boxing participants, seconds, food crews and all sorts of people responsible for their role in running a successful sporting event. The main ring was surrounded by eager officials, timekeepers, judges and bodyguards for deterring any rough-house treatment toward any boxer. Not all crowd members were happy losers.

A huge rectangular light hovered closely above the main ring shadowing the rest of the facility in darkness. It was an eerie place. With so many criminal elements present, no one ever knew if they would experience an altercation. Suddenly, the announcer grabbed the overhead microphone and began shouting loudly. The cupboard door suddenly flew open. Stale fresh air blew in. Davidia was released from her confines.

'Quickly, the announcer is introducing everyone.'

The staffer had kept his word. He and Davidia stood to the rear where they could view the whole scene before them. At the mention of any name, a great roar erupted. The sillier the name, the louder the roar became. Twenty would-be brutes paraded like prepared meat packs itching to slam bone-hardened fists into a solar plexus with pleasure. Forget a six-week cruise. Delivering pain was the preference. All were expected to be huge hulks with small IQs; however, there was one participant covered in a complete body suit and was considerably far smaller than the whale counterparts. At the mention of the name, The Shadow, the crowd choked in surprise. Undersize individuals weren't allowed to compete. No one considered the oddity had any chance of success; after all, tonight was open to all, all males though. Bulk, hulk, bad breath, sweaty torsos and filthy language were a breakfast competition feast with tonight being prepared for one huge smorgasbord party. Each name held a superstition about it that hid the boxer's emotions. The bell sounded. Bout one was on. Most bouts lasted three rounds of blood lust. Thick rags held by the well-trained staff mopped up the body leakage of blood, sweat and tears. The canvas floor became a stained abstract painting with all the pounding, feet shuffling and body scraping embedding body fluids across its surface. A mad roar erupted each time a body thudded onto its surface. The first few bouts had the normal brutish outcome of injuries and expected results. The air was filtered with mild hysteria as many supporters screamed colourful language at the combatants.

Suddenly, it was the turn of The Shadow. There was little support. The crowd jeered abuse and linguistic put-downs. The ring was alive. The announcer almost laughed so loud his voice got lost amongst the noise.

'In the red corner we have Thug, a two-hundred kilo, well-bred, beef steamroller and in the blue corner we have The Shadow, an eighty-kilo, one-punch loser.'

The crowd became ape-like, whooping up with sheer delight at the prospect of a one-round, blood-thirsty smashing. The svelte-like "young man" was the smallest competitor ever to grace the ring. The mob acted like a braying bunch of loonies. A chant of kill, kill, mince and spill erupted. No one dared not engage in the outrage.

It was noted that the small competitor only wore one boxing glove on the right hand and on the left hand a thin, satin-fingered glove. This allowed complete finger dexterity. Fingernails had been deliberately shortened and unpainted. There was no point in giving off clues to The Shadow's true identity. The body suit only added mystery to the bout. The southpaw stance wasn't that well-known in the boxing fraternity.

The David and Goliath battle began with a grunt, swing and a miss. The Shadow ducked. Thug chased him around the rink, spitting, yelling abuse and using his tree-trunk legs to kick. The boxing match disintegrated into a street brawl scenario. The Shadow was agile, quicker than a ferret ducking down a burrow, weaving and creating frustration. A glancing blow to a shoulder sent him reeling to the floor. Thug seized the opportunity to floor-drop onto him; however, The Shadow darted quickly between his legs, engaging two round objects by head-butting them as he made it through. Before the agony groans were loud enough, he had jumped onto Thug's back and pressed a pressure point in his neck with a solid index finger. He was out for the count. The crowd were stunned. The huge, hapless hulk lay prostrate on the floor. It took eight staff members to remove him from the ring. The Shadow didn't celebrate the victory. The less attention he received the better.

'How about that!' yelled the startled announcer.

The crowd were silent. The betting ring was in meltdown. The bookies looked foolish. They had made a fortune and the crowd were upset. The favourite was pole-axed by an underfed opponent. There was a mad scramble to place bets on The Shadow's next bout, against him. The crowd didn't believe that beginner's luck existed past one bout. Their confidence had returned via their wallets.

Davidia wondered also how it was possible that someone so small could beat someone so big in a physical encounter. Where was grandma? She knew she was in one of her memories, but had no idea where grandma was. Nothing she could see gave her any indication. As far as she was aware, she was the only female in the arena. A toilet break beckoned. That was an unexpected obstacle. There was no way she could enter the female toilets in a totally male environment. She took the plunge and bravely entered the men's toilets. Fortunately, the crowd had eyes on the bouts and she was not observed. The line of men's urinals reminded her of horses being led to drink. A cubicle was free. She dashed in and as quickly as she could completed her business. As she was about to exit, in the cubicle next to her she noted a frilly pair of pants around two quite attractive ankles. The walls between each cubicle had a perving height, if one was so inclined. She looked again and, like a magician's deft of hand, they had disappeared. In their place was a pair of black leggings similar to what she saw The Shadow wear. Both of them exited simultaneously, both in theme dress, and the shock of seeing each other caught their breath. It was a deadly moment for both. Discovery. Davidia sensed something. Her staff rod became heated. The Shadow didn't say a word. There was something quite feminine about him. Davidia placed a hand out for a grasp. It was not reciprocated. She then took a punt.

'Is that you, Michelle?'

Suddenly, The Shadow took a step backwards not knowing what had happened. It was impossible to know who she was. The game was up. She would be booted out of the competition arena and suffer some serious damage for falsely impersonating a male. A crisis had arisen. Davidia knew she was female. It felt right.

'I'm a female too,' she risked saying. 'Your secret is safe with me as I hope my secret is safe with you.'

The Shadow felt relief.

'No one must know. Why are you dressed in theme? No one else is.'

'It's a long story. We better leave here in case we get questioned for loitering. Good luck with your next bout.'

The girls exited safely without any revealing or embarrassing questions. The Shadow readied for the next bout. Davidia resumed to her viewing station. The din was almost unbearable. There would be a few visits to the hearing specialists after the day's entertainment had completed. The airwaves were awash with anger. The announcer strode forward once again and introduced the next match. The air was tense. Nobody left their seat no matter the duress to do so.

'In the red corner we have The Arm Breaker who has won his last ten bouts within time and each by a knockout in, would you believe it, the first round.' The announcer drawled out the introduction, creating mild hysteria. 'In the blue corner,' he looked over sheepishly, wondering what word to elicit from his personal dictionary, after all, this was part theatre to describe the newly discovered elf, 'we have The Shadow, who surprised us all with his jungle animal movements.' The crowd booed. Poor losers didn't accept failure too well.

'You'll be minced in seconds,' yelled a crowd comedian.

'Smash his face and break both arms,' was another comment.

'Kick him in the nuts and pulp his miniscule brain,' said another angry arm-waving crowd bully.

It was full of them. No one wanted The Shadow to win. The crowd didn't care if any injuries sustained were life-threatening. They wanted blood and a return on their rock-solid investment. Speculation was for the losers whoever they might be. The Shadow sized up his, or was it her, opponent, now that we know that it's grandma under there. The Arm Breaker wore the largest pair of boxing gloves, each the size of a pillow. It was doubtful if they were packed with soft eiderdown. He moved forward, took the regulation boxer's punching bag stance and stared at The Shadow, who smiled. His southpaw stance was a conundrum because his left-hand wore a delicate glove with exposed fingers that if it hit The Arm Breaker, it would crumple into a mass of broken bones. It was the smile that undid him. The crowd were delirious with revenge, that they didn't see the delicate subtle facial movement which was enough torment for The Arm Breaker. He wondered if he was fighting a sissy. He became enraged and swung a hay maker from the bleachers. It caught The Shadow in the guts fair and square. Was it over already? The Shadow cleverly feigned the pain and grimace, but had moved in the direction of the fist's momentum and grabbed it with his body and swung like Tarzan Of The Jungle on a fat, thickish menacing vine with a huge bulb at the end. He was lobbed to the other side of the ring like a trapeze artist and landed on all fours. He growled like a jungle cat. He was in theme. His prey turned with spittle dribbling from its distorted lips. The Shadow felt the pain of the punch, but camouflaged it well. He darted around the ring like a Peter Pan fairy, leaping, cartwheeling, rolling and tumbling like a spongy ball. The crowd were incensed at the stupid antics. The Arm Breaker roared and beat his own chest. He couldn't beat The Shadow because he was too quick. Suddenly, he ran with rage at The Shadow. He thought that he was being treated with disrespect – he was, but who cared. A fight is not a tea-party with plastic cups and four-year-olds, even with niceties. The Shadow moved sideways and in doing so, brought up a left fist that thundered into The Arm Breaker's six-pack, which had recently blown out to a keg. The ripple effect of disturbing his guts stopped him momentarily. The crowd roared. This was real action.

The Shadow smiled again. Mind you, it was all in the eyes. An enraged male huffed and puffed. The Arm Breaker took the boxing stance again and poked out a few lethal jabs menacing The Shadow's face, hoping to pummel it into submission or at least land a telling blow. Many glancing blows bounced off The Shadow. It was apparent that The Arm Breaker was winning the war. The Shadow seemed to be tiring. At the next blow that missed, The Shadow grappled his huge opponent and their heads almost banged together. The Shadow whispered in The Arm Breaker's ear.

'You swing like a girl.'

He then bit his ear. It was a superficial cut, but in a hysterical state anything was possibly said.

'The Shadow bit off his nose. You cruel bastard!' yelled an irate, visually-misinterpreted patron.

Whilst the crowd abuse worsened, The Shadow once again applied the pressure hold. Calm pervaded the ring. The Arm Breaker momentarily tottered back and forth acting like an inflatable human. The crowd swayed with him. Bang. He thumped the floor with an angelic look as if he was relieved the bout was over. It wasn't heaven where his mind was. The Shadow had won again. The crowd bayed for his blood. How dare the elfin-size bastard beat their selected champion of the day? Their pockets hurt more than their abuse. The Shadow was ushered from the ring with bodyguard protection. Everyone was livid, except The Shadow and Davidia.

'How about that!' yelled the announcer.

'How about bloody what? The fight's rigged. It's not possible a person that small could decimate a giant.'

The crowd were obviously biased in their assessment. The facts are the facts.

Davidia had watched in awe. Gee, grandma was good. She visited the change rooms where huge, smelly, sweaty men went through their processes. It was too late to stand on moral ceremony. There were so many battered body parts present. Whatever was sighted didn't affect grandma. He/she was one tough cookie. The Shadow sighted Davidia and feigned disinterest. She walked over to Davidia.

'Get out of here. It's too dangerous for you. They can smell fear and anything feminine.'

'Then why can't they smell you?' asked Davidia.

'I'm covered in oils and male body products. You aren't. Quickly, you have attracted the attention of The Mongrel.'

A huge male headed toward her. Davidia steadied herself with her staff rod. Slirander felt the tremors through the stone floors covered in male mess. She was ready to rod someone. The staff rod became red hot.

'What are you doing in here? Take off your stupid costume. No one who isn't a competitor can be in here.'

He put his hand out to grab Davidia. She raised her staff rod as a defensive barrier. The Mongrel touched it and received third degree burns to his hand. The expletives matched the audience's earlier efforts. Davidia fled to safety back to her viewing station. Fortunately, The Mongrel had fought earlier and lost, otherwise he would be disqualified by injury. The Shadow kept to himself, careful not to engage in male banter, or be prematurely bullied by others who were all sore losers. His final opponent sat sullen, withdrawn and morbid, biting his fingernails in anxiety. His mental state was awash with uncertainty about how to defeat The Shadow and acclaim the audience's appreciation and adulation. Was it to be that someone had finally defeated the shrimpish male? It was all conjecture. Grandma sat silently. He knew his unpopularity had reached fever pitch. Would he make it out alive? Self-preservation was more important than a lynch mob wanting a piece of you, so a plan was formulated. The fight wasn't to be rigged, but what other name could it be called?

Grandma was never going to leave the boxing rooms in one piece if victory was his. The change rooms were emptied except for the two final protagonists. The Shadow walked over to The Axe Head who almost quivered in fright at the approach. It was fortunate he wasn't seated on a rounded toilet pan otherwise it would have been filled.

The Shadow leant over and whispered something in his ear. It definitely wasn't asking for a date. A nod, cessation of finger biting, sitting up straight and a smiling growl came from the change rooms. The whole auditorium shook. It was on, the final. No one knew what The Shadow had suggested. This time, the mad crowd had switched betting allegiances. It was time to bring home the bacon, baby.

The announcer grasped the microphone for one last time.

'How about that!' he roared.

The sound-led crowd were at home in their jungle.

'In the red corner we have Axe Head, who has never left an opponent standing upright with their head intact.'

The crowd roared again. If anyone was uptight with domestic issues today, they were released as a therapeutic medical marvel.

'In the blue corner we have The Shadow, who has beaten the best so far. Will his persona be revealed after the fight?' The crowd continued with the deafening din.

'Blunt his blade,' yelled an enthusiastic bet changer.

'Give him a swing and a miss,' called out another big bodies betting deserter.

It seemed the money was on The Shadow. It also seemed a huge disaster was only one bout away. The fighters eyed each other as if a stare could actually hurt. The Axe Head grimaced, not in pain, but in what happens if he wins? Will he be skinned alive? The Shadow didn't care. His escape plan was sorted. No one knew what it was and until a moment ago, neither did the author. She looked toward Davidia. What a great fall person and patsy she'd make. Did this mean that Davidia would become the target of dissent, but at what personal risk? Not all grandmas are nice all of the time. Well, she wasn't really Davidia's grandma, so any risk to anyone else was worth a shot to save your own skin. Davidia's staff rod began to glow. It meant danger. Davidia couldn't release it. It felt like an arm extension. The ding of the bell diverted all attention to the championship match between the Chopper and the Elf.

A ten-second circle of set-up, then The Shadow launched a barrage of actual punches, mostly right-handed, into The Axe Head's ribcage. He lurched backwards on unstable jellied legs as he absorbed the power hitting. He thought that the little chap can certainly hit hard. He rallied to foil another onslaught. He lunged forward and slapped The Shadow so hard, he rolled over the canvas causing skin burns on his buttocks. The crowd didn't yell so hard this time because their adopted thug was now The Shadow. They thought that their investment was shrinking. It was, but they didn't know it. The first round was a game of follow the leader and hit me if you can. The bell rang to end the round. The crowd weren't actually gripped with excitement; however, it was underwhelming.

'How about that!' the announcer yelled again to generate crowd enthusiasm.

'How about fighting?' someone yelled.

'My pet chook with one leg could hit harder than that,' yelled another.

There was a large group of unhappy punters ready to biff anyone if a brawl erupted.

The bell for round two rang out.

'Go get him,' said a supporter, but for whom?

The Shadow knew that it had to be this round or not at all. He checked his coordinates for Davidia and calculated the distance between them via the swinging ringside light. After a few tepid efforts at fighting, The Shadow did his jump on the back and had his finger prepared for pressure application. Instead, he missed his mark and poked The Axe Head in the eye. The crowd booed loudly.

'Fight fair,' they yelled.

The Shadow whispered, 'It's time.'

The Axe Head pretended to topple over and just before he did,

The Shadow grabbed the overhead light. He ran to one side of the stage and used The Axe Head as a launching ramp, swinging like Tarzan back and forth. His agility was mesmerising. Before anyone realised the truth of the matter, he had managed to swing near Davidia and landed next to her. In a flash, he pulled off Davidia's head disguise and disappeared over the back and exited the building.

'What a coward,' said Davidia, incensed at being unfrocked as a female and grandma running out on her leaving her to face the mob alone, well almost.

This meant that Axe Head had won the bout via disqualification of The Shadow and the punters all lost their money. No one was happy. Even the announcer had a final, 'How about that!' before the mob headed Davidia's way. She sensed immediate danger. For her there was no escape. The crowd had her surrounded. They were furious that a female had been present in their midst. They hoped she wasn't a reporter, anyway. The expected headline next day would read something like, 'Tragic accident at fight.'

'Get back,' she yelled, 'or you'll be sorry.' She was clutching at strength sentences. It was a defence mechanism.

'Or what?'

'Just you see.'

At that moment, her staff rod, which had been glowing red for a while, turned white hot and spat out darting sparkles which burnt when landed.

'That's a bloody sparkler. It can't hurt anyone.'

That brave punter tried to wrest the staff rod from Davidia. It spat again and he received serious degree burns and was flung backwards into the crowd. He had received a mild electric shock. Slirander was warming up. There was no time for any more pleasantries. A huge shaft of light streaked from the top of the shaft, momentarily blinding everyone. In a flash, it disappeared and so had Davidia and Slirander. The boxing crowd were left financially stranded by grandma. She had also endangered Davidia. Her thoughts of a gentle loving grandma were becoming distorted and coloured.

There was no sign of grandma.

*

'That council meeting has been going a while,' said Slirander as she fiddled with the black and white memory ball that Pole had recently handed to her.

'I feel that I've missed something. Have I been anywhere recently? I'm sure I have.'

Davidia wasn't convinced that she'd been there all the time. Hadn't she experienced another grandma memory?

'I haven't noticed,' said Slirander.

'Did your grandma ever … ?'

Davidia couldn't remember at that exact moment what it was she had forgotten.

'I've been waiting for Pole to return from the meeting.'

Davidia shook her head.

Now, what was it?

7   THE DECISION

'Our memory structure has recently been interfered with. Those two new memory intruders have upset the memory balance and our ability to carry out our duties as we should,' said the head memory councillor, who spoke slowly and deliberately to the crowd who absorbed the severity of the comments.

'Does anyone know how they managed to arrive here? Has someone had a horrific memory experience that invited them? Whatever the reason, I feel that our community isn't safe whilst they are here. We can't have distorted memories which aren't kept in the format that they were received. That isn't our job.'

'I had a thunderous headache when I ate my last memory. It misbehaved so badly I almost choked eating it,' said a crowd member.

'What should we do about them?' asked another.

A few murmurs could be heard. The memory keepers were public servants of the mind. They performed by rote. It was obvious that the girls were an unintended problem. Pole listened intently. He rose to speak, but never got the opportunity to express his opinion. The rainbow-coloured Pollital structure shook involuntarily. Had a mental earthquake erupted? Had everyone present shed too many leaves simultaneously causing the ground to shudder, or had an unexpected surprise arrived amongst them?

The Pollitons wandered outside to see what the interruption was. Everything seemed normal in Pollital. It was a strictly regimented existence with all this memory storing; however, rarely did anything disrupt their efforts. Perhaps today something had occurred that was unexpected. They returned inside to determine the outcome of Slirander and Davidia. It wasn't going to be nice. It was decided that it was far more important to continue storing memories, which far outweighed the importance of standing for any interruptions. The girls' fate was sealed. They too would now become a permanent memory for others who had known them to this early stage in their lives. They had no idea there were plotters against them. Pole was disappointed. He enjoyed meeting a future memory from those that he stored. Now that situation would close and he would return to his duty. He sighed heavily.

*

'Throw it higher,' encouraged Davidia.

The girls were tossing memory balls to each other as they waited for Pole to return. When he saw them playing catch, he was furious. He almost ran, but settled for a quick walk toward them.

'Stop that immediately,' he yelled from both mouths.

'We were being gentle,' oozed the tepid excuse by Davidia, having been caught out displaying childish tendencies.

'It's too dangerous. You have no idea what you might unleash if it isn't eaten and stored correctly. Once, another memory-keeper misbehaved and those unleashed memories were lost forever. The owner of them suddenly forgot those precious elements. It's a huge responsibility we carry. Somewhere in here we have stored some of your memories already, which you can recall at any time. Don't ask. They are not here in grandma's memories.'

'So far there's been nothing to fear,' said a defensive Davidia.

Slirander had felt a movement in her aura. She detected uneasiness within Pole like he was afraid to tell them something.

'How did the meeting go? Is there anything of interest for us?' questioned Slirander.

Pole shut both mouths in defence of blurting out the truth. He shuffled on his feet. It wasn't a dance. 'What to do? What to do?' he muttered. His moustache of eucalyptus leaves rose and fell on a lip hinge as his airwaves were tortured for a response which he didn't want to pass on. Eventually, he knew the truth must come out because every memory is an exact truth of that memory owner's thoughts.

'You are *persona non grata*. The memory council voted that you must either return to your own world, or if kept here, you will wither and disintegrate without ever producing another memory of your own. We don't possess in our world any of the sustenance that you need. Sorry, that's it. What to do? What to do?'

A weary Pole stood before them. He appeared deflated.

'Not welcome. What a lot of rubbish. We are two fine young girls anyone would be proud to be friends with. Let me see your memory council. I'll explain a few home truths.'

Davidia had kicked her thought-overflow bucket and was ready to fly the verbal flag at anyone. Not welcome, indeed! Well, there was one occasion when at school she was invited by another girl, who had eyes on a matching male, to her home for the afternoon. It was to be a special girl's chat about male personas at school and how to catch their interest. Unbeknown to Davidia, the other girl had invited two young men, fellow students as well, to play the latest video games on the market. It was a carrot a male couldn't refuse. They arrived, rang the doorbell, gained entrance and oh, to find the parents were out. The two males saw Davidia and immediately the other girl had the ice freeze flowing. They paid Davidia the attention that she thought was rightfully hers. The afternoon was short and ended with trepidation about whether the other girl would ever speak to her again. Welcome one moment, unwelcome the next. What to do? What to do?

The atmosphere was tinged with sadness at being rejected. It was more annoyance for Davidia. Slirander had a less emotional outburst bubble. The scenario is to now decide, before it is thrust upon them, what to do? what to do? That decision came soon enough. A group of senior memory-keepers approached them. They all shuffled at the same pace. There wasn't a hill to climb to slow their progress. The memory-controller had a fungi beard instead of a leaf one. Age and time had allowed it to flourish. They stopped. The girls put down the memory balls and waited for deliverance. Whatever the outcome, Davidia was prepared to fight it all the way for grandma's memories.

'Are these the tall objects that are causing concern?' said the memory-controller.

'And what objects are you?' said a terse Davidia in response.

'We are the memory-keepers and it has been decided that you need to leave grandma's memories. You are ruining history.'

'No, we're not. We're learning history. Isn't that what memories are for, to recall historical events in all of our lives?' Such a clever response.

'That's true, but usually it is done outside of being in a memory. In here you tamper with the truth. In the outside world, memories are related by the giver of them whether they are true or not. We don't judge what we are given, we keep them. Not every memory has a need for recall and over time many disappear, lost in the void of a person's mind. So, what is given to us must be kept in its pristine form, otherwise memories are just a distortion if it is allowed to mess with them from the inside. That would be too dangerous. Nobody would ever again have a real memory.'

Davidia and Slirander nodded at the wise words of wisdom.

They only wanted to understand grandma for their thesis. Slirander spoke.

'We are in my grandma's memory. We are tracing family history so we are more knowledgeable about her life. There are many missing gaps and we want to fill a couple of them for my parents' sake. Distortion isn't our end game.'

The memory-controller had never experienced dialogue of such sense before because the girls were the first ever and only memory visitor that he had met. Even with good manners and logical explanations said with humility, it was still an impossibility to stay. The memory die was cast. It could not be altered.

'You must still leave, regardless of your goodness. We hope that all your intentions are good. Seize them.'

'You're just a puny shrub,' yelled Davidia, with an elevated voice. 'You'd burn well on our open fire.' Someone was angry, which wasn't assisting the cause. 'If you land one twig on me, I'll snap it off.'

'Davidia, calm down,' said Slirander. She didn't want a forest fire.

'How dare they arrest me? I've broken no laws.'

'Unfortunately, we have. We turned up in grandma's memory. That in itself is a mental misdemeanour.'

'I'm not going anywhere.'

Suddenly, Pole rushed forward with a very small, yellow coloured ball. It looked delicious, possibly mango flavoured. It was hand size. He threw it to the girls and, naturally, there was a spat over who caught it. They were such a competitive pair. Davidia snatched it. Her nails scratched Slirander's hand. Her involuntary slap sent Davidia reeling in surprise. The yellow coloured ball bounced erratically with excitement at being tossed so high. It didn't return.

*

'Treat the gentlemen with respect. Remember, that every small whim must be attended to. Be attentive. Listen to what they say because to them it's important, but to us it's income. Make them feel at ease. Never rush and whatever service is performed, do it with good grace and manners. We aspire for repeat business. That way we will all keep our employment.'

The madam of the establishment was training the new employees in the art of emotional income massaging. During the Second World War business entrepreneurial opportunities were rather limited, so a thriving personal experience service was formed to make ends meet. Imagination and ingenuity were born again and again and again.

*

The street frontage of an old building was painted in bright red with a huge slogan emblazoned across it. It was called "A Department Store for One Stop Shopping". The public was appalled that such an eyesore could exist in their city. It was the significance of the colour often found in gender attire that caused the furore. The public thought that it was a specialty shop for small parcels no decent woman would be seen purchasing. It was assumed it was a men's only establishment full of products not normally considered for sale to the female population; however, it did strike interest. The misconception was the colour. Public outrage flourished. The newspapers were full of offensive attitudes to the building. After a week of verbal carpet criticism, the owners couldn't understand what all the fuss was over. It really was a department store as advertised. The colour was an unfortunate choice. When the truth was revealed, there were a lot of red newspaper staff faces that matched the building that they had abused in print. It had all been one huge mistake in selecting the colour. The owners decided to paint it light beige, which blended perfectly into the streetscape. What was all the misinterpreted fuss about? The colour red, establishment and other indicators could register a certain business profession where privacy was important.

*

Davidia found herself outside a small shop front with an advertisement for pleasure seekers. She thought that it was a clandestine travel agency for adventurers. It was further down the street from the previous red building, but did anyone notice? The building wasn't attractive. The putty around the glass windows seemed temporary at best. The glass was frosted with a myriad of scratch marks across its surface in a splatter pattern as if someone was imprisoned and tried to scratch their way out. The leadlight colouring above the door had faded. It was too tall to peer through. It had the feeling of unpleasantness. There must have been a reason that she had landed there. She didn't have long to wait.

A young woman dressed in a neck-to-ankle waistcoat with threadbare sleeve-ends, and hemline-wear with trauma and greyness often associated with cemeteries, walked by with a brisk gait and an infectious smile toward her. If it was a real "disease", then everyone should have one. The daylight was more pleasant in grim times when a smile glides past. She stopped, spotting Davidia staring in the window, or at least trying to, thinking she's young to go travelling alone. Perhaps she's lost?

'Are you seeking something?' asked the young woman.

Davidia fidgeted. Was she? She wasn't sure what it was though.

'Is this a travel agency? I like travelling.'

'This isn't the type of place for young girls.'

'What sort of place is it? It seems mysterious.'

Above the leadlight window was a red light-bulb which wasn't switched on. It blended nicely on the unnoticed scale. At night; however, it lit the doorway so no one would trip and be the subject of public litigation. This section of the street, Davidia noticed, was less prestigious than further along. Foot traffic was almost absent during daylight, but during the evening many patrons visited the area. Were they all lost too? The red light acted as a guiding star, like a compass point indicating a direction. The young woman was about to enter the premises. She had a key. Maybe it was an art gallery of some sort.

'Excuse me, I have an appointment. Nice meeting you.'

The door was opened, closed and Davidia was left in the street pondering. Across the road was a fish and chippery fuelling the airwaves with fatty smells, delicious vinegar aromas and the inevitable fishy scents. Davidia didn't dare touch the sides of the doorway. It had a greasy slime layer. As she pushed the door, a small bell tinkled. An older-aged male with a greasy apron, huge moustache and a Santa paunch greeted her.

'I have no time for beggars. Please leave,' he said sternly.

That's ridiculous, thought Davidia. Me, a beggar? A bugger occasionally, but definitely not a beggar. She took affront.

'Sir, I am no beggar.'

'You are wearing beggars' clothes. Can you pay for your order, that's if you can make one?'

'I can certainly pay my way,' she replied indignantly.

She rummaged through her pockets in her jacket only to discover that they all had holes. Her shoes had exposed toes and the heels were almost worn out. The old coat draped over her was riddled with running threads, burn holes and not a decent stitch to hold it together. Davidia was surprised that she was so appallingly dressed. At home, her present outfit would be binned as unusable rubbish or rags to wash the family cars. In the current times, any clothing was valued due to its scarcity.

'No money, eh?'

It was looking dire. She had no funds to pay for anything. How would she survive if flat broke? There wasn't a solution staring at her at present; however, there was a suggested solution she could be staring at across the road that she was oblivious to. Conditions were harsh. It was getting late in the day. She was alone. Where was her friend, Slirander? She felt abandoned.

'Can I sit here for a while? A friend of mine works at the travel agency across the street. I'll wait here until she comes out.'

'Do you work at the travel agency?'

'Not yet. I'm new to the area. They might offer me employment via my friend.'

'Let me know when you start. We could work something out.'

Davidia felt the sudden interest in her well-being quite odd. Are all men strange at times? Her hair hadn't been washed for some time and had entwined together like rat's tails. A hairclip was hidden amongst the unkempt mess. There was nothing else up there in her dirty follicle forest. She unclipped the hairclip and in doing so, pricked a finger. The small amount of pain was ignored at the euphoria of actually possessing something that she owned. Warmth generated around her body as if a blanket had been thrown over her as reassurance that she wasn't alone. She felt that Slirander was near. The hairclip began to open and shut in the palm of her hand. Was it in Morse Code? Davidia watched it carefully, hoping it wasn't dangerous. She tried to close it and it latched onto a finger. Its grasp was unbreakable.

'Who's that whispering in my ear?' she said.

It wasn't a lost flea or fly trying to escape, but rather more of a droning hum. Sound generation was understandable.

'Be careful. This town is dangerous. Selecting the right friends is crucial.'

'Is that you, Slirander?'

'Be alert. Select your friends carefully.'

'I know it's you.'

'Select your friends carefully.'

'I always do. What are you on about? I know how to choose friends. You're one.'

The hairclip released its hold. Davidia rubbed the indented digit, returning it to its normal shape. There, perfect hands once more. The shopkeeper was studying Davidia and was already building his travel dossier on her. Nothing was mentioned about legal age or poor selection of future job choice.

It was nearing dusk.

A dull, red light across the street awoke. It flickered for greater impact.

The foot traffic in the area seemed to be busier with a definite absence of females. This must be the business end of the street, the Wall Street section. Davidia noted that the travel agent began to receive adventure travellers as the sign said. Suddenly, the front door opened and out strode the "friend" that Davidia had met earlier. She wondered if she could be grandma because she hadn't met anyone else who fitted the description. Before she had disappeared, Davidia dashed across the road and accidentally bumped into her due to her haste. Both fell onto the pavement. Davidia's coat flew open to reveal a young woman in her prime. That meant nothing to Davidia, but her friend noted its attributes and immediately summed up its advantages. Both got up, brushed off any dirt. It didn't matter, their coats camouflaged it anyway.

'Aren't you the girl that I met earlier?' said the young woman.

'Yes. I was thinking of a travelling adventure when we met.'

'Have you ever travelled before?'

'No. My parents have been rather strict on education coming first.'

'What age are you? I think there might be an opportunity to travel.'

'I'm eighteen,' lied Davidia. She was mature for her age. 'I don't have any money and thought that there might be an employment opportunity because everyone knows that travel is a growth industry. Are there any jobs available?'

'Where are you staying?'

'Nowhere actually. This is my first day in town.'

'So, you don't have any friends here? Does anyone know that you are here?'

'I have one friend. I'm sure she knows where I am.' She fondled the hairclip.

The young woman liked what she saw. She thought that Davidia would be very suitable to an upmarket office situation and, at the moment, the travel office lacked a specialist. Davidia could become that person. Employment would be assured with bonuses and accommodation. Sleeping on the street wasn't a pleasant available alternative.

'Wait here for a moment. I remembered that I left something important at the office.'

The young woman returned to the travel agency. Five minutes later she emerged smiling. She signalled to Davidia to come forward. Across the street the shopkeeper waved and smiled. He flashed a ten-pound note. What a dickhead, thought Davidia. She didn't know how accurate she was in her quick assessment.

The travel agency door opened. A large male with the shape of a walnut greeted them politely. Nice manners are a good first impression. They entered a long dimly-lit corridor that stretched almost forever. The carpet was threadbare. The paint on the walls had exhausted its use and peeled everywhere. The many small rooms that interrupted the clean flow of the walls were numbered like prison cells. They were all shut. Davidia wondered what sort of travel agency had so many offices. It must be really successful.

Unfortunately, a door had inadvertently been left open. Davidia saw a naked man, a pile of clothing and a lady rushing around the room also naked, obviously to pick it up. Could it be his wife?

'Is this a laundry facility? I saw a man and a woman with no clothing in that room.'

'Laundry is one of the many services that we provide. It's too costly to wash elsewhere in town, so we assist our staff members as part of our employment contract.'

Further along, Davidia heard the repeated phrase, 'Oh, my God!'

'Are those persons praying?'

'Religion is sometimes taken too seriously, so we have introduced singing lessons, such as you heard, as praise to the Lord for use in Sunday sermons. Not every traveller sings to the same tune, but that one is a real specialty.'

Further along, other groans, moans and slapping sounds echoed from behind closed doors.

'It sounds like someone is ill.'

'That's our sound department perfecting sound effects for the local radio station for vampire hour. We have a special contract to scare travellers.'

Davidia was most impressed. If war was happening outside, it certainly had no effect on the successful business practice inside. A few moments later, a huge room beckoned entry. Its walls were well-padded like a mental health institution specialty room. Large couches oozed with deep felted pile and when brushed, it felt like sinking one's hands into pools of pure satin. It had a heavenly touch.

'Wow! What a beautiful room. What is it used for?'

'This is the staff lounge where all employees relax after their short exercise bursts.'

'Where's the office where the travel attendants sit to serve the customers?'

'Once you shower and freshen up, your new employment will commence. That room over there is yours. There is clean linen and spare clothes for you to wear. Please put them on. We'll talk further, shortly.'

Davidia was so excited at having a shower, fresh clothes and accommodation. Her new friend seemed nice to take her in with an employment offer. She entered her room. It had a shower in one corner and a large double bed, fully sprung. She bounced up and down a few times in girlish enthusiasm. Her new clothes were neatly laid out on the bed. When she picked them up to admire, she noticed that various items had holes in them where they normally shouldn't. It didn't tweak that she would be wearing erotic gear. It didn't look too bad. Shower first. The water was tepid with poor pressure. She just had sufficient time to complete a proper wash including hair when someone entered the room. She peered from behind the shower curtain. It was a male. It wasn't the shopkeeper from across the road. This one was well-presented with a thin tie, tight pants, pointed-toe shoes and a cigarette that hung from a corner of his mouth like a dead slug. He sat on the bed. Davidia felt that her privacy had been invaded. She was naked and her clothes weren't within arm's reach.

'Excuse me, you shouldn't be in here, sir. This is a lady's room.'

'That's precisely why I am here.'

'Could you please leave so that I can get dressed?'

'I quite like it here.'

'Are you my employer? That young woman who brought me in here said that I would meet my employer. She's giving me a job.'

'I will be shortly too.'

'It would be better for us all if you left, let me get dressed and then we can talk terms, deal?'

'Sounds okay, but I'm willing to pay plenty. My wad is thick.'

He left. Davidia hurriedly dressed. She was incensed at her privacy invasion. She was going to sort it out and meet that young woman to explain what had just happened. She didn't think that he was the adventure-traveller type. The clothes she put on made her look cheap. She didn't care, it was problem solving that she was after. She walked into the lounge room and noticed it was full of men and women in various stages of undress. There seemed to be a large staff employed. Travelling was a popular pastime, but to have so many in the one place was a surprise. Were they stranded or just waiting for their particular trip to depart? She walked up to one couple and asked,

'Are you taking a trip?'

'It's the trip of a lifetime.'

That sounded plausible. Suddenly, her hairclip began opening and shutting as it perched on the side of her head. It fell off. She caught it. Once again, the danger warnings whispered into her ears. Slirander was warning her. Incidentally, where is grandma? She had to be here somewhere. Davidia was in her memory.

On the other side of the room there was grandma, or was it, fully-clothed, glasses resting on her nose and writing something down. It must be her booking itinerary. She seemed very busy. Davidia approached.

'I had a male stranger in my room. I felt uncomfortable. Why was he there?'

'It is so that he would become a fellow travelling companion.'

'He was too old and smokes. Where are the people my age? Are they on the same trip as me?'

'You are travelling solo.'

'How come I'm doing a solo trip when I only asked for employment with the opportunity to travel?'

'Give me a moment.' The young woman turned away.

'When do I start my new job?'

'You almost did.'

'No, I haven't. You haven't provided me with any training or told me which desk I am to sit at. Where's my office?'

Davidia was standing near a mirror on a column and glanced at her reflection. It bounced back at her in a curious manner. A young girl stood there in leggings, suspenders and a tight form-fitting top made from a see-through cotton design. She was dressed similar to Dr Frank N Furter from the Rocky Horror Show. She jumped in surprise. To the left or to the right, it didn't matter. In her haste to find the young woman, she had paid little attention to her new attire. Everyone else had. Eyes feasted, tongues wagged and wads of money had a growth spurt like many desires. Then it dawned on her. Maybe this isn't a travel agency after all, but a casting couch for movie moguls to assess new acting talent. What shows could she be in? Her mind was dizzy with expectations. The young woman returned to Davidia. That delightful smile she had seen earlier in the day had been distorted into a heavy scowl. Davidia was the innocent.

'Behave! You have been selected employee of the day and there are many people interested in travelling with you.'

'I don't see any set-up for a travel agency in here. There's no desk or office. Why are all these people half-dressed? They aren't travelling in that condition, surely? This isn't a tropical rainforest and outside it's minus three degrees. I only asked for a chance at being a travel agent and not to be dressed up in clothes with missing sections as a rather thin version of Porky The Pig.'

A crowd of males encircled her. She was trapped. Would Slirander's grandma be involved in anything seedy? She had to know. The only question that undid grandma in her memory was mentioning her name, because it was impossible for her to know it as she had never met her in the real world. What else could she do?

'Michelle, can you please advise the going rate for an hour's effort?'

Davidia had finally twigged that she wasn't going to get a desk job in a travel agent, nor would she be travelling anywhere soon. Her excitement at employment had waned after re-entering the lounge room full of pretend swimmers in their one-piece clothing costumes. She gathered it was some sort of gala performance which she didn't particularly want to join. Grandma's eyes almost became Asian in appearance. Pain played dangerously behind them.

'Who told you my name? No one here ever uses their real name. This agency uses aliases to protect the staff.'

'It is Michelle, isn't it? A friend of mine told me.'

'I told you not to use my real name. You put lives in jeopardy by revealing that private information.'

A crowd of attentive listeners turned their heads toward the conversation, wondering why there was tension brewing. Fortunately, the level of sound was too low for others to have heard what had been said. It was assumed to be either a pay dispute, about working conditions, or room location. Davidia did present excellently for the intended purposes of the establishment; however, she didn't intend complying with that set of rules. She had her own agenda and her prospective employer wouldn't like them.

'Well, what's it to be, me telling everyone your real name, or you giving me a desk job? Better still, I have decided I no longer want to travel anymore. I am leaving. I need to collect my things first.'

Davidia whirled around so quickly to depart, the loungers all thought it was a mating display. They clapped and whistled and dreamt of a future encounter. She stormed off to the room she first visited to collect her rags and change into them. No sooner had she entered the room, when she heard the dreaded click of a door being locked. She was imprisoned and in a simple travel agency. She peeked through the keyhole to observe an angry scene involving the dead-slug smoker and grandma. She was convinced it was her. The stutter over the name said it all. Money had changed hands. It appeared that the dead-slug smoker had a huge wad and he believed that he had paid for certain rights.

Suddenly, Davidia's hairclip fell out of her hair again. She was getting sick and tired of replacing it; however, when she felt it this time, it was shaped as a door key. As the door was unlocked and the key was withdrawn, Davidia placed her key in it and it remained locked. Heavy pounding began. Davidia quickly changed into her rags and stood near the door. She saw a horribly taut face spitting real dribble a sponge would strain to hold. A male charged at the door. At the point of impact, Davidia opened the door and the hapless traveller flew past, landing on the bed. Davidia slipped through and relocked the door. Dressed in rags, she wasn't as appealing as before. She made directly for the corridor and hopefully to safety. Grandma rushed over only to receive a five-fingered sandwich providing her own red sauce. She landed bum down on the floor bruising her petite buttocks.

'Why, you little bitch,' she swore. 'I'll teach you a lesson. I'll rip your hair out.'

Training was over for the day. The corridor was dark as she ran toward the opening. Grandma was in hot pursuit. Then she remembered all those scratch marks on the front door that she had seen whilst outside. Reality dawned upon her. Maybe she will add to the patterns? She was almost there, when the huge walnut appeared as blockage. He was a turd in a large passage providing an impassable blockage no medicine could budge. Grandma was yelling rude words in a constant rage, sounding exactly like some of the behind-closed-door travellers. There wasn't any tour bus to catch today. It wasn't leaving the building. Davidia stopped short of being manhandled by the walnut. Grandma drew near.

'Please open the door,' said a breathless Davidia. 'I am no longer interested in travelling. It was a mistake to meet you, Michelle. I don't know for sure what multi-skilled operation you are running, but it definitely isn't travel because there are no customer service desks. Where could I sit? Besides, I'm almost sixteen.'

Grandma couldn't believe what she was hearing. Was this young girl so naïve as to not understand the establishment's purpose? She cleared her ears.

'We can't let you go. You will put us all at risk.'

Davidia thought that this isn't one nice granny. What would Slirander think if she knew the truth?

'It's time that I left. Please stand aside, otherwise I will put you through that glass door,' she said to the walnut.

He grunted, smiled, folded his arms across his chest and began to laugh so loud, a small tremor was created. Grandma dived at Davidia. Her hairclip was in one hand. She defensively slashed at grandma to defend her off and scratched the back of one hand. Her other hand let rip a flash upper cut into her solar plexus and forced any wind in her system out of the escape hatch between the two bruised buttocks. A young girl lay writhing on the threadbare carpet. She turned to the walnut who was still laughing.

'Little lady, that door is shut. Scratch your way out if you can.'

He picked up Davidia like a dust rag and stood her in front of the scarred door. It was triple glazed and impossible to bare-knuckle its collapse. David punched it, kicked it and wore down her once immaculately manicured nails, which was most upsetting, as she desperately tried to escape. She was nearly done. Then that hairclip caught her attention. Just like Slirander, it always wanted to be noticed. She took a few deep breaths.

'It looks like I've lost and you have won. Could you please look away as I say goodbye to the outside world? I need a moment of reflection. I'll return down the corridor after that.'

The walnut and a hurt grandma nodded in agreement. She was theirs. What a catch and future treat for their travellers. They both felt good about themselves.

A few tears welled up where she had poked herself in one eye. There was no need to overdo the damage. She dropped to one knee hiding the lower section of the glass panel from view. She withdrew the hairclip and scraped it over the glass surface. It bit, dispersing paint flecks and creating further patterns. She pressed harder. It bit again and again and again. Slowly, a circular groove appeared in the panel. Time was running out. The hairclip had acted as a glass cutter. Slirander, you genius!

'That's enough contemplation for the moment. Get up.'

Surely grandma hadn't recovered from her bout of stomach wind. Davidia had tried to press out the glass panel, but it needed greater pressure than she could exert. The walnut was the ideal candidate to give it a good kicking. In a moment of almost insanity, Davidia kicked the walnut in the shin. It had no impact. Her almost toeless shoes had no firmness. Once again, that incessant hairclip needed handling. The message was to bend down and place it between her toes as a toe knife, a very small one. Davidia stood up. She had to big-note herself, didn't she?

'Are you prepared for this?'

The walnut wasn't good at childish games. He let her have her way. He stood there waiting for the inevitable failure of a tepid foot prod. Imagine his surprise when Davidia kicked him with a potent weapon. The toe knife had penetrated his tough hide and instigated enormous pain. In his rage he ran at her and swung a tree trunk sized leg. She was agile as an elf. It missed. His foot landed on the scratched glass door panel and it splintered the glass, blowing a hole in the door. Davidia darted for the opening. She couldn't make it with the rag coat. She flung it to one side and escaped into the cold outside. It was pitch-black. The flickering red light could only identify a silhouette.

'That bitch,' screamed a seething grandma.

Her bonus might be cut after the loss of her prized traveller.

Davidia was cold and miserable as she sat down crying at her near incarceration. She thought that the next time that she travels, she'll book it online. The kind shopkeeper from across the road offered her a place of refuge. She took one look, suddenly turned and kicked him with the toe knife. It thudded into the wad of money he held in his hand as an inducement to enter. She withdrew her foot. It was pounds richer and even the cold didn't worry her because she could now feed herself.

Thank goodness she knew how to use a hairclip.

A hissing sound followed her. A bright yellow light lit up the street. A small yellow coloured ball was floating toward her.

She heard someone call, 'Catch!'

*

A crowd had gathered around the girls. It seemed that all of Pollital was there to witness an event. Davidia was displaying her stubborn streak. The Pollitons weren't unreasonable in their understanding that they had to leave grandma's memories. So far, the girls had interfered in a few points of memory. It was time to stop the potential for ruining many more. The crowd moved closer.

'Is that my hairclip?' asked Slirander.

'I suppose so. I must have borrowed it.'

'It's quite a useful item, isn't it?'

'It has its uses.'

Davidia hadn't told Slirander anything about the recent memory. The danger associated with each new experience was becoming more severe and she began to wonder if another one would lead to a more serious situation. She had been fortunate to date. A loud chant erupted. It was the Polliton's eviction chant. It was simple, silly, some would say stupid and nonsensical, but effective.

> To do, to do, to do is to do,
> To don, to don, to don is to don't,
> To go, to go, to go is to go,
> To get, to get, to get is to get
> B bye, b bye, b bye.

The girls were suddenly immobilised. A large transparent film had them embalmed like a vegetable wrapped in rice paper. They experienced weightlessness as they floated slowly over the landscape to the drop zone from where they had originally appeared. The grass below was soft and welcoming, probably to a cow, but not for the girls. They were being dumped as unwanted memory garbage. Was this the end of their thesis research? They were sure that there was much more to discover. It was hopeless to say anything angrily because they were sealed tight. Davidia was incensed at the treatment. If she wanted to be so tightly hugged, it had to be by a male. Nothing else should get this close.

They stopped, hovered and were then lowered to the ground. Their cocoon only opened from the bottom and they slid like two large slugs into the soil. They saw Pole. Was that a tear he shed? Then complete darkness and a gentle thump. They were back in grandma's room of waving hands except this time it wasn't the palms that waved, but the back of the hands. Davidia brushed the back of her hand over the wall before the correct print was found. Once again, she passed through the waving hands wall followed by Slirander. They were now in grandma's secret place intact. The waving hands wall all began to clap. Davidia took a bow again. Still no flowers.

There must be more to this grandma. It seemed that their journey had been cut short.

'Which wall next?' asked Davidia.

'That one,' said Slirander.

8 Hessian

'Why pick the one covered in hessian? It doesn't look that inviting,' said Davidia.

She thought that the other stone and slate walls would be more interesting. They seemed to have depth and strength, which she understood were some of grandma's qualities learnt from her memory experiences to date.

'See how it flutters, yet there is no breeze in here. It's alive, but it isn't,' replied Slirander.

When she was a child, her grandma regaled her with fantasy stories of strange beings and places. Her imagination was a minefield of ideas which related well and some not so well. A frightened little girl often crawled into bed under the covers hidden in a world of darkness dreaming of fabled monsters not found in any modern-day children's books. Where did she get them from? Grandma would tuck her in by running her hands lovingly over the covers, ending with a couple of soft pats and caring words. That was one of Slirander's memories that she had rediscovered whilst researching grandma.

'Are you sure? There must be a breeze in here somewhere. Inanimate objects don't have a built-in motion motor. They need something else to move it. I'll show you.'

Davidia took five steps toward the wall, yet she wasn't any closer. She did it again and still hadn't gained a millimetre. It appeared that the environment, in this case the hessian wall, was moving whilst she was stationary. Was that possible? She didn't believe it was so. She turned to Slirander with her arms outstretched in surrender.

'I know that it's hard to believe. That key must be the most difficult of them all to find. Grandma never told a secret, so we'll have to locate it ourselves.'

Davidia decided to run at the wall. Failed. She tried to jump both forward and backwards. Failed. She crawled along the floor slithering like a snake in case there was a laser ray she had to crawl under. Failed. Slirander held her hands together as a bolster when Davidia put her foot in it and was catapulted forward in an attempt to jump over it. Failed. That damn wall hadn't moved, nor had Davidia made any impression on getting any closer. Her frustration was about to vent itself.

'What if it doesn't have a key?' asked Slirander.

'What do you mean that there's no key? There's got to be one. You said so yourself. I'm exhausted. There must be an easier way. Is there a map to this place? What about a remote?'

'Keep looking.'

'Keep looking,' mumbled Davidia.

She was angry at their lack of success. It was time to rethink their approach. Davidia stood back and studied the room once again. She scanned all walls carefully. Slirander walked around prodding and poking her fingers into and onto every wall surface, crevice, bulge, indent, undulation, feeling for that "found it" moment. Every centimetre had been touched in some way.

The floor received the same detailed treatment. Not a bloody clue was evident.

'This is doing my head in. Are you sure there is a key?'

'My grandma was so secretive. I assumed that there is one.'

'We've searched high and low and didn't even find a sniff of any key on the stone and slate walls, which makes me doubt that there is one, otherwise either of the other two walls would have opened. Why can't we get close to that particular wall only? There must be huge secret memories in there, if it's so well protected. I'll try once again.'

An insect suddenly flew past Davidia. She was standing as close as she could to the hessian wall that was allowed. She leant over, in a touching-your-toes moment, to avoid being the obstacle that flattened the flying pest. To her surprise, she couldn't straighten up again no matter how hard she tried. Temporary paralysis had gripped her body. She was now a letter C shape with both ends of the letter touching the floor.

'Slirander, come and help me. I'm stuck. I'm not imitating the Pollitons' height.'

'What did you do? Have you pulled a back muscle? You probably lack fitness to bend over like that. Here, I'll try and straighten you.'

No sooner had Slirander touched her friend's arm, she was thrust forcefully into the same shape. They were a pair of Cs, if anyone had seen them. They had to strain to look sideways at each other. What a predicament! They were temporarily disabled and both detested their new selves.

'What a bloody mess! This it totally, and I mean totally, stupid to be bent like an arch. It certainly strains the spine.'

'It only happened as soon as we made personal contact. There must be a message in it. Maybe there's an emotional connection with grandma.'

'If there was, I couldn't read the bloody thing from this position. I can't even stand, sit or move. I don't want to think what would happen if I was caught short.'

They were like two amusement park pieces stuck into the pine bark mulch at the local playground. They wriggled and wriggled, but were stuck hard and fast. In their emotive whinging and displeasure, neither had noticed that the hessian wall had slowly moved toward them.

'What's that tickling my back? Do you feel it?' Davidia asked.

'It's got a rough edge and is heavy. It smells like a bag of wheat chaff that you feed horses with. It feels close.'

After another moment, the hessian wall had consumed them into its secretive world. They were in. It felt different to a moment ago. The air had an edge. It was dark and gloomy in the landscape of silhouettes. It felt like an abandoned and deserted forest. The trees had a sadness about them. The predominant colour in this particular environment was rocket grey or unstable black. There was sufficient light to see their way around, but not too clearly into the distance. Their exit from this section of dreamtime was a small hessian covered, well-hidden cave behind the movable rocks. To relocate their exit, they had to trace the movable rocks' movements in the forest. Not an enviable task when you may be taken well away from them.

The girls hobbled, hunched over, into the forest of thin dark shapes. They still couldn't straighten up. What was the load they bore on their backs to cause the arching?

'This is no good for my modelling posture,' whined Davidia. 'My feet are dragging through the ground, ruining my new recently purchased footwear. What is this dreadful place? I don't think there are any good memories in here for grandma. No one is advertising to come and get a good memory.'

'I have heard that grandma had a period when she couldn't remember some time of her life. Mum and dad called it "The Missing". I don't know if it's true or not. I don't ever recall hearing about this place. I only met grandma properly when she was much older than a young girl. I wonder what happened in here.'

'For one thing, I'd bloody well like my back straightened. This is the pits being fifty per cent of my normal body height.' Davidia was bored with the smaller her.

'Now you are complaining. We're stuck for the moment. There must be a solution somewhere.'

'It won't be stuck on a billboard. There's probably none here. Have you noticed that we can observe the vegetation much more closely? Too bad I'm not going to be a botanist. We might have to eat it to survive.'

The girls fumbled their way along. It felt like they had walked hundreds of metres; however, they had only moved a few steps. Where were they? No life form erupted into any greeting. The thin, dark trees all stood singly and alone. Was it a forest of mirrors that gave the impression of a larger space?

'I'm exhausted. Now I know how a chook views the world, unpleasantly. I'm sitting down, if I can.'

Davidia made it to a small mound, rotund in shape, and attempted to sit down. The mound moved sufficiently for her to be unable to sit. She had to view the mound through her legs and reverse to it like parking a car. Because of her C shape, it was difficult to sit correctly and she could only perch her most valuable sitting asset on the edge. At least it relieved the pressure on the rest of her body. The relief was only temporary. The mound started to bubble like aerated chocolate. Davidia got quite the surprise. She fell off. Slirander had been watching and noticed that the mound had moved. Maybe it was home to a mobile animal.

'Get your fat arse off me,' said a belligerent, nasty-toned voice. 'You shouldn't be here. You're trouble.'

It spat a section of granule-sized rock at them. It littered the forest floor.

'Such rudeness. What's your problem? Too small, with an inferiority complex?'

'Not at all. That shape you have warns everything here to avoid you "less damnation befalls them".'

'How come then that we are the lucky ones to speak with you?'

'You touched me with those rounded shapes. See, I'm round too. We match.'

Davidia thought for a moment. There was ample time to think as long as she liked. She wasn't going anywhere. She did wonder where she was, though. Slirander verbally approached.

'Can you tell us where we are? Is this place a memory field?'

The mound thought also. How did she know what it was? Nobody had ever guessed that before. It had to carefully weigh up the contents of its verbal response in case its words released the dangers that may be underneath them.

'This is a memory field. Long ago, the Pollitons lived here and stored the memories of an individual. She had so many to store. A whole forest was designated for that purpose. I think it was grandma, yes, that's it, grandma. What a feisty, troublesome lot of memories. There was interference in the storage that blackened the minds of the Pollitons and they ended up here, buried but not forgotten.'

'So, this place is called Pollital then?'

The mound was stunned that the two odd shapes knew its name.

'Yes, this is Pollital. How did you know?'

'My grandma must have mentioned it,' said Slirander, coyly.

She didn't want to say that they had visited Pollital and could have caused the scene before them.

'You have a grandma. Isn't that a co incidence? This is the field of a grandma's memories. You could be related. How exciting to have a visitor. How did you get here? No one has ever visited before. You are a first and look at you, trouble already.'

'Are we standing amongst all of grandma's memories?'

'No one is sure all of them are in one place, but I'd suggest there are many here.'

'Are we able to visit them?'

'No. These have been sealed for safe-keeping. Nothing is to disturb them.'

'Surely there's no harm in locating one. We are doing a thesis on grandma's age and thought that some of her memories would be helpful,' said Davidia.

'Do not disturb anything. This is a treasured place. Interference with the past is a warning signal to the future. You have been forewarned. Do not disturb anything. I need to move.'

'Before you go, how do we become straight again? We normally stand upright and not bent over like this.'

'You certainly have the stance of an early practising, old-age individual. We don't know any name for it. Nothing in here has come in that format. Sorry, can't help.'

The mound became silent. They could be in a cemetery of dead thoughts or a forest of memories. The colour of the forest didn't worry them. There was the pressing problem of standing straight again. Where was the antidote to being arched?

*

'This is still the pits,' said an irate Davidia. 'I need to stand up. This bending over is really hurting my back.'

'Me, too,' said Slirander. 'There must be a solution in here somewhere.'

Her happy day wasn't all that happy. They were allowed into a memory section of grandma's memory and wondered if the pain they were experiencing was worth the effort. The scene around them didn't engender a happy memory period. It seemed all gloom and doom from their surrounds; however, perceptions can sometimes be misleading.

'Those tall, thin shapes might hold the answer. Remember those round coloured balls Pole ate? Each one stored a memory. There may be something similar in here. We just have to find it.'

The girls ambled forward until Davidia hit her head on a silhouetted tree trunk at its base. It didn't hurt because of the slow pace of movement.

'What now, another damn obstacle? Move or I'll kick you if I can.'

That was impossible, arched as she was. She would have to reverse up to the tree and use her heel as the weapon of possibility. Slirander joined her. All they could see was a variety of sinuous tree roots escaping into the soil. What to do? what to do? entered their minds. Were they alone? Was Pole using extra-sensory perception to contact them, or was it just an imaginary thought?

'Did you feel that thought?' asked Davidia.

'Yes. It felt like Pole was wanting us to do something, or was he warning us? Grandma's memories certainly aren't straightforward like how to look after a pet, or bake a cake, or wash the weekly pile of clothes. We need to find whatever it is that will guide us to what I don't know.'

'Let's sit down.' Davidia tried. She couldn't sit comfortably. 'I'll lie down instead.'

With her C-shape body, she lay up against the tree trunk but around its base. It was circular. Slirander did the same. Both were now on their sides on each side of the thin tree trunk. There was no such thing as inner sprung dirt. At least there was a moment's reprieve from backache. Instead, they now had side ache. Their bodies were becoming a whinging machine. As they struggled to get comfortable, their hands and feet touched momentarily, making a complete circle of contact around the thin tree base. They didn't feel anything except acknowledgement that their feet and hands had touched. They had unintentionally made a circuit.

'No, you don't. Get your filthy paws off me. I'll snot you in the kidney balls. I'm not to be molested,' yelled Davidia.

Two hessian hands had taken residence under her armpits,

which had been recently shaven, and started to lift her upwards. On the other side of the tree, the same thing was happening to Slirander; however, their feet remained on the ground. Their bodies were being slowly stretched and straightened. There was no pain and soon both girls were standing upright back to their normal occasionally belligerent selves. They couldn't believe it. The only marks left were a red rash where the rough-hewn hessian hands had held them tight. Whose were they? What had freed them? They looked around. No explanation was evident. What had happened to the tall, thin tree? They now stood higher than it. Were they in the land of Small Tall or Tall Small?

'That feels better. I'm myself again,' said Davidia.

'Thank goodness we've returned to normal,' said Slirander. 'I was feeling that grandma didn't like our intrusion into this section of her memory and we are to be punished for it, somehow.'

They still had difficulty believing that they were once again normal.

'You think that was amazing. Try this,' said a disguised voice. At least that's how it sounded.

The girls couldn't locate the source of the sound.

'Show yourself,' said Slirander this time.

She thought that she should be the front foot person in her grandma's memories. In this set of memories, she could participate as herself whereas in the previous set, she was a foil and support for Davidia. Also, in the earlier set, Slirander hadn't been born, but in this set she existed in the real world even though she was very young when the hessian set of memories were formulated.

'You can see me; however, I can't see me. I'm everywhere you both are. I permeate your total being. You have brought me back to life again. I hope it's worth it. I hope you find what you are looking for. Remember, a mirror reflects real life, but what does a memory reflect?'

'Are you our conscience?' said Slirander.

There was nothing further to see or hear. Davidia had also drawn a visual blank. Suddenly, their legs itched. The tall thin, or was it now the small tall tree, began growing its tree roots around their legs. Was it an escaping memory or a Polliton trying to be resurrected? The growth was sinuous, like veins. Before they could grab a proper leg hold, the girls bent over naturally this time with the possibility of returning to their full height and tugged at them. The dreadfully persistent twiggy roots weren't giving up without a struggle. Davidia tried to uproot a few. Was that a scream for help? They were becoming so bloody annoying the girls used a joint kicking strategy to release them. That didn't work either. It was as if the forces of evil lived in the soil. They didn't want to compost or be a buried memory. Soon they were almost covered and entombed in a tree root coffin where any insect, any form of bacteria and the thousands of specie of fungi would have a field day dissembling such huge life forms.

A treat like this was a rare opportunity. The entombment was almost complete. None of the tree roots had a nick, cut or any snapped roots during their growth. The final pattern was to be a facial turban in a circular python-like growth commencing at the base of the neck. It reached the girl's mouths. *Ce le vie!* It was *déjà vu* that tomorrow may never really come just as yesterday won't be repeated. Davidia's growth pattern was sightly quicker. Fertility had nothing to do with it. She was slightly shorter than Slirander.

When Davidia was a small child at kindergarten, she was in the sand pit playing by herself building the most magnificent imaginary castle where the prince and the princess would live happily ever after. Another little girl with an envious and misbehaviour streak came over and pushed over her castle. Davidia cried. All that effort lost in a moment. The other girl didn't care less. Davidia rebuilt her castle. This time the same naughty girl pushed Davidia instead. Her little fingers slipped upwards near Davidia's mouth. Instinctively, Davidia bit that set of five as hard as she could. The little girl screamed in agony. Her five little fingers had tooth indentations which took a day to disappear. Her castle wasn't destroyed and a lesson had been taught and learnt. Apparently, by year end the two girls were the best of friends. Go figure.

As the tree root began to cover her mouth, Davidia opened it and bit down so hard that the tree root snapped. She could have sworn she heard a cry. Another tree root became ambitious and Davidia bit that one in two also. At each attempt, the tree root found it impossible to shut her mouth. What a formidable weapon to attack! At the pain of losing its continuity, the tree root began to wither.

'Slirander, bite it when it gets near your mouth and break it in two. Mine has given up. It's releasing its grip. Hurry, you don't have much time.'

As a child she used to stuff dirt into her mouth, eat garden slugs, snails and any non-stinging flying insects. Tree twigs weren't really edible or pretend edible food; however, to save herself, she pretended she was a hungry termite and had a feed. The tree roots retreated in agony. Both were slowly released.

The tree that they had been standing around began to sink into the ground taking them both with it, tree roots and all. It was a memory tree and the girls had triggered its release by biting the tree roots. They were being sucked underground. The memory forest was real. It was over in seconds. Where had they gone and more to the point, was it possible to escape? Danger might begin with the letter D, but it can also have serious unfavourable outcomes. Had they triggered disaster, another D word?

*

'What an unpleasant feeling,' said Davidia. 'I feel that I have been raked by small clods of dirt as we were funnelled here.'

'It was a tight squeeze, wasn't it?' replied Slirander. She too had felt uncomfortable.

'What is this place? It seems to be a cemetery, or that's the vision created by those structures.'

'I don't believe that this is a real cemetery. I think it's the town of Tombstone. Grandma occasionally mentioned that she loved westerns and often talked about Cowboys and Indians. It must be this town. She described it to a T.'

'What would she be doing in a western town? She hadn't visited America, had she? Did the family know?'

'There are many missing areas of grandma's life and this could be one of them. Mum and dad often spoke of mystery as normal. My family is full of it.'

Had Slirander discovered one of those missing memories and was about to experience it? The girls noted that they were in western attire with leather coverings over dirty, dusty jeans which had pale cheek patches where they had often sat on a horse. A large hat hid their ponytails. They were both packing, when neither of them had ever used, let alone touched, a firearm. It was a six-cylinder *Colt 45* used for defence or attack, whichever worked for the owner. If confronted by a gun-toting hombre, they may have to use them. Perish the thought. They didn't walk with both thumbs stuck in their belt. They were two city slickers on a stage set in a western movie, or they had hoped they were. The drinking age was above their age limit. If they had wanted a drink, no moustached, unshaven, unwashed male would dance on ceremony in refusing them a drink, if they had wanted one.

'What's that odour?' asked Davidia, sniffing the airwaves of new smells.

Slirander didn't want to offend, but someone had to tell her.

'That's you.'

'It can't be. I've never smelt like that before.'

'You are in the West. Showering is at a premium.'

'Phew. I'm glad I didn't live in those times without my perfume team. Close encounters could be rather unpleasant. What are we doing here? Are we going to shoot someone, rope a horse, arrest a drunkard, drink in a saloon, or just look gorgeous in rough western clothing? I hope we are in a grandma memory. Tombstone by the sheer nature of its name doesn't engender a night club party atmosphere.'

'Something will turn up. It always does.'

Slirander searched for any indication that grandma was there somewhere. They swaggered down the main street past Slab MacMillans, the undertaker, The Gay Variety Saloon which served more than drinks and the Sherriff's office with a 'Howdy doody' to the sleeping law representative. It all seemed so ordinary. Even the horses look exhausted standing still. What a boring town. The most interesting item of discovery was a few children washing in a horse trough.

It was midday, twelve noon. The sun had positioned itself in the dead centre of the street. A hot trail of heated, agitated, dust ran through town. It was actually stationary, but indicated a danger marker for those intent on solving a dispute with weapons. That never ended well. The acid tongue of two young girls wasn't considered a dangerous weapon in those times. How things have changed in the modern world.

'Hey, you two with the ponytails, get off the street,' yelled a dude, standing on a porch outside the saloon.

He had a stalk of wheat dangling from one side of his mouth. It was a saliva manufacturer and when full it was spat into the dust which then rolled into a collective parcel of moisture. No one rushed anywhere near it.

'Why us, dear sir?' said Davidia, in character. 'I don't like no big boy pushing me around. Use your manners in front of a lady.'

'You're just goddam kids, for crying out aloud.'

'That may be so, sir, but I still like manners. Perhaps sir needs to be taught a lesson in how not to spit. It spreads germs and is such a disgusting habit.'

'Don't antagonise him, Davidia. Can't you see he's either spoiling for a fight, or else he's clearing the street for one. Don't make yourself a target.'

'He was so rude.'

They begrudgingly obliged to avoid being the centre of attention. They stepped up onto the boardwalk. Their hobnail boots thumped loudly as they walked in unison to their own rhythm. It could be the making of a soundtrack for a spaghetti western. They decided to enter the saloon where most reprobates and good citizens hung out, usually drinking, playing cards or changing clothes upstairs, pretending it to be a serviced apartment and unisex retail store. Two new women in town caused a stir.

'They look rather fresh,' drawled a patron, as he eyed them carefully.

'I reckon that pert little tail needs some taming,' whooped another.

'Wacha doin' in here, ladies? Are ya lost?' said another.

The crowd started whoopen and hollerin', throwing their hats into the air in excitement at the fresh female influx that had wandered in.

'They look like two little cows that need milken,' suggested someone.

That did it. Davidia didn't mind being a butt joke, but some of the raucous repartee peeved her positively awfully. She didn't have to stand being ridiculed in front of grown men with childish behaviour. Her stubbornness and pride were about to be aerated.

'Excuse me, kind sir, the one with the nose as long as his ears. Did I hear ya call us cows, did I? Now I might not take offence to some of ya chat, but I do when you know I only have two teats and a cow has four, so how could it be we're cows, you being a farmer and all. I suppose that thing between your legs is a knowledge pen, when I clearly know it can't write. Will you apologise, dear sir, or do I have to give ya an embarrassing whippen in front of everyone.'

The crowd was stunned. Davidia had oscillated her hips as hypnotic ploys as she moved to the rude section of the bar; well, that could be anywhere. Her bravado was hidden under her large hat. As she neared the perpetrator of ridicule, she lifted her trouser up one leg and jangled a spur. She spun it like a roulette wheel. Whilst the eyes were fixated on a pair of imagined frilly panties with a spinning spur, she whipped out her pistol, safety catch on, and gestured menacingly by rolling her bottom lip along the barrel.

'Now, ya see, my little friend here is like my daddy. I listen when he speaks just as you might now.' She turned the gun in her hand and swirled it like Wyatt Earp and re-holstered it, in case matters got worse. 'Now, I'm going to walk to the end of the bar and if I don't hear that apology, I surely will reduce your knowledge pen to a pencil stub.'

The crowd was breathless. No woman had ever before challenged comical Bill; however, this was no laughing matter. Slirander was petrified to the spot. Was this her dearest friend acting out a dangerous fantasy as a gunslinger? It was almost unbelievable, another danger word (Davidia) with the letter D. Bill's nerves were shot and shortly he might be too. Davidia made it to the end of the bar. She stopped, slowly turned around and stared down her challenger. She tried to spit, but her throat was too dry. Her hand shed beads of escaping sweat. She stood astride thumping the hobnail boots into the floor for thundering effect.

Her neck rolled in a circle, her eyes lit with fire, and Bill, well he had nowhere to hide. He didn't want a demise, his or hers. It was only words he had used, regrettably. The scene was set. Suddenly, the piano player tinkled a honky tonk tune and the crowd returned to the bar. Davidia and Bill had avoided a serious confrontation.

'What was all that about?' said Slirander relieved that Davidia didn't exit Tombstone in a wooden box.

'He was so rude.'

*

A feminine boudoir is usually the domain of a classy woman who knows how to core an apple, strip the cover off a pea pod and how to "mango". It was the place of a woman who has street cunning even the gutter rats didn't have knowledge of. Her outfit of shock and surprise hid a vulnerable mind. It was all about presentation. An attractive, mid-forty-aged woman had lain eyes on the two newbies who happened to be in her saloon.

She had followed their brazen behaviour and the ensuing kerfuffle; however, they seemed to possess an innocence long lost in town. The possibility of risk and harm was ever-present. She thought that they needed a motherly figure and protection, or was there an ulterior motive for such kindness?

'Young ladies,' she yelled from the top of the stairs. 'Come up here.'

Davidia and Slirander saw a striking female with the confidence of a queen.

'I wonder what she wants,' said Davidia. 'She might want to sell us into some form of slavery. I've heard about that.'

'She looks like the boss. Notice how everyone nodded when she yelled. Tamed animals don't behave like that when someone speaks. Let's see what she wants.'

'Righto, pardner,' replied cowgirl Davidia. She was really stepping into the memory theme. Slirander sighed.

'Excuse me, sir, I need to climb the staircase,' said Davidia, trying to brush past an adoring crowd.

'I'll be up in five minutes,' a patron commented.

'Up what?'

'The stairs.'

'You aren't a stalker, are you?'

The cowboy full of cheap whisky didn't quite understand the stalker word.

'Nope,' was all he said.

'Our parents would detest us being in amongst this cowboy filth. They smell, yell, swear and wear unwashed clothing covered in dust. They just aren't our normal style. The sooner we are out of here, the better.'

'Stop whinging and let's see what the overdressed mannequin wants.'

At the top of the stairs a charming lady greeted them. Her gloved hands hid a callous-free, delicate pair of hands. She greeted them warmly, but with the eyes of mistrust. Were they to be her competition, or just an innocent pair of young ladies out of their depth?

'My name is Mrs Crupe, and you are?'

'Davidia.'

'Slirander.'

'What is the purpose of your visit here? You are too young for these here parts. Trouble is always a close neighbour in the west.'

'We are, umm, lost. The stagecoach driver dropped us off here instead of Dodge City. We were to visit our aunt, but he got lost. It was suspicious. I think he was paid to drop us off here. We can't think of a reason why though, can you?'

Mrs Crupe choked a guilt cough. She waved her arms in

a street direction "this way" sign. They took a few steps and entered a large room. Inside, it was a smoke-filled haze. Neither girl smoked. Lighting was dim to avoid facial recognition. It was a gambler's den. They noticed a couple of young women croupiers dressed in can-can outfits with aspects of their clothing missing. They passed through and out of the other side of the room and ended up in a dormitory style accommodation. A dozen beds, six on each side of the room, lined the walls. It was basic with no privacy and the cleaning agency must have had a year off. The girls were appalled. Davidia remembered the insane asylum and was experiencing Ground Hog Day emotions all over again.

'What is this place?' asked Slirander.

'Your new home.'

'My new what?'

'Your new home. It's the best in town for workers. You girls are my new cleaners and this is where you will live. Pay is food and accommodation with one free day a month.'

'But we aren't cleaners.'

'You are now.'

'What if I refuse?' said Davidia, being stubborn.

'You won't.'

'Why won't I?'

'This town didn't get its name for no reason.'

'Davidia,' said Slirander, 'play along. We're here for a reason. Remember?'

That silenced dissent for the time being. Mrs Crupe left them alone.

'I'll be back in five minutes.'

'If that's your grandma, I'm not liking her. She can't push us around.'

'In this time, she can. We are in her memory and in a town and country that my family have never known she had visited. Firstly, we must determine if it's her and after that we might need to leave. I have a bad feeling being here. We might have to use our guns. My aura isn't in good health.' Slirander knew her feelings well. 'Further, how we get out of here will be a contest I have no way knowing the outcome of. Try not to upset everyone we meet.'

Davidia listened. A well-trained ear was a useful learning tool.

'I'm going to powder my nose,' she said and quickly darted out the doorway, along a dimly lit corridor – lantern light was a poor conductor of good vision – and crept up to the door with a Mrs Crupe sign nailed onto it.

She peeped through the keyhole. Mrs Crupe had a whip in one hand and was hitting something out of eyesight. There was the whip cracking sound followed by a dull thud. Davidia thought that she must be practising for an upcoming competition. Suddenly, someone took her by the scruff of the neck, opened the door and threw her like limp washing onto the floor.

'The little brat was eavesdropping. What shall we do with her?'

Davidia glanced around and could only see a wooden horse that had been thrashed by the whip and an unshaven man with long fingers gnarled by manual labour, standing over her as a prized pelt. She had thoughts of kicking like a horse, but restrained herself until she had learnt more of her predicament.

'What's the meaning of this?' Mrs Crupe bellowed.

The clothing that framed her body became taut with anger. Each stitch was about to separate.

'I tried to find the toilet and as I passed by your door, I heard frightening sounds. It sounded like indoor thunderclaps and it scared me, so I took a peek to see what it was. Now I'm on your floor, which really does need cleaning.'

'Impertinent little bitch. Keep your nose and pretty face out of my business.'

Davidia had noted a hint of a familiar accent an American

doesn't have. Her impersonation of an American had fooled everyone so far and she wasn't questioned about, 'Where do you come from?' with an Australian accent. She had a delicious, impudent thought.

'Are you from these parts? I detected a hint of a flavoured accent from somewhere which may suggest otherwise.'

Davidia was asking, without knowing it, for a belting. Her verbal footsteps kept standing on someone's verbal toes and they hurt.

'Get out. Take her back to the dormitory and prepare her for work.'

Davidia was directed back to where she started and pointed toward the toilet area.

'If that's what you were looking for, use it. Five minutes to change and I'll have those guns.'

The girls were left floundering with curiosity. They were stuck in a working memory in a deadly dangerous town where no one's safety could be guaranteed no matter who said what. Five minutes passed. They had changed into their working gear of frilly pantaloons and large skirt with a window of missing material across the breast area which was displayed only when they leant over. No one looked at the fluffy suds in their buckets anymore.

'This outfit is a little risqué for cleaning,' said Davidia.

'I agree. We don't have our guns and I have a dreadful feeling that they may become our new best friends. We'll have to retrieve a set each from somewhere. Let's do the cleaning job and be prepared to leave the saloon at a moment's notice. I must find out if Mrs Crupe is grandma.'

'I hinted that she had an accent from somewhere else.'

The tall man came back. He took them and their sudsy buckets to a backroom.

'Clean in there first.'

Without complaint, the girls did as they were told and completed an excellent job. When finished, they looked around, snooping into drawers and cupboards. They were empty. The tall man returned. No prize or thanks was given for an excellent job. What a rude bastard! Were most people in Tombstone rude? Their agenda had to be fed so the cleaning and waiting game had to be played out.

'Clean in there.'

It was Mrs Crupe's office. Without question they set to and once again did an excellent job. It was rather hard to understand as when both were at home, manual labour was done by a foreigner. It was surprising that they both did the manual work without whinging. There is a first for everything. They should take back that character trait and add it to their capability list.

'Stand guard,' said Davidia, 'whilst I snoop. There might be a clue desk or cupboard. Secrets are bound to be hidden somewhere in here.'

Slirander kept peering around the door for any intruder. Davidia didn't understand the financial papers strewn as litter on the desktop. After a few minutes, she was surprised that there really was nothing of interest. One would have thought that the manager of an establishment had something to declare. Nope, it was as clean as a baby's backside. Was grandma a myth? Loud footsteps headed their way. A sleazy cowboy struggled with a crazed bottle that didn't want to be friends. Its contents washed the walls. Stains dribbled to the floor. There was a mixed stench in the air of spilt alcohol and bad body hygiene. There wasn't a hospital nearby to manage bad smells as an illness. The inebriated gent spotted Slirander. His face split almost in two with a grin. His dental arrangement didn't engender any form of a close embrace.

'It's my turn,' he drawled.

'Your turn for what?' said a defensive Slirander.

'To wash me. I paid good money downstairs. My dollar ain't going to waste.'

'But we are employed as cleaners.'

'Exactly my point.' He fell down in a dishevelled heap.

'So that's the catch,' said Davidia, who by now had lifted her bucket as a weapon and was ready to swing it. 'That damn Mrs Crupe is thinking that we'll wash that filth.'

Before Davidia had further time to engage in outrage, Mrs Crupe materialised.

'I see you've met Freddy. Pick him up and escort him to my office. He's my husband.'

That comment shot through Slirander like a bullet through the heart. Married, grandma? No one in the family knew about this. Did they have any children? Was she her mum's mum? Was she really her grandma and if so, was this pile of crap, her grandpa? Suddenly, being in grandma's memory was wreaking havoc with her historical understanding of her past. Was it now in jeopardy? Her mental health was erupting like an exploding puss sore. Yuck! Slirander didn't suffer from migraines, but her first experience of it had just arrived. Davidia could sense her friend was suffering. She had to do something. What to do? what to do? There was Pole singing inside her head again. Was it advice or just a subconscious jingle?

'Excuse me, Mrs Crupe, is that Freddy really your husband, or did you say that to avoid any embarrassment, if he was seen entering your private quarters and not your private parts?'

Davidia had verbally over-stretched her thoughts and realised her verbal offence. Mrs Crupe smiled just as an executioner does, hidden under his hood, when the guillotine is about to separate a lifelong connection in reducing one's actual height.

'That will do for now. Leave us alone. I'm single; however, to preserve one's face things are said aloud to inform gossips who repeat that as a truth. It's a lesson learnt for you both.'

It was said with lack of anger and was just a piece of good western motherly advice. The West is all about preservation.

'Thank you, Michelle,' said a cheeky Davidia.

As Davidia walked away from Mrs Crupe, she turned her head for the assassin's charge. She could sense a stiffening of Mrs Crupe's corset and noticed her tightly-bound breasts rise so high that they almost popped out of her outfit as two whoopee cushions and watched her fists meld into rocks. Mrs Crupe strode forward wondering how in the hell did the two strangers know her real name. It had never been mentioned by anyone before. She had to solve this dilemma.

'Where did you get that name from? Who told you?'

'It is correct then?' said Davidia. 'The stage coach driver who dropped us off in town, told us to stay with a Michelle. We're here. You're here, so we assume it's correct. Is there another Michelle in town?'

'There is not.'

'We come from a land down under. Have you heard of it?'

Once again, the girls sensed real danger this time. Mrs Crupe had a small pistol tucked in her boot and bent over to retrieve it. Davidia knew then that Doomsday had arrived. Without any further dialogue, she swung her sudsy bucket so hard, it knocked Mrs Crupe into a horizontal position, dazed with a head wound. Davidia snatched the pistol and told Slirander to run.

'You hit my grandma. How dare you?' Slirander took a swipe at Davidia who retaliated with a well-placed kick.

'Stop being so bloody stupid! Grandma or not, she was going to shoot us. I might love my grandma, but I'm not taking a bullet from her. You should do the same.'

The girls high-tailed it out of there. They ran down the stairs into the boozy swill. The dreadfully out-of-tune piano effectively rendered everyone tone deaf. The path to the door was replete with male obstacles, the full torso and not a small component of it, as they moved carefully through them. Slirander accidentally bumped a belligerent, literary, dictionary-read gentleman.

'Ya shit. Come here, I'll smack ya arse.'

He mistimed a swipe, hit a fellow cowboy and a brawl erupted. Suddenly, bodies flew about in swirls all trying to land a punch. The girls made it to the swing doors and burst out of there into the dusty street. It was completely empty. The moment that they passed through the swing doors meant that grandma's memory was now at risk.

'It's about time you faced your fate, you snivelling waste of space,' said a six-foot, tall, nasty hombre dressed in a full black ensemble, the colour of the demons of death. 'I'm givin' you one last chance to avoid a lead sandwich. Back down and I won't fill you full of holes.'

He spat, kicked the dirt, patted his holster and stared down the street as if hypnotised. There was no one else in the street except the two girls. It was a fearful moment. Davidia, ever the drama queen, approached the fearful episode with her usual skills of humility.

'Are yer talkin' to us, Black Bart? I don't know about no apologise, but I certainly know a man when I sees one. I reckon you got the feel for it.' Davidia sauntered toward him. He didn't flinch.

'One more step, Fast Fingered Fanny, and you're dead meat. The vultures will feed on your carcass when I is done with ya.'

Was this real, a shoot-out with an outlaw? Davidia grasped the small pistol tightly. She flipped the safety catch. She drilled into his eyes as she approached. Beads of sweat ran down his craggy face. He could have been Irish.

Suddenly, a woman was heard screaming from the saloon. Mrs Crupe had also run into the street cursin' and hollerin' words a lady shouldn't use. Grandma certainly knew how to communicate with the public. A crowd of rabble virtually tumbled into the street behind her. It was the back-up crew to an audience for the showdown.

'Let her have it. She stole my gun, the little thief. I'll put her in a plain wooden box with pleasure.'

Slirander turned to Mrs Crupe and used her range of verbs and nouns to great effect.

'You old cow. She's my friend. No one hurts her. Stick this up your arse.'

That's not a pleasant place to place any unwanted intruder, dead or alive. Slirander lashed out with a spur, having learnt to reverse kick thrust and it went where suggested. A wail of pain erupted. There was one nasty, writhing female on the ground who she was related to. Well, you can't pick family. Davidia had made it to arm's length with the patient Black Bart. Davidia believed he really didn't want to shoot anyone; however, he had a reputation to uphold.

'Are yer gunna look at me all day or are ya doin' summit about it?'

Before he could answer the threat, a huge crowd ran down the street chasing Slirander, baying for revenge. Black Bart could see the girls were in trouble. Quick as a flash, he unhitched his horse, flung Davidia up first, then Slirander behind, and smacked its rump. It whinnied and neighed, but knew its job was to run and it did. Straight out of the end of town a huge dust cloud was all that could be seen. Black Bart tipped his hat and allowed himself a smile. It had been years since he had last done that.

*

'Has this horse been programmed? It seems to know where to go. It must be well-trained,' said Slirander.

It was a dream horse transporting the girls to elsewhere. She would love to have been an equestrian, but cost and time made that difficult. School didn't provide a pony club. Suddenly, a huge ravine opened up in front of them. The horse jumped. The girls screamed and the ground shook. They shut their eyes. The horse was no more, but they felt they were still in existence. How could that be? They looked at their feet and found that they were sky-surfing with ski-cloud shoes. It was deathly quiet.

Where were they going?

*

Grandma must have made it back to Australia after all, because Slirander was two generations later.

What a lady! Or not?

9 Prison

The girls were floating amongst the memory clouds using their ski-cloud shoes with great dexterity. Their V formation was an instant winner. Clouds parted willingly to allow them through. They had no idea where they were in the memory set nor if they were near the memory forest. Grandma had certainly kicked up her heels in surprises. Was there another one ahead? After a while boredom, that great mate of those who don't have their smartphone handy, had arrived. Davidia wanted direction, not misdirection, and began to moan as if it was a practised art form.

'Where are we going? I'm sick of floating aimlessly. I need to be grounded,' said Davidia, with tones of, what's next?

'I can't see the ground from up here. Have you noticed that we aren't falling closer to the earth? I hope we aren't stuck up here as cumulo Slirander and nimbus Davidia.' Slirander was alert for any new experience that didn't involve life risk.

'It's just our luck to be fluffed up. Look ahead. There seems to be a huge wall heading our way and down there next to it is that ghastly memory forest that almost dumped us in the Tombstone cemetery. We must be floating in a circle coming to ground like a glider. No wonder we didn't think that we were going anywhere. The ground always appears to be the same distance. Maybe our eyes need checking.'

'You can see the outline of the Pollital that we remember. It's so strange how it has altered so significantly since we visited the memory ball set. Maybe there are different memory sets all managed by the Pollitons, but each one is presented differently.

We could be in the anger section by the appearance of that forest.'

As they neared the wall, a long, thin, spaghetti strand tree branch headed directly for them. It came from a black sinister memory tree embedded in the memory forest. It was a snake of the air. It didn't hiss or poke out a feeler. It knew where it was headed.

'Look out, we're being threatened again,' said Davidia. 'Where are my secateurs when you need them? I'd snip it if I could. That would teach it a lesson to stop being bothersome.'

In the air there was only one way to fall – downwards.

The tree branch split into two, then three and four. It attached itself to the girls' ankles and began to pull them earthwards. They struggled. It was a lost cause. Their ski-cloud shoes faded without raining. It was impossible to stay airborne without them. Begrudgingly, they began to descend into the darkness below. The memory forest sent fears and chills along the spines of all its inhabitants. It was a bleak landscape. There was thought that there would be no happy memories amongst them. They hadn't encountered any. Thump, they landed. The tree branch released its grip. As it shrunk, it took another form of a short shrub that left leaf litter and detritus as it shuffled. Is it possible? They thought that they had recognised Pole. A moment later, once the eyes had acclimatised to the dark surrounds, they peered closer. It certainly was a familiar bush, but it wasn't made of fresh leaves but older, crinkled and curled ones all destined for fine composting.

'Well, we are down safely. Thanks to whatever you are. Have we met before?'

Davidia was curious to at least know their saviour. A thank-you wouldn't go astray either. Did it speak? It did have two mouths.

'You are in danger in this forest. Nothing but unsavoury and risky memories are filed here under each tree. You have been warned not to disturb any of them, but you didn't listen. It isn't guaranteed that you will escape this forest. Items of doom patrol the area. No one can tell what form they take. Be wary of whatever you meet. I might even be one. It is at great personal risk that I saved you from the endless floating with those ski-cloud shoes. They are part of a never-ending story. I've had my time. I'm exhausted.'

The short, stubbly bush disintegrated like sand particles disappearing on a beach. A small patch of black soil was all that was left of a smattering of good advice.

'Did you believe it? We don't listen? What a bloody cheek. I heard every word.' Davidia was annoyed at the inference her ears weren't tuned in or on.

'I don't think it meant hearing, but listening to what was said,' replied Slirander.

'This place creeps me out. Remember that wall we saw, I wonder if someone lives there. It's worth exploring. We might locate a nicer memory than being shot at. Now, which direction was it?'

'I'll lead you there, if you want,' said a nearby sound.

'Who's there? Show yourself. You don't scare me.'

'Down here on the forest floor. I'm a litter leader.'

'A, excuse me if I'm in the lost books, a litter leader. Is that a person who reads small books?'

Davidia hadn't quite heard the original comment. It could have been in Japanese English.

'A litter leader. I lead rubbish from place to place.'

'We're not rubbish. We're girls who are not to be messed with. How come you exist in this gloomy forest? What sort of memory are you?'

'Yours.'

'No, you are not. These are grandma's memories and we are on tour. Do you have a name, nothing else seems to?'

The question was ignored. The litter leader wanted to lead, so why weren't they following?

'You must follow me otherwise you will be stranded. It's not far.'

'Slirander, should we follow or not? How about exercising your aura?'

'I feel it's safe. It doesn't feel like a doom item. Where else are we to go?'

It was decided to single file to the wall. The litter leader began heartily, but after three steps, fell over, quite dead. At least a track led ahead and so they continued. After a dozen steps – it seemed like hundreds – perhaps it was – they embraced a huge wall. There was no red carpet, or even a black carpet, to greet them. They stood dwarfed by one side of an assumed rectangular edifice. They stood back to study its structural composition and accidentally stood on another small rock mound. It moved.

'Unfortunately, we meet again. Trouble is brewing with you two. You need to leave the forest. The memory forest is revolting with the disturbances created by your presence. A nasty memory may ruin your stay.' The mound began to move away.

'How do we get in?'

'You shouldn't. Don't you listen to warnings? If you must, pull that twig jutting out of the wall. Reap what you wish for.'

'We aren't interested in presents.'

The mound disappeared quickly. Davidia pulled the jutting twig. They waited. The wall began to move toward them like grandma's hugging embrace. It parted around them, then closed. They were now inside a large expected rectangle, but the other three walls were missing. A siren sounded. Sounds of rushing everywhere was heard, but nothing could be seen. Voices barked instructions in the harshest of tones. Responses flew at random. They felt in the middle of a mad rush hour at a commuter station at knock-off time. Was all this in their imagination? Nothing made any sense.

'This is weird. There's nothing here?' said Davidia, confused by rushing sounds with no objects of movement to be seen.

'There has to be more to it. We could be in a disaster memory. Tread carefully. The last time we were sucked underground. This memory research is fraught with uncertainty. Watch out for memory mines. A trap could have been laid. One false step and it's prosthesis replacements, or worse still, no more us.'

Slirander was obviously concerned. Grandma's past should possibly remain that, in the past. She hoped that they didn't discover a memory too dreadful to repeat. The girls were stranded in an open space without any clues to its reveal. A moment passed. The stillness sent whisperings around their minds, tempting a move.

'What are you here for? Nothing exists except the past. Open a catastrophic memory and fall in. Don't be afraid. The past cannot be repeated. You are safe.'

The same repetitive thoughts harassed them until Davidia couldn't stand the teasing anymore, besides, repetition was tedious and boring. Where was the real action or at least some form of movement? There was no need to act like a monument, stone slab or deadwood; something had to give.

'This bloody grandma nonsense has gone too far. It's annoying the crap out of me. I'm taking a step in that direction. Nothing could be too dangerous that we can't handle.'

Davidia took three steps towards the west. In the story it makes no difference what the direction was, just that it was mentioned.

'Hello there,' said a doomy voice. 'Please enter my memory.'

'Hello there,' said another doomy voice nearby from another direction. 'Please enter my memory.'

'Hello there,' said a third doomy voice. 'Please enter my memory.'

They looked around and a sea of opening and closing holes greeted them. The ground surface was aerated with questioning holes all wanting them to visit their particular memory. They stood still daring not to move. Suddenly, an overhanging dead tree limb darkened by years of memory storage, wavered above their heads. It had watched with interest the dilemma of the two objects caught in the field of most dangerous thoughts. Nothing had ever disturbed any past thoughts, now, changes were felt. The girls had upset the past and it wasn't happy.

'You must choose a memory hole as there is no other escape from the graveyard of memory gaps. Nothing has ever entered there, before. Are you a bacterium, or have you lost your memories? These memory holes belong to a grandma. Nothing else is ever to visit. Are you grandmas? I've never seen the owner of a memory as it is impossible as only their memories are retained here, not their original form. We don't appreciate any visitors. It changes our permanent serenity. I need to attend to my dark thought responsibility. I don't want that one to be unleashed. Choose carefully. Nothing good will come from any selection made. My limb aches from all this hovering. Memory advice is all about how you use it. You must now make that dreadful choice, otherwise all holes will combine into one and you will disappear permanently into the past. A one-hole choice might give you the opportunity of survival. No one knows because it has never happened before. Bye.'

The dark tree limb returned to its destiny. It had exhausted its verbal fuel supply, but fortunately for the girls, it had warned them. Did they take any notice of its warnings? The holes kept repeating the same question like a small child presenting a tantrum to get his or her own way. This wasn't any supermarket aisle of embarrassment. This was a memory dilemma the girls had to decide for themselves. The atmosphere began to darken. Demonic thoughts seemed to avail for mental suction. A conscious decision had to be made immediately, otherwise a wrong choice was a certainty.

'How do we decide which choice to make and if we choose one too far will the others let us pass?' asked Davidia searching for a "friendly" hole.

Slirander shut her eyes and had a flash thought. Colour. It was about colour. Only black or grey existed here. Colour seemed a stupid idea, but why did it manifest in her brain? Her family was full of unexplainable phenomena. This might be one of those moments.

'Pink. Select any opening with a pinkish tinge,' she said.

'I suppose memories do wear lipstick. Many of mine do. My mirror often says so.'

'Look. That one over there is signalling. It certainly is agitated. It has a pinkish tinge.'

'How do we signal to the other holes that we have made a choice?'

Slirander, in a wizardry moment, stretched her arm straight and a tiny light ray spat from her finger. It froze the hole. Suddenly, all the other holes ceased aerating the ground and closed over leaving that one space open. The girls quickly moved toward the frozen gap. It wasn't very large. Slirander put a foot in it first to see if her leg disappeared. Fortunately, it was still attached.

'Why don't you unfreeze it?' said Davidia. It seemed the obvious solution.

'Hold hands. We need to go together.'

Slirander raised her arm again and another light ray spat from a different finger. The hole unfroze. It enlarged enough to take them both and moved around them so that they stood on an isle in the middle of a gap. The sound of rushing commuter traffic emerged from the hole and, whoosh, they were sucked underground into another memory.

What would this encounter bring?

They doubted it would be a Christmas celebration.

*   •

'Move it, Charlene, or you'll be in solitary confinement again,' barked a large-framed woman with large, darkened lips, hair upheld in a bird's nest arrangement with a few trailing hairs shaping her face as an annoying flicked item, and dark-blue stained coveralls frayed at the leg ends. There was plenty of material surrounding a substantial torso that moved to the speed of, "Do I have to?" This was one of the prison staff officers wielding their power and weight in a daily confronting situation.

Mandy was administering her official duties when Slirander and Davidia arrived as new inmates incarcerated for impure thoughts. They had been arrested as memory pests and the sentence for such a diabolical belief was life imprisonment. The thoughts were never properly explained.

'Watcha staring at, darlings? Haven't you seen a real woman before? Do that too often around here and you'll end up as dinner fodder for any knife-wielding maniac. Believe me, this establishment is full of them. You two are so darn pretty you'll have no trouble making "new friends". Be careful when showering. That is when you are at your most vulnerable. Don't misbehave. The cure is worse than the sentence.'

The girls had arrived at the processing centre where they were stripped, measured and given a "fresh" set of clothing washed in recycled sewerage water. They had landed in a prison for the bewildered; well, at least they were. It was busy as rush hour as they passed the huge dinner hall where food behaviour was a test of bad manners. Everyone present seemed to have megaphone voices. Competition for seating and food often boiled into downright violence. The girls were shocked at the sight of the amount of physical turmoil. It didn't quite have a party atmosphere. Often a prisoner visited the infirmary via a return to their cell. Sometimes, they were expelled from another exit to compost at the end of a briefer sentence. There was a permanent space set aside for those who finished their sentence early. It was a cemetery. Apparently, release from this prison was rare. No explanations were given. It would be a confronting stay for the girls and far more dangerous than a finger paper-cut. They were walked along a corridor of open barred cells with limited privacy, which was only looking the other way. The guards could monitor them more easily in case they were up to any mischief or altercation, which often occurred.

'Here is your Hilton accommodation. Don't spend too much time in front of the mirror. It's a waste of time and temptation for others. Remember, there are no friends in here. Trust no one. Make yourself comfortable. It won't last long.'

Mandy left them to their own devices once the cell door had been locked.

They were placed in cell number eleven. It consisted of two bunks, each with a mattress that felt it was filled with dirt compacted so densely that sleeping on cement was a close relative. The private ablution seating was an exposed hole in one corner with a stone rim protecting it. A damaged wooden desk with three legs was propped up against the toilet rim, otherwise it would be floor waste. The blanket each was given was so thin that running a hand on the other side of it without it touching was easily silhouetted. A pillow was formed from the clothing you didn't sleep in. No toiletries were allowed except for the remnants of a dirty cake of used soap, which, by the look of it, had been poorly treated. There was no need to sniff its aroma. One look said it all. Toilet paper was almost alien and conversations were in soft tones unless you wanted an earful of unwanted abuse. Air conditioning and heating was the same open window for all four seasons. The bed uprights shook when touched. Sleeping soundly was problem based with the shaky bed movements. The girls sat on the bottom bunk, wondering what happened to civilisation. They were now two unsavoury convicts protesting innocence at all times. It was a black mark against their good personalities. The shape of their bodies registered disappointment, fear and lack of confidence as they slumped forward.

'What a shit-hole!' said Davidia. Her future words needed a full mouth rinse before being offered as comment. She felt that bad. 'This is a stuff-up. I'm ready to go home already and we have just arrived at our all-inclusive holiday destination.'

'It is a dump, isn't it? It stinks so foul. The other inmates appear to be a violent lot. Grandma must be in here somewhere,' said Slirander, also fearful that they had landed in a right mess. Even the nasty comments on Twitter never gave her the woeful feeling she had experienced upon arrival. 'I might have to draw on some family history if we are to survive and escape from here, but not via the cemetery. I'm claustrophobic.'

'How do we fill in our time? We can't sit all day, or is that it? Some exercise and breaks must be provided. This thesis on grandma might mean that we have uncovered one unknown memory too many to our own detriment.'

Davidia felt soulful. Even when the door is down and closed tight, there's always the possibility of a crack appearing through which to escape. There were so many cracks in their cell they'd never find their way out. They had arrived at the prison prior to dusk and had passed the food hall with its cacophony of sounds on their way to holiday heaven.

'Hey, you two. Get your cute arses out of there. It's dinner time. There mightn't be anything left, but protocol says we have to give you the opportunity. Move. I won't ask again.'

Mandy unlocked their cell door. She had many keys on a key chain slung around her waist. It was so heavy that her pants slid downwards exposing her bum crack. No one knew if that was a mating signal or not. That theory hadn't been tested. The girls cautiously walked the corridor, their complete range of senses on full alert. Mandy thought that because of their youth, trouble would follow them like a trained pet. She had no empathy for either of them. Over the years it had been worked out of her.

The food hall was in full function. Inmates, all female, sat together. They belched, farted, swore, spat, slurped, urinated occasionally, hit another in violent outbursts, kicked and scratched in cat fights and food kindly described as gruel on a garbage lid was freely thrown. The mess on the floor was voraciously cleaned up by those hungriest and who may have missed the rotted offerings in the first place. A space was found for them.

'Raise that fist and I'll stick my foot so far up your arse, I'll kick your teeth out.' Mandy knew how to handle the rabble.

A few inmates begrudgingly moved.

'Are you Mandy's pet teases? I'd like to have some of what she's getting,' said an inmate, whose eyes registered lust which apparently wasn't on the dinner menu.

'I'm sorry for the intrusion,' said a very polite Davidia. Disarm the aggressor and act caringly. 'This is our first evening visit and we didn't know the prison protocol. I hope we don't upset you again and if we do, we apologise for it happening. It's a pleasure to meet you. My name is Davidia and this is my friend, Slirander.'

Davidia and Slirander felt they were feted like mini celebrities.

The whole food hall was staring at them. They were the youngest set of inmates. It was impossible to recognise any comfort amongst all the beaded looks. Fear wasn't allowed to be shown. It was a sign of weakness; however, the girls didn't feel brave amongst the other inmates. How would they know if grandma was amongst this lot? They tentatively took their seats.

'No point in waiting. There isn't any table service here. Get your own,' said a bad-breathed inmate who they were sure was on some dopey stuff.

They carefully made their way to the self-service trays, selected one each and moved along the food chain counter to ask for some food. One look at it told them it wasn't appealing. Thud! A large spoonful of sludge hit their tin plates. It was grey and a substance dribbled out of it like dish water. A battered spoon was the utensil of choice. They nervously made their way back to their seats. Unfortunately, a beast of a woman deliberately elbowed Slirander's tray so that it flew like a frisbee across at least two tables splattering the inmates with the intended shit meal offering. The tables were suddenly upturned and a surge of abusive language and threatening women headed her way. It was pandemonium. Suddenly, Mandy interrupted.

'Leave her alone. You all remember what it was like when you first got here.'

'We weren't animals then,' replied a snarler.

'Give them time to settle. No one wants solitary confinement, do they?'

Mandy eyeballed them all. They all knew not to cross her. Past examples of retribution had resulted in broken bones, missing teeth, the occasional knife wound, time on crutches relearning to walk properly, and her language was a tad intimidating.

'I told you that you have no friends in here. Don't make me repeat it.'

The dinner hall settled; however, many eyes had observed the two "innocents" and were anxious to make their acquaintance for whatever reasons of their own. No good would develop from that collection of ideas. Slirander sat down minus her food tray, but still held the battered spoon in her hand. No one noticed the anger she had transferred to it and the fact that she had placed it in her pocket. It was thought to be lost amongst the disruption. Why she put it there was an automatic reaction with no obvious explanation. It was now bent, but in a different way to the other inmates' spoons. She turned to Davidia who had a stunned facial expression. What? Eat the rubbish labelled food. She almost dry-retched at the first mouthful.

'It gets better with time,' offered another inmate grinning at the prospect of another's pain and discomfort.

Amusement was generated by other's misfortunes. It was an endless and dangerous list. What was to be Slirander and Davidia's contribution?

*

'Guilty,' echoed across the courtroom as judgement was passed on the hapless trio of protesters.

Grandma and two friends had been caught up in a protest against the persecution of women and the banners that they held were admonishing the current government for poor behaviour and attitude toward them. The main city street was full of agitators when the police presence swamped them like the plague and rounded up every female they could. Many made it to safety; however, some were not so fortunate.

'Get your bloody hands off me,' grandma yelled, as she was shoved into a "Divisional" van. Her two friends were stuffed inside like pillow fillings as the van became crowded. 'If you touch those parts of mine again, I'll sue you for assault and sexual harassment.'

Apparently in the rough house treatment of the arresting procedure, securing a hold on a wriggling female anatomy from behind under the armpits, often a tenuous grip at the best of times, was fraught with uncertainty and so hands had the capacity to slip and secure a hold elsewhere. That caused the assault comment. Had it been a personal emotional moment, then no assault comment would be mentioned, but perhaps a range of more pleasant-sounding words would have emerged.

'Sentence is three months,' said the judge, as his gavel struck its wooden sounding board with a resounding echo.

That sound sent shivers down their spines. Revenge would be a salad eaten cold if it could be returned. The law currently had the advantage.

*

'How are we going to find grandma amongst this surly lot?' questioned Davidia, who was beginning to realise that they could be in serious trouble with the prison rough.

'We'll know,' replied Slirander, 'there are ways.'

'Well, they aren't written on any chalkboard that I can see. I don't like it here.'

The girls decided not to eat the food offered. Their body reserves would last a few days as a fasting diet. Slightly overweight wasn't a complaint item, but if it left its carriers, there would be no complaints from them.

'Return to your cells. It's lockdown time,' bellowed Mandy.

The food hall was quickly cleared. It was silent except for the creaking walls and ceilings which spoke their own mysterious language as they headed toward decay.

The cell doors clanged shut as keys jingled and jangled their lock-up message. They were like rats or guinea pigs held in a hostile environment.

'Where's the damn light switch?' said Davidia.

Unfortunately, she had no holiday reading material to devour or enjoy. There was no library either.

There was not even one lousy, cheap, if necessary, candle to see with. Fire was refused in case an arsonist inmate attempted to burn the place down. Deprivation was rife. No wonder anger was an every day and night visitor. It was all about coping mechanisms to last through each day.

'There's no light switch. We'll just have to retire early, try to sleep and start our search properly tomorrow for grandma,' said a sensible Slirander.

She didn't want to be holed up another day longer. Her taste of prison had left a worse taste in her mouth than the food she didn't consume. She could sense Davidia's mild distress.

'It's an outrage that we are in prison,' said Davidia. 'It's a miscarriage of justice.'

'Davidia, snap out of it. We aren't actually in prison ourselves. We are in someone else's prison memory. Got it! Research, remember. We have to find grandma if she's in here. It's also possible that she's left this memory and we are too late to prove she was here. This could become a forgotten memory and if we don't either locate her or escape, we're doomed. The memory forest had missing elements and I hope that we haven't entered one of them.'

'Stop your moaning. It has disturbed me being here. I'm frightened. There seems to be so much nastiness and danger in here. We'll both have to be real careful tomorrow. Let's make sure we don't separate, otherwise we could both disappear or become entangled in unpleasant activities.'

'Will you two shut-up? A lady can't sleep with all yer jawing.

If I don't sleep proper, youse will regret it,' said the neighbouring cell reprobate.

She had been interned for murder. Apparently, she took a dislike to her partner's mistress, disposed of her and replaced her affections with hers. That didn't last long either. The new mistress disappeared also because her attentions had drifted elsewhere. Now she was permanently housed away from society, but not from still being a danger to others.

'Apologies for the noise.'

There wasn't a need to make enemies. It was a natural progression anyway to bad behaviour behind bars.

That evening, the girls struggled to sleep. Sleeping on cement with an open window, no heating and thin-wearing clothes had left them tired and listless the next morning when the brightest part of the day was when the sun shone through the window. Nothing else was going to shine today. A shit-hole doesn't change its form overnight.

The girls awoke. They sat on the bed. They stared and yawned. It was an active beginning to the day. At home, neither slept in day wear clothes. This was a first. They missed their early morning shower, refreshing perfumes, clean clothes and appropriate body spray. Ah! Memories of their own. Slirander was about to stand up when she fiddled in her pocket and withdrew the bent, battered spoon.

'Breakfast in bed, is it?' snarled Davidia.

Slirander ignored the comment. What was its purpose? She wasn't going to sharpen it into a weapon for self-protection. However, during the night, it had absorbed from Slirander an innate strength and certain abilities, not easily explainable. It became a spoon guard to protect the girls. When threatened it acted in their defence. How, was only determined by the actual threat. So far, one hadn't occurred. The day was but a pup.

Days in prison lost their true meaning. They were no longer days of the week. It was shower day, free time day, dinner day, exercise day and so on. Today was danger day because it was shower day. It was labelled a dual-purpose day, a time to be on guard for your best defence.

'Get out. It's shower day for you filthy, smelling tripe to clean yourselves.'

Mandy was giving out instructions. Self-esteem wasn't promoted. Belittling the inmates was verbal practice each day. It was used as an emotional control mechanism. It generated hopelessness amongst the prison population. The cells were unlocked. The decibel level rose with greeting each other.

'How did you sleep, bitch?' said an inmate, using prison vernacular.

'The same as you, bitch,' was the automatic response.

It was a popularly used term.

Crowds milled in any open space. The girls were directed to walk toward the showering room, which shocked them. The females filed in. The doors that guarded the entrance had their fair share of battering. Emotional outbursts often resulted in structural damage. It was an open floor plan with no privacy and hot water was only a dream. Twenty at a time were selected to disrobe and walk ten metres, under the watchful eyes of the adoring crowd, to stand in line like a police line-up and proceed to fight over the one cake of soap to be shared by all. There was not a remote possibility to reduce one's body stench without a nice smelling soap remover. The girls were in the second group so that they could observe the protocol. They were petrified of being naked in front of any crowd and especially an evil lot such as was present. Not all adoration was complimentary or wanted.

'None of them have their clothes on,' said an astonished Davidia.

'There's nothing wrong with your eyesight then?' replied Slirander.

Her thoughts were more focused about finding grandma.

'Do we have to do that too?' Davidia wasn't pleased.

'It's prison rules. Follow them or suffer. Be as quick as you can.'

The girls observed the first draught and tried to look away. There was something impelling that stopped them. It was Mandy with her baton forcing each face to stare straight ahead. There wasn't any pleasure in prison. Twenty sets of buttocks weren't a good breakfast entrée. Slirander began to fidget. Her hand touched the bent spoon. She suddenly realised that if it could do that then maybe she could locate grandma. Carefully, she extracted the spoon when no one was looking and uttered a silly chant.

What to do? What to do?
Become invisible for a moment or two,
Seek grandma amongst the butts,
By tapping those who aren't with red welted stings,
And return with good news to bring.

No one noticed that a flying object sped past each and every female showering and landed a prefect red welt on every left buttock. It stung and identified each strike. Slirander counted twenty hits. Grandma wasn't amongst this group. The animal-like behaviour was best left undescribed as many of the women slapped those next to them and a shower melee developed.

'Out. Next.'

A mad scramble was made for that precious cake of soap. Davidia and Slirander had never before disrobed in front of anything except their mirrors. It was a foreign experience.

'Stay together,' warned Slirander.

They were quickly lined up. The water was turned on. Forget the cake of soap. Goosebumps formed as big as apples, well almost, as the frozen water did its best to imitate a cleanliness application. Slirander sent the bent spoon on errand two. Once again, a series of twenty red welts emerged on left buttocks. There was no grandma in group two.

Before the mutual admiration society approached them, they exited as quickly as possible. They were too focused on getting in and out before noticing the crowd reaction to two lovely, young girls. They dressed in the same smelly garb that they had entered with.

'Grandma wasn't amongst that lot. This last group is all that's left.'

Group three were all lined up. Slirander sent the spoon again. Two thirds of the way along, one left butt was bare, with no red welt. The spoon returned to Slirander's safe-keeping. It had further use.

'That's her,' said Slirander, excitedly. 'It's odd looking at grandma in this manner, but we may have found her.'

'Out,' called Mandy.

Everyone retreated into their day wear, which was their all-the-time wear and moved to the food hall once again. It was morning break where a limp tea bag, which had been dunked many times, and a mouthful of stale bread formed the daily sustenance. The girls edged near grandma who wasn't aware of her two youthful stalkers. She sat with her other two cohorts.

'Push in,' said Davidia. 'Bad manners thrive in here. Someone will just become disgruntled if we shove in.'

The girls sat directly behind grandma hoping to interact with her. Eventually they did, but not to their pleasure. The crowded table was infested, with everyone wanting a piece of the conversation. It was the surprise that had the girls aghast.

Slirander and Davidia were close enough to butt in, if they tried, and so they did. The prison memory was wearing thin and they wanted to leave if possible, but only after meeting grandma.

Grandma seemed to control the table conversation. Everyone hung on her every word.

She was extolling the virtues of protest and how the judicial system was biased against women. Naturally, large cheers went up. Tin mugs clanged and the many grunts heard signified basic education had been lost on some. Davidia made a dangerous mistake. She corrected grandma. It was a controversial comment.

'It's not true that the law is biased against women. There are more men in gaol,' she said.

It was said loud enough to be heard and interrupt the table adulations.

Suddenly, silence reigned. That was almost an impossible feat, but no, Davidia had somehow managed. Grandma waved her hand. Two medium sized females stood up from their seats and each took hold of an arm. She faced grandma.

'Would you repeat what you said?' Davidia did.

Grandma stuck her fist into her guts and sent her sprawling on the floor to the delight of the crowd. A third person withdrew a small knife fashioned from another missing spoon and held it aloft, waiting for the signal.

'Let me gut the bitch,' she sniffled. Her hands shook, Davidia shook and Slirander shook. 'I haven't had this much fun since my fiancé messed the kitchen floor. It was delicious.' Once a maniac it's hard to change personality.

'I prefer that you don't hurt my friend,' said Slirander. She held her bent spoon tightly. It was receiving mental instructions from her. It became magnetic and white hot, but had no effect on Slirander. 'Kindly put your weapon down and walk away. Do you agree with that, Michelle?'

'Youse never told us your name,' said an inmate. 'That's a sissy name. They call me Bluey because that's what I does.'

Grandma flinched at the mention of her real name. Why that should be so, was a mystery. Extraordinary scenes erupted with her next comment.

'I don't know who she is. Do her in,' she ordered.

The maniac with the knife raised it to the strike position. Saliva dribbled effusively. She looked like a slobbering dog. Her eyes had lost any depth of expression except darkness. Slirander nudged her bent spoon which flew out of her pocket and attached itself to the other spoon, wrenching it from the assailant's grasp. In the process of attachment, it ejected a shot of pure heat which burnt all of her hand turning it red and it began to peel like an orange. The scream filled the hall with fear. Slirander's spoon returned with the nasty prize. She quickly took a hold of it.

'Does anyone else want to try?' she bravely questioned.

No one else was prepared to take up the cudgel. She looked directly at grandma.

'Why did you want to hurt my friend?'

Grandma hissed and snarled at her. She acted exactly like the others with the herd mentality. By this time Davidia had recovered from her prostate position and squared off.

'You don't deserve any children. Is your name Michelle? No one heard your previous answer.'

'It would be appreciated if you could let us know,' said Slirander.

She had a feeling about grandma and she wondered whether she had sensed it too.

'Yes, and no one before has dared challenge the dominant leader in here. It's a dangerous place. You have just written your own death warrants. Don't leave the prison without one. There's plenty of room for you two outside.'

'Is that with or without the legal process?' replied Slirander.

Clever answers were not appreciated in prison. It just makes a bad situation worse. It was stalemate. On the one hand, there was grandma playing boss giving dangerous orders and on the other, the two girls whose only fault was to find out grandma's name to determine meeting her in a memory. Maybe this was a forgettable memory? The hall was full of treacherous emotions which seethed like bubbling soup. It had become a very unsafe environment for the two girls. They knew they were in danger and surrounded by the agitated crowd.

'I don't like the look of this,' said Davidia. 'I feel we should leave, but how? I would feel far safer in that crappy cell than in here. At least there'd be a wall behind our backs instead of this unstable crew intent on harm. Perhaps that's their enjoyment, hurting others.'

'No one will harm us, of that I'm sure,' said a confident Slirander. 'Excuse me, we need to return to our cells, so please allow a pathway through the crowd. We need to plan our escape.'

She said it to the general population who were stunned with the cheekiness of it.

'You'll never leave here and if you do, it won't be alive,' an inmate called out.

It was ignored, though noted.

To leave the hall, it would be akin to running the gauntlet as they did in ancient times with each inmate holding a stick to bash the passers-through. No one moved. Slirander had to be proactive once more. She brushed the bent spoon again and it flew around the room buzzing heads as an annoying flying pest, leaving a small dot of hot liquid on every person. It slowly oozed over their scalps scalding them like a hot chilli. The pain was sufficient to distract them from the girls leaving the hallway. As Davidia passed grandma, she gave her a withering look.

'You don't deserve a granddaughter. You actually tried to have us killed. My opinion of you has certainly altered.'

Grandma's eyes glazed over. She didn't understand the reference; besides, she was single, in prison and rehabilitation was yet to be achieved.

'We aren't going to that cell again, are we? We need to escape from here. What about the cemetery? There might be an exit from there,' said a nervous Davidia.

'That would be most unlikely. It's the end of the train ride of life. I doubt if there's an escape hatch for souls to slip through. I prefer the solitary confinement rooms because they are dark and we can escape without being seen.'

'How can we escape from there? There is only an entrance door, not an exit one.'

'Look at it as an opening and closing of that space. Quickly, Mandy is nearing us. Do something to get us tossed in solitary confinement.'

'Why is it always me that has to provoke animosity?' muttered Davidia.

She had to use unfamiliar prison-speak to create a reaction. Would it be enough?

'Hey, large arse, you want to try some action on this?'

Davidia ran her hands up and down her torso like a model extolling the fine features of the latest designs. Her hands rested on a couple of important locations which didn't go unnoticed. Mandy began to sweat. There were few sweets on the job and she was sorely tempted. She approached Davidia. Little sweat drops formed above her lips. Nothing was said about anywhere else. Her hope of laying a hand on her took a twist as Davidia landed a beautifully placed kick to her stomach. It created involuntary wind turbulence and one giant worm was writhing on the stone floor.

'You nasty little bitch, you'll pay for that. It's a week in solitary for you both.'

Mandy stood up and bashed Davidia with her baton. It left her buttock with a nasty, perfectly shaped bruise. She was grabbed by the neck and frog-marched all the way to one of two dark cells. Slirander was thrown in the other. They were pitch-black inside. Once the heavy steel door had squeezed shut, it was like a sealed sound cage. The animals inside were tense. Davidia felt the walls. They were all solid stone. The floor was likewise. Once the eyes had adjusted to the dark, all she could make out was a ditch for a toilet and a wooden bench upon which to sleep, sit or nap. There was no water or any bedding. It was stark. She called out to Slirander. There was dead silence. There was no way of telling time or how long they would be cooped up, if they stayed the journey to release.

'Curse Slirander's grandma. I might never get home again.'

A pearl shaped teardrop escaped from her welling eyes and made a damp spot on the floor, which she couldn't see. At that moment she felt sad and lonely. She sighed.

What was Slirander up to?

*

In the solitary confinement cell next door, Slirander had paced out her environment and noted the hopelessness that it presented. The cell was small and believed to be escape proof. The stone walls and floors were of a thickness any mason would be proud of. There were no cracks to pick at, no loose bars on a window, because there was no window, and its two-stone thickness made it almost impenetrable. How was a girl to be released from this? The door was sealed tight. Slirander couldn't change form because she was in the memory as herself. To do so meant her end; however, the bent spoon that accompanied her might just be the difference. It was talented in many ways that explanation would take far too long. Better to enjoy its journey without question.

'It is up to us now,' she said, speaking in the dark to the bent spoon as if it was her pet. 'Remember what we thought on the way here and what you must do.'

The bent spoon didn't speak, but responded with a movement of its scoop.

'Me too. What to do? What to do? Drill the wall between the cells.'

Slirander had instructed the bent spoon to act as a drill bit and attack the mortar around the stones between her and Davidia's cell. The escape plan was to bring Davidia into her cell, reseal the wall and then escape from there. She had discovered a weakness within the wall, but it was only from within her cell. Slirander gently turned on the bent spoon by rotating it between her hands. It instantly revved with excitement. Soon a small hole appeared, then a larger one, until the mortar around the stones had been loosened. Davidia heard the droning sound, but put it down to general mental noises as her head was swimming with imaginary sounds. She ignored it. Slirander took the bent spoon in one hand and used it as a battering ram against the stones. Miraculously they moved, creating a gaping rectangular hole, and crashed onto Davidia's cell floor. The sound echoed but couldn't be heard outside.

'Playing builders, are we?' said Davidia, not realising that freedom had been given a chance.

'Davidia, climb through,' encouraged Slirander. 'There is a way out from in here. Hurry.'

Davidia did as suggested. This time she did listen to what was said. Once through, the two friends were reunited. The stones were replaced by the bent spoon attaching itself to them and one by one dragged them back into their original spot. In the dark, no one could tell that they had been removed and replaced.

'Am I glad to see you,' said Davidia. She hugged her friend, something she wouldn't do whilst in the shower. 'How do we leave here? I can't see a bright exit sign or any doors. It's as tight as a fish's arsehole. Believe me, I've looked. The fish certainly know what a tight spot is.'

'Meet Bently, my super spoon. It will get us out of here.'

Davidia felt the size of Bently and the dark hid her expression of disgust and disbelief.

'A small bloody bent spoon is our saviour? Thank God I'm not in an insane asylum, I might believe it,' she muttered to herself. 'What's its party trick?'

'Have faith. What to do? What to do? Drill a hole in that wall.'

Bently couldn't see clearly in the dark, so Slirander placed it in the exact spot her mathematical skills had told her was the weakest point in the room. She let Bently at it. A continuous droning sound was heard. Small pieces of rock and dust particles were dispensed from the hole like a wombat excavating between its legs. A few minutes later, Bently returned red hot and in one piece. Slirander bent over, another thing not performed whilst in the shower, and peered down the long hole to the outside wall. There was clear daylight. It was a small and tight hole similar to the fish's whatnot. No one could escape along it unless you were a small spider or dust mite. Slirander mumbled some silly chant to herself and before another word was uttered, her fingers extended into the hole and disappeared. A moment later she had a thin tree trunk in her hand. It was another memory tree which she managed to pull inside the cell. Her fingers returned to normal. She tied a huge knot of thin tree branches and it acted as a plug in the hole.

'Pull,' she yelled.

The thin tree trunk didn't want to be uprooted as it protected a memory. It had to return to its upright stance. It tugged as hard as it could. Slowly the cell wall began to crumble and an opening appeared large enough for an escape. Davidia was amazed that her talented friend had conjured up the impossible. They wouldn't be discovered as they were on an outside wall. Another week, and only then will anyone realise an escape was made and ruin the reputation of the prison. They weren't concerned about the murderous grandma.

Were they prepared to meet her again?

Once outside, they were in the memory forest, which didn't seem as doomy as when they had first visited.

'We're safe,' said Davidia. 'Thanks. I was not enjoying my holiday in there.'

'Me neither,' replied Slirander. 'We aren't truly safe from this memory yet. We have to actually leave it behind.'

Suddenly, a huge tree root dangled in front of them. Was it a tease? Was it lost? Had its memory responsibility escaped? Was it searching for something? In an act of haste and for no better reason, Slirander yelled out to climb it.

'I'm not Davidia and the beanstalk. Besides, I'm afraid of heights and we don't know where it goes.'

'Get up that tree root if you want to survive. It is our escape route.'

'Don't push me about.' Davidia had regained her stubborn streak.

'If you won't, then I will.'

Slirander grasped the tree root and swung up it exactly like a close animal relative does in the forest.

In a flash, she was gone. Davidia was alone. The tree root began to withdraw. Davidia had to engage her stubborn streak and swallow humble pie – even that wasn't on the prison menu

160

– and imitate Slirander. She was a hair's breadth at being left behind. The upwards climb was difficult and she had to pass through clods of clingy dirt. Her hair became an entangled mess. Pop! She had made it to the surface. Slirander was waiting.

'Glad you made it. We have climbed out of that memory tree and are now once again in the real memory forest. I'm not sure where to go next.'

'What about an exit?'

10 ESCAPE

'I think my visit to grandma's memory has worn thin. Twice we've been under threat in this section of her memory. Those memory trees hold nothing but danger. Have we missed all the nice ones? Even her lower key memories held risk. I doubt if any fun would be generated in here.' Davidia was contemplative about her recent experiences.

'It has been difficult, but we did agree to follow her journey,' replied Slirander.

She wasn't actually defending grandma's past. She was justifying why they came in the first place. They had discovered a few surprises. Were there anymore they would encounter on their attempt to leave?

'This gloomy place is so depressing. My memories don't hold anything like this. Which way is out?'

'I'm not sure. It all looks the same to me.'

The darkness of the memory forest brooded over them like a heavy burden. Every tree was thin, black and lacked any real colour. None of them offered any assistance. Would a voice materialise and lead them to safety? They began the walk to nowhere. The ground was squelchy under their feet. They were fearful that a memory might escape and encapsulate them. A footprint lasted as long as the next one was made. Davidia grabbed a tree trunk and raised her feet above the ground. There was no shoe imprint left at all. That's how it should be in another's memory. Only the person's memory imprint should remain. Davidia continued the journey.

'I'm sick of this. Exactly what are we looking for? There aren't any doors in here or exit signs, so how do we know where we are going? It's like a bloody maze. I can get out of them, but in here I'm not so sure.'

'I must admit it's a bit confusing. I'm as lost as you are. Do you remember how we got here? Surely we can find that entry point again.'

'No, you won't,' chirped a voice. 'You had been told not to upset the memories and did you listen, no? You have signed your own eternal warrants.'

'Get real. We aren't staying in here for eternity.'

'You have no choice. The memory forest has spoken.'

'You mean a damn tree is telling us it's over; life as we know it.'

'You will have to adapt. There is no real food in here. You may continue to wander aimlessly. Everything is the same.'

'Which one of you smart-arsed trees is taking the mickey out of us? I've a good mind to uproot you and see what memory you hold. Is it you?'

Davidia was boiling into rant mode. She searched for any sign she was being spoken to. There was none. In exasperation, she kicked the nearest tree as hard as she could in a fit of frustration. A splinter broke off. A cry of pain could be heard. That memory tree was now imperfect. It had been tampered with. The other memory trees were agitated that their perfect symmetry of shape and being whole had been ruined by a damn sixteen-year-old girl whose memories were much shorter than the one she had just damaged. The memory trees all suffered the inflicted pain.

'Are you satisfied now? Something terrible is going to happen in here.'

'Such as what? I've got a headache. Give me some intelligence for that old furphy. None of these memory trees are capable of anything other than standing guard over a piece of someone's history. I need to be home.'

'I feel trouble heading our way. We've disturbed something unpleasant.'

'So far in here, it has all been unpleasant, so what's the difference this time?'

'I'm not sure, but it doesn't feel good.'

The girls stayed alert. They didn't want an unfair advantage taken over them by not being prepared.

'Those trees are beginning to shake. It wasn't from anything I said. Maybe it's a memory eruption. Who knows?'

'I suppose bad memories can try to overtake the good ones. This memory forest is littered with the bad ones, if not all of them.'

What to do? What to do?

'Did you say something, Slirander? I thought I heard Pole. He wouldn't be in here, surely?'

'I heard it too. It must be a warning of some kind.'

A distant sound was heard. It wasn't verbal, but a low monotonous howl was growing closer. It hadn't been planted by them. Maybe the trees did? It wasn't an uninvited visitor much like the girls. The sound didn't increase in intensity. The trees began to shake. Their tree roots became exposed. They began to topple over, but never released their grip in the soil. No memory had escaped. The forest now was a bent over affair with the girls being the highest structure in sight. Two skyscrapers in mini land. They wondered what that was all about. Nothing had attacked or reprimanded them, even though they may have deserved it. No contact had been made either. It wasn't an alien force, was it? Grandma's memories were full of surprises and intrigue. They waited. There wasn't anywhere else to go. Time couldn't be measured. Day or night just became two nouns of memory. They might be in the land of the lost and forgotten. The girls felt anxious and were searching for a solution. Where was that bloody exit? They sat on a bent tree trunk and snap, it split in two. That was a huge mistake. What not to do? What not to do? whispered in their ears.

'How were we supposed to know that? We're tired and need a rest,' said Davidia to the whisperings. She thought that she was haunted.

'I feel trouble brewing. The trees have bent over in subservience for some reason or another. There may be a memory overlord in here. My mum told me that grandma was a mystery wound up in a corkscrew. One never knew what would happen next with each twist and turn that she lived.'

'She was probably an alcoholic. Corkscrews only open bottles of various types of alcohol as far as I know. I could be wrong, but in this memory maze anything is possible.'

Suddenly, the tree that they were seated on collapsed and sadly uprooted like a hair follicle tugged from its growth space. The girls crumpled to the forest floor. Once again, tree roots encircled their bodies.

'Not again,' said Davidia, 'more biting of tree roots. Isn't anything edible in here?'

They were held fast, yet felt that they were slipping away into another underground world from the past. Grey monotonous strobe lighting guided their path. Where had they ended up this time? Grandma's memories were exciting but quite tiring. Nothing easy projected from them.

'It's another damn hole in the ground. It's like a game of snakes and ladders and we don't really know who the snake is. I doubt if it's a gold miner's digs we have ended up in.'

'It's a cave of some sort,' said Slirander.

'I'm not going down an underground hole for anyone. Speleology is for the stupid. I'm staying up here in the light.'

Davidia wasn't subjecting herself to tomb-like stress in any set of caverns.

'There doesn't seem to be anyone else around. Look outside. That may clue us in.'

Slirander wasn't sure of their bearings. They were in a cave, but where? There was no one else around. The landscape outside the cave was a barren, sandy desert even a camel would baulk at crossing. What would any grandma be doing in a rotten place like this? It had to be some sort of punishment, didn't it? Sane individuals would avoid it like the plague, or was this an internment home for the two memory disturbers? What a conundrum! They had no idea where they were, or where they are, or where that was, or where it might be, or where things had got skewed. It could be one or all of them. Whatever it was, it had the corkscrew feeling of being screwed.

'Where in the hell are we?' said Davidia, standing at the cave entrance surveying the horizon, for what, she wasn't sure.

'It's got me puzzled too. Do we have to make a choice between a cave or desert? Neither of them seems to lead anywhere. We might have overdone the grandma memory thing. This memory has certainly thrown us a real problem. There are no other inhabitants in this one so far, so what is it all about? There is not even a possibility of any engagement with others. This certainly isn't a holiday spot like the last memory.'

'And look how that turned out. There's a real mystery about this one. You don't think grandma met with aliens out here in the desert, do you?'

'I wouldn't put it past her. The more I learn about her the more I don't seem to know. People are sometimes experts at hiding the past especially if you don't want anyone knowing about it. If it was an affair, I can understand that, but this, whatever this is makes me unsure if I really knew my grandma at all.'

Slirander was having secondary thoughts about her lovely grandma. So far, she had been an eye- opening world of surprises.

Would she compile her thesis on what she knew prior to visiting her past, or include the new fascinating areas of knowledge she had now experienced with her? Who really was grandma?

What to do? What to do? once again rang in her ears.

'I don't know what to do,' Slirander yelled in her top decibel range.

There was no echo. The grains of desert sand shrunk in fear to avoid the wind blast. She let a tear slip past an open eyelid; in fact, it was group therapy time and a few other self-made teardrops joined in the wet party. Sadly, her face was striped with wet streaky lines, like drawing a line in the sand with a stick, which gave her a zebra look. The gentle drip, drip, splashing sound was all that could be heard. Davidia felt the same, but didn't want a facial leak. Was it hopeless for the two memory seekers? It certainly seemed that doom, another D word, might become a permanent unwanted companion. They sat forlorn and lost as Slirander continued to cry. It was a pensive moment. To be home with family, her own bedroom, fresh food and lots of perfumes and clothes was a wish list not found in grandma's memories.

What are they going to do?

*

'Make for those small hills over there. I should camp there for the evening. Go, Sandstrom,' said a desert dweller delivering good tidings between oases.

Tidings was the official title; however, in reality, it was only gossip that it delivered. In the lonely parts of the sand dunes, its utterings were mental relief and word fertility for any inhabitant. It gave hope for the beleaguered. News of something else always cheered them up. Sandstrom was a large grain of sand that it sat on like a magical carpet. They had travelled the annals of time together on a never-ending circuitous route.

This was a desert rat, despised by many because of its appearance. It was treated as an outcast destined to roam the sand dunes with Sandstrom, its transporter. Its mangy coat was moth-eaten and hardly qualified as a coat, more like a second-hand waste garment. Its tail had most of it missing due to unappreciated gossip being passed along. In human terms, it was no larger than the smallest pinkie and well adept at camouflage. Its eyes rotated from right to left, then left to right, confusing anyone who tried to eyeball it when difficult words were expressed or something said no one liked to hear. It was a verbal legend of the dunes, often whispered about in hushed tones of, 'Does it exist?' They made no sound when travelling because all gossip was saved for the next "whatever" it met. It was headed straight for the girls and the cave. It was a safety rest stop on its travels and normally, a gossip-free zone. It had a name, but what use was it when no one cared to speak it. Simply, the word "rat" had sufficed.

*

A small puddle had developed at Slirander's feet, no larger than two thumbnails. The cave floor was of solid rock and kept the wet teardrops as captives. In time, evaporation would remove them.

'It makes a nice reflection,' said an imaginary sound. Slirander was thinking of woe.

'It certainly does,' she replied. 'Is that me in there? She doesn't look pretty.'

'She does. You are in a mental camouflage moment. It will change.'

'I'm so in the shit in here. There is no exit, but thanks for making me feel better.'

'You will have a visitor shortly. It will be fine. Good reflecting.'

The mental sounding ceased. Slirander looked around. All she saw was a thoughtful Davidia waiting for her to finish the sobs. She nodded, which is one of the head's movements. What visitor?

'We are receiving a visitor shortly.'

'From where? Thin air? Shall I wear a skirt? It's hardly likely out here in this bustling metropolis.'

Davidia doubted her friend, based on the nothingness of the area.

'I am surprised myself. Wait and see. Who knows what transpires in the memories of others?'

Slirander was certainly in a reflective mood.

*

'I can feel that something is not empty,' said the rat, sniffing the air.

His sensitive nostrils had picked up girl scent, a most uncommon odour. What was it doing here? Did it belong to something? It sniffed again and confirmed its first analysis was correct. What an interesting situation. It was the second time that it had sniffed girl scent, but this time it was quite different, fresher, in fact, and not so far away.

'Sandstrom, I think we may have company shortly. What a delicious thought.'

There were other existing things about which it could divulge what it knew and pick up more interesting tales.

'Now where did I pick up that similar scent? Whatever we meet may want to know. It could be one of them. I'll file that in my memory. The cave is nearby. We can rest again soon.'

The modest hill in which the cave and its new cave dwellers were currently in residence, appeared in front of them. It was a bump on the landscape, much like a camel's hump. Sandstrom pulled up out front. It could see clearly what was in there. It sniffed. Fear was absent, but company wasn't. An approach was made. In they went. They were amazed to see a tiny oasis on the cave floor. Was it a miracle? It hadn't rained inside the cave ever, so how could this have happened. A tiny tongue flashed at it for taste. It was fresh, clear and tasty.

'We'll stop here tonight,' it said.

Suddenly, it turned and noticed the two giant walking monoliths above. They were mobile but seated. It was question time.

'Can you communicate,' it said. 'I'm down here by the oasis.'

'Did you say something, Davidia? I thought I heard a squeaky voice.' Slirander couldn't see the source.

'I'm down by the oasis,' it repeated.

'I'm sure I heard a voice of some kind.'

'Sandstrom, fly up there,' it pointed. 'Is that better? Can you hear me now? I'm in front of that round moving shape with the rolling eyeballs.'

Davidia squinted and saw a minute flying object. She looked closer.

'It's a miniature flying rat. I didn't know that rats could fly. It must be a new breed. Excuse me, did you just speak to us?'

'I most certainly did. What are you doing in here? You're foreign.'

Who cared what they were talking to or what about?

'We are looking for a grandma. Have you seen any lost ones lately? I mean this place should be full of them.' Sarcasm began to seep into pointed commentary.

'I don't know what a grandma is. Do they have a particular look?'

'Not really. Perhaps you have seen someone who has similar features to us.'

'Perhaps I have. I've scented something similar, but not actually seen it as clear as you two. It was partially covered. It isn't far from here. My apologies, I forgot to introduce myself. My name is Migraine. I believe it's French,' he said proudly.

'You mean migraine as in headache?' said Davidia.

'No. No. It is French, it is sounded so.'

Before a tetchy argument ensued, Davidia sensibly thought, why not, let Migraine believe it's migraine (me-graine). She couldn't be bothered arguing over semantics. It had hinted at a familiar scent. Could it be grandma? The girls were paying attention to the flying speck.

'Where did you say you scented a similar smell? Surely there couldn't be another like us in a barren place like this. What exactly is this place called?'

Migraine had to think for a moment. In all its travels it had never thought before of the names of areas it travelled in.

'I'm not sure. No one has asked for that. It's …' The ground suddenly shook. 'That's a warning. It often happens. The caves are often a disgruntled lot. I better continue my travels.'

'Aren't you tired and in need of a good rest? You certainly look like you deserve it.'

Migraine thought again. It did feel rather tired. There was that delicious new oasis that it'd recently discovered, plus there was no fear or threat to its safety, so the rest option had appeal. It landed next to the teardrop oasis. It had reduced alarmingly. Evaporation was its enemy.

'Did you see that the oasis has shrunk? Where did it go?'

In its realm, each oasis was a permanent waterhole and it was surprised to find that this was a temporary one. It was a gossip first. It would be keen to extoll the thrill of such a discovery to others throughout its travels making it a more eagerly sought-after speaker to all. Maybe the inhabitants in this memory might not think it was so disgusting after all.

'They were only teardrops.'

'What an unusual name.'

'Exactly what are you? You haven't told us. We're waiting.'

Davidia was anxious to know what Migraine was and its function in grandma's memory.

Migraine thought again.

'I'm a tidings sharer. A mobile information relator and a first-class gossip. I hear, remember and relate verbal data from each place I visit and pass on some or all of it at my next stop to the listening group. It's exciting to transfer this knowledge. What can you tell me about whatever it is you are?'

The girls weren't interested in giving free advice before they knew whether it was actually worth it. Their school motto was Receive to Give, so that's exactly what they proposed.

'We have a proposition for you. If you tell us about that other scent and where it is and how we get there, we will personally produce for you another teardrop oasis and make you the gossip envy of any memory.'

Migraine couldn't refuse the enticement. He went on to explain that over a small sand dune not far away, he had passed a Bedouin camp consisting of a few camels and half a dozen tall shapes with dark bushy masses hanging in front of their turbans. Each carried a huge sabre almost as tall as themselves. They were camped at Peski Oasis, refuelling for a long day's travel. A small tent was guarded by two of them. It was impossible to see what was in there; however, a fly-by produced an interesting scent which hadn't been sniffed before. It was simply amazing. Being so small, Sandstrom flew in through a small gap and Migraine saw a shape that look like the two girls'. It was tied up in fashionable satin scarves revealing two fearful eyes. It was either a slave or a captured shape that they were taking to the markets to sell. That was Migraine's take on it. She could also have been a royal princess being secretly smuggled across the land to avoid a relationship from betrothed marrying. Whatever the reality of it, the girls wondered whether that was grandma. It was their only lead so far. They wondered why there weren't many more inhabitants.

'How do we get there and which direction is it in?'

'You must walk in that direction where the sand is furrowed. You must move quickly before the wind changes direction. It isn't far. The horizon is tricky. Beware of the environment. It's harsh, unforgiving and difficult to walk through. I fly, so it is easier, no?'

The girls weren't sure of the advice.

'What happens if the wind blows, the sand furrows away, redesigns it, or flattens it into a huge sandpit before we reach the end of our journey?'

'Ah, no! It is over. *C'est le vie.* What else can I do?'

'It's worth the risk. The exit might be that way also.'

'I thought we'd have to exit via the memory forest. That's the impression I've formed whilst in this unpleasant memory section,' said Davidia.

If an exit actually existed and one hoped there was, it was impossible to know the whereabouts of its existence. It would be a trial-and-error exercise, one which might jeopardise their safety. The girls agreed to the risk.

'Thank you, Migraine. This is your reward as agreed.'

This time both girls were forced to shed tears, made easier by thinking of the dates that they could experience in the future, yet not be able to make it. Two small pools of teardrop oases formed on the cave floor. Migraine was so impressed. These were the first above-ground oases that he had ever seen formed from such strange mobile structures. Normally, they were produced from an underground water source. His gossip potential had immediately increased by witnessing this new phenomenon.

'That's enough,' said Davidia, 'my eyes are starting to hurt.'

'I wonder how far we have to walk. The horizon is pancake flat and there is nothing but sand between us and it. I'm not sure of this memory; however, let's go and leave Migraine to his new interest.'

Slirander was just being cautious. She didn't want any stuff-ups or walk into an unknown situation she that couldn't handle.

'Are you a Polliton?' asked Davidia, as an afterthought.

She didn't think the comment would have any impact. How wrong was she? Migraine suddenly developed his namesake and began writhing on the cave floor.

'What to do? What to do?' he repeated involuntarily. 'How dare you release my secret? Nothing here knows my true identity, so how do you know it?'

'It was a guess, that's all,' said Davidia.

'A damn good one, I'd say. Now I cannot travel anymore as a tidings traveller since my secret has been openly spoken about. You have ruined my forever gig. Why did you visit this memory? If you ruin it, it's over also for you both. There is now not much time for you to escape from this memory, but it will be much tougher than before. The memory had been warned of dangerous interferers in its keeping, but the keepers had no idea what the problem would be. Now we know it's you two.'

'You mean that there is an exit somewhere?' said Slirander, hearing the comment.

'Every memory has an exit.'

'Where is this one?'

'It's …'

The ground shook and the cave roof fell on the two newly created oases. Amongst the dust, Migraine disappeared. They were alone again. The furrowed sand line was still visible. The girls quickly began walking toward it. Would it disappear also and ruin any chance of locating grandma?

174

*

The sand underfoot had the feeling of being held by two hands. Each grain was an impediment to easy walking. The girls trudged slowly toward the horizon, dutifully following the furrow suggested as their guide. A small sand dune is supposed to appear on the horizon as their bearing point. They looked around. The whole damn desert was full of small sand dunes and the horizon in every direction was identically labelled – flat.

'This is a great pickle we're in,' said an exhausting Davidia. Short breaths seemed to be the day's breathing pattern. 'It has a similarity and sameness. Nothing stands out except us.'

'We just have to keep moving. If we stop, the sand will envelop us and we might become the sand dunes that Migraine was talking about.'

'We seem to have walked a long way, but covered very little ground. It's impossible to tell what we've done except feel lost. It makes me wonder whether we'll escape from here. Home is certainly drawing me. I might have a dose of homesickness and lacking interest in grandma's memories.'

'If we make it back safely, we'll make this memory the last one to search through.'

'Good idea. Now let's get out of here.'

It was becoming darker the closer they walked to where the horizon was supposed to be. It didn't matter how far or for how long they walked, the horizon would always be out of reach. Instead, they needed a bearing. The furrow was slowly disappearing. The darkness made it impossible to see clearly into the distance. Suddenly, they saw a distant light flicker. In the desert, the night skies were clear for astronomers to observe without city lights distorting their vision.

'Was that an omen?' said Davidia. 'Weren't the men with the Bible guided by a bright light?'

'Stick to reality. It could have been a shooting star flashing past; however, it seems more man-made than heaven-sent. Those lights are campfires. Someone has lit them for night warmth. I doubt if they are to guide an aircraft onto a landing strip. This is a sandy desert.'

Their path had been set. They crept closer. Only the darkness hid them. Shadows menaced the ground for sure-footedness. The nearer they approached, sounds could be heard. None of it was in English. Maybe they'd discovered a new language? The mind is a tricky area at the best of times, but in the desert its imagination is heightened. They had no idea what they had happened upon, so surveillance was the best form of discovery. Davidia's scouting skills might be useful. Could she emulate The Blue Rat?

What would she have done? A disguise. That's it. A disguise. There wasn't any drapery store nearby, so it was the clothes that they stood in that would be its own disguise.

'Stop,' whispered Davidia. 'I can hear speaking in a foreign language. It's coming from that way.'

Davidia pointed carefully to a singular tent with two guards standing outside. The huge angular sword each wore would certainly gut a human. Davidia patted her mini muffin-top just to ensure her stomach was still strategically placed on her body and it wasn't available for any rearrangement. The girls observed their adversaries and were watchful about their movements. After a period of time, nothing had altered. Frustration began to set in as well as the cold soulless night of the desert sands.

'We should be warming ourselves near those fires and not here hiding like a sand lizard,' said Davidia.

'It's not possible to barge in and take a seat. We need a strategy.

Move to the far side around there,' Slirander pointed, 'and see if we can get really close.'

'Who said that you were in charge? I was a Scout, so I'm clearly a leader.'

Davidia was having control issues. Blue Rat or not, she had the management zeal. Slirander ignored the bleating because her focus was not on self, but grandma. Reluctantly, Davidia agreed to move around. The dark was their cover. The light of the campfires gave the impression of power. The grains of sand were proving to be an irritant. They permeated each piece of clothing and footwear creating the body itch. It had to be ignored, otherwise they could be discovered. Both girls were now near the tent around the back. The guards were at the front. The tent opening was there. The walls were made of canvas. A sharp knife could slice through a wall like shucking an oyster. Who had the knife? Nobody. Suddenly, a mosquito-like buzzing sound flew around their head spaces annoying them endlessly. Fancy, mosquitos living in such an arid desert? They wouldn't have lasted too long.

'What to do? What to do?' whispered in their ears.

'I'll bloody well what to do if I catch you. Piss off! We have a rescue mission unfolding and you are so annoying.' Davidia was on song with her verbal assault.

'Keep quiet. We don't want to alert the guards. What's bothering you?'

'A damn mosquito keeps droning at me.'

'Where is it? I can't hear it.'

'Take out your ear plugs. The pest is nearby.'

'I still can't hear it and I don't wear ear plugs.'

'It is still here. I sense it. Listen.'

There wasn't a sound. It was as if the desert slept. Was the annoyance only imagined?

'Need any help?' a light, squeaky voice offered.

The owner of it couldn't be seen because of the dark. It surprised them both. This was the first time in any dream where other help had been offered. Davidia was immediately suspicious. Slirander kept an open mind. Her sensitiveness was more acute than Davidia's. She waited for further contact.

'Who said that?' whispered Slirander. They waited.

'It was me,' said the voice. 'Remember me, Migraine? I wanted to ensure that you had made it safely to the horizon. You haven't got there yet.'

'Are you to be a help or a hindrance? This is a dangerous situation for us all.'

'What is it you hope to achieve?'

'To meet someone.'

'Approach the guards then. They'll speak to you.'

'It isn't them we seek.'

'Then there is nothing else for you here.'

'What makes you say that?'

'Intruders are never welcome to interfere with the laws of the land.'

'How are we intruding into the laws? We're not solicitors, felons, thieves or criminals who need the laws, so I don't see how we are intruding.'

'It is your presence. This memory is in turmoil now that you have visited and must not be tampered with. You must leave, if you can.'

'A few minutes ago, you asked if we needed any help. Now it seems to be the opposite. That is a light threat you mentioned. Which is it, help or hindrance?'

'I'll give you a migraine you won't forget if I find you,' piped Davidia.

She took a round arm swipe as a cricket sweeper and hoped

to strike what was causing the girls' uncertainty. A whoosh of air was all that was heard. Migraine realised that he was at peril with the girls. If he was swatted, then that would permanently alter the memory. His last parting shot was, 'I warned you.'

'The cold is a killer. I've never spent any time in a desert. I suppose it's cold every night.'

'We must get inside that tent unseen. If there is someone in there, then it must be grandma. She certainly has gotten herself into some dangerous memory spots. I wonder how bad this one will be. Whatever would she be doing out here? She's not royalty. Mum and dad had never revealed any desert circumstances. Perhaps she's a prisoner? Davidia, you can distract the guards by offering yourself as a person of interest, or perhaps a lost traveller, or even a princess. You've often whinged that no one treats you like a princess at home. Now is your chance.'

'What stupidity treat are you eating? Those guards look like heavyweights with a "don't mess with me" look. They'd eat me for supper.'

'Remember, you are a young, clever girl. Men can be putty in your hands if you play it right. What was that guy's name at school, the one you tricked into taking off most of his clothes on a blind date by playing cards of Strip Jack Naked and you threw them out of the window moments before your parents returned home. He exited through the same space just as quickly. Now, you had him hook, line and sinker. Think of the bush brigade as two older, larger, fooled males. They all eat from the same breakfast plate when it comes to attractive young women. They are always hungry.'

Slirander had massaged Davidia's ego perfectly. In the dark her red cheeks rouged up with confidence. Yes, she did have the goods required for interest. Yes, she was attractive and clever. Her confidence had an upwards spiral. She smoothed her sandy clothes, tightened her scarf around her head just so the face was clearly shown and felt down both sides of her body. Her shape was all there. Who wants to know?

Was she ready or not? It wasn't a child's game, but the idea of it assisted in focusing her approach. How would she explain her sudden appearance from out of nowhere, looking well-fed and being at this particular oasis? Not more mistruths, or no, it would be an imaginary recall. After all, she was in a memory and when recalled they are not exactly as first remembered. She was safe to embellish any story as long as it seemed plausible. She was like a hamburger, ready to go.

She stood tall and revealed herself from her hiding place. She strode forward toward the tent like a walking, mummified silhouette. The sand made no noise upon her approach. She didn't want to scare them like frightened hares, so she stopped short about six metres and stood still hoping to be noticed. Had she worn her favourite perfume; she would have been immediately scented. Desert showers didn't happen too often. A moment passed. The camp fires flickered nervously in the darkness, casting sinuous shadows as their light passed by the palm trees. Davidia was standing in between shadows. A guard glanced in her direction and motioned to her to come forward. He must have thought that she was a slave girl adoring the night sights because he showed no fear or anxiousness about her presence. Davidia moved forward trying to be as relaxed as possible. The light display on her cheeks didn't reveal her skin as white, but rather olive, an acceptable colouring for desert dwellers. The speech and understanding would be the real issue. To her amazement, the guard spoke in English.

'Hey, you there. It's after curfew. What is your business being outside? It is banned. Return to your tent immediately.'

A hand rested precariously upon a huge sword. It didn't have to convey its message by being removed. Davidia had no tent. She suddenly dropped her head and expressed her best sheepish look, staring back from two dewdrop eyes, flicking her eyelids as if they possessed an affliction. Her eyelash waves were like two miniature beach towels, or so it seemed. Her brainchild was to act childlike and pretend to not understand.

'Is that my tent? I'm lost. I went for a walk and I'm sure that someone turned off the lights.'

She raised her arms in surrender to not knowing where she was.

'That is not your tent. Tell me where your tent is located and I will direct you there. It is not safe out in the open. Marauders and thieves regularly attack oases like this one. One must be on guard at all times. Your safety depends on it.'

If Davidia could lure one guard away, then Slirander could slip into the tent and confront the inhabitant.

'It's this way.'

Davidia left with the guard. Slirander now had to use her own ingenuity. How long would Davidia's ploy last and what of its consequences?

*

The guarded tent was as insignificant as all of the others. Slirander noted that there were guards outside each tent and all were ferocious looking. She waited until Davidia was well clear, enjoying a guided tour. She crawled along the sand dunes like a desert python moving sideways for speed and silence. She had nothing sharp to cut the tent; however, that was an oft used tactic and easily detected when attempted. Could she dig underneath? That would take too long and, besides, digging in dry sand is refilling the same hole attempting to be dug. Her only venue of entrance was through the front door flap. How would she enter unnoticed? Her sleuthing skills weren't that expert. Another moment passed. Then she brilliantly remembered the temporary paralysis touch her father had once shown her. It lasted only a few minutes before wearing off. It meant close contact of the body kind and usually with less clothing than the swathes of cloth hiding the body. Slirander said a spell and a finger became sharpened like a pencil. She stabbed herself to ensure it functioned properly. The trick was to jab it into the forearm of a person just below the elbow. The shock of the jab stunned the receiver temporarily and they were powerless to perform any human function other than stand still. Firstly, she needed to see that forearm. A sixteen-year-old now had to act maturely beyond her years to attract the male insect into her trap. She swirled her scarf around her head, revealing only her face. She also looked olive-skinned in the fire shadows. She approached the remaining guard.

'Don't you look handsome this evening,' she said, with eyes downcast.

The male guard tensed, not that it had been a while since an attractive woman had confronted him, but rather his guard position was under threat. His hand felt for his sword and not his dagger.

'Who are you? It's after curfew. You should be home with family.'

Slirander thought that she soon might be.

'I thought that you would enjoy the company of a femme fatale, if I knew one,' she teased.

'Stay there. It's a dangerous environment here. Go home before risk attaches itself.'

Slirander moved closer.

'I love a man with large … ,' she paused, 'forearms. Maybe you can show me yours. Mine are smooth and silky.'

She guided the sharpened finger along her forearm leading his eyes in a hypnotic trance. Her skin was blemish-free and it felt like silk. The guard felt edgy. It wasn't his large sword, or his small dagger that was moving like an unseen desert serpent. There was a persistence he felt with this female, so in an act of conciliation and bragging rights about his forearms, he raised his cloth sleeve. Slirander reacted like a real desert serpent and stabbed him quickly without any pain. The glazed look indicated he was under her spell, another one. His body was paralysed. He stood as stiff as a palm tree. Slirander seized the moment. She entered the tent. What would she expect to find?

'Is this a bed and breakfast? The tour guide told me this was my accommodation for the night. This is tent number fifteen, isn't it? Are you a fellow traveller?'

There was already an inhabitant in there. Slirander wasn't told she had to double up with an older woman (going with the travel theme).

An older-aged woman sat there cross-legged with both hands facing upwards just under her chin. She reacted by throwing an object at Slirander which she held in her hands. Was it incense, a small vial of poison, or a miniature knife? It was a handful of gold dust that settled like the gentlest of gold snowflakes around her. The women stared at each other in a thought battle. Neither knew what was in each other's head, but complimentary was doubtful. The staring lasted a few seconds more.

'This is not public accommodation of any sort. This is my private quarters. You have not been invited. Please leave.'

The acid response could etch into her skin quite easily. There was an unpleasant, dangerous feeling around the cloth manne-quin; well, that's what she appeared to be.

'So, you're not a prisoner, a slave to be sold or hiding from a boyfriend?'

'Where did you get such preposterous claims? There is funny dust around. Have you been inhaling recently?'

The question was pointed, but not as sharp as Slirander's finger.

'There was talk amongst the tour travellers that we would meet at this oasis a strange and beautiful woman who was a member of the King's entourage. You mean it was only just gossip? I'm glad then I didn't invite the whole tour group over once I was settled. May I ask your role and how you got here?' Slirander was keen to know more. She decided to let a family comment slip out. 'You have the same features as me. Perhaps we're related?'

'No one has the features of the King's charge.'

'Could I become a King's charge? I'm much younger and fresher in every way,' she goaded.

It was obvious Slirander had almost worn out her welcome.

'Yes, you could, but it's a miserable lifestyle. I sit all day, eat prepared meals and when the King wants a play toy, I'm summoned. That's all there is to it. I was visiting Cairo as a traveller, like yourself, when someone noticed me in the marketplace with my fine white skin, blonde hair and full contoured shape. I was kidnapped and I am now on my way to a life of servitude. This trip is a training run of subservience. I dare not put anything out of place. My head needs to stay exactly where it is.'

'Can't you escape? I never knew you were in Egypt, I mean, I'd never been to Egypt before, either. Can I help in any way?'

'No. Go before the guards discover you. Death awaits us all, but for some in life it comes earlier. Don't waste your time as a deceased person.'

Slirander hadn't asked her name, so she didn't know that it really was grandma. She had to try and name a name.

'My name is Slirander. What's yours?'

'It's Angel Flower.'

'That's not a real name, is it? It seems made up.'

'The King names all his charges. It's the least I can do is to accept it whilst I plan.'

'So, it's not Michelle, then?'

Grandma's face went rainbow, then purple and then sauce red under her scarf. She became enraged. She stood up from her seated position and began to have a body tremor.

'Who told you? No one in this camp knows it. Have you been sent as a spy? The sacred vow of not knowing has now been broken. You have invoked the death demons. Guard, remove the invader with your sword.'

Slirander knew immediately that no accommodation or beverages were to be offered to a weary traveller. The tour was over. Her life was now at risk. She exited the tent. Fortunately, the guard was still incapacitated, but the groans from various body openings suggested movement was coming. Other guards could be seen running toward the tent, swords raised ready for that fatal swipe. Slirander didn't fancy being a French guillotine citizen at that very moment.

Where was Davidia?

*

'This is dangerous place. Not safe for girl out on her own. Is your tent near here?'

The guard escorting Davidia had good manners and treated her with respect, having assumed that she was one of their own. They had walked quite some distance. Davidia had no tent to go to, so she had to improvise with the truth. She kept her eyes peeled for an opportunity to turn to her advantage, or at least benefit her in some way. A group of tents were set up outside the oasis perimeter and Davidia was about to say that she was with them when the guard raised a hand and pointed in that direction.

'What is it?'

'Stay away from that group. They deal in death. They sell weapons and treat women badly. You look good. It's not possible you know them.'

Davidia thought, what a vote of confidence in her tastes when she was about to use them as a ruse and say she belonged. Another plan was needed. A deadly mistake had narrowly been avoided.

'It's a lovely night for a walk, don't you think?'

'I'm not here to walk. I'm here to return you to your tent. Where is it?'

The guard was becoming agitated. He had other guard issues than stroll under the stars. He began searching in earnest for that elusive tent. It wasn't camouflaged, hidden behind a rocky outcrop or on a nearby sand dune. It didn't exist. They had almost circled the oasis and if that happened without finding her tent, a real problem would erupt.

'This is as far as I need to go,' said Davidia. 'My tent is down that side street. It is safe for me from here. My family will be pleased to see me. Thanks for your care.'

'There is no tent down there. It is all houses.'

'I am a visitor to my family and in their front yard is my tent. You can return to your guard duty. Your person of interest may need your protection more than I do. I'm almost home now.'

Davidia encouraged the guard to return to his duty. Any longer with her and explanations might be delivered by force on a sword tip.

'You go, I watch.'

Davidia slipped silently into the laneway, moving lightly and quickly checking over her shoulder in case she was followed.

Fortunately, she wasn't. She waved as she disappeared behind a wall into someone's mud brick front yard. It was large enough for a real tent, but an imaginary one can fit anywhere. The guard left her alone.

'Trespasser! Get out of my yard,' yelled an irate citizen who had an intruder on their premises.

'My apologies. I got lost down these side streets. I was being chased by a ruffian and had nowhere else to hide.'

Davidia bolted. Like Slirander, she was running somewhere as well, but where?

*

The girls were entrapped at the oasis in the middle of the desert. To run into the dunes meant certain death from being lost and lack of food and dehydration. The fabulous life duo would definitely come to a close if that happened. Fortunately, it was still dark and at times shadows played tricks on the mind with what it actually saw.

The girls were excellent sprinters, but running over sand slowed down the impact of speed. Slirander ran into the desert against any better judgement. In the dark, she could disappear for a short period of time. Davidia sensing that running around the streets was rather pointless did exactly the same thing. At least she wouldn't be chased out there where danger lurked everywhere if one believed superstitions. A sand dune might appear as a huge, man-eating slug. A sinewy shadow could be an assassin ready to strike. The night sounds might be an animal on the loose. Whatever, it was represented as, it was their immediate salvation.

The girls had both dived behind the same sand dune slug spitting and spluttering grains from an almost-swallow. The shock startled them both. Had they been found for execution by the guards for transportation as body entertainment for bearded males? Heaving heavily, Davidia ventured first contact.

'Who's there? I warn you, if you try anything silly, I'll run you through with my sword.' She waited.

'And what stupidity that would be,' came the response from Slirander. She waited.

'Is that you, Slirander?'

'Of course, it is. I see you didn't run out on me.'

'I wouldn't leave you behind; in fact, I don't know if there is anywhere else to go. We are stuck in a sandy desert kilometres from anywhere. It's not safe at that oasis either.'

'Wait until it's light and we can assess our situation from there.'

'This grandma of yours is nothing but trouble. I'm beginning to wonder more about her life with all these hidden components. She's certainly been an adventurer. Maybe our lives might follow a similar pattern. There's still plenty of time.'

'She's proving to be quite unusual. Wait until mum and dad hear about her exploits. They'll be surprised. It makes me wonder where mum was born, perhaps in a dugout canoe floating on the Amazon River, or on the side of a mountainous Nepalese village in a small brick house, or in some other foreign land in a hospital. It's quite exciting, isn't it, not knowing? In the meantime, we must find the departure lounge from this memory. We've outstayed our welcome.'

'The guards might search for us in the morning. We're both good female catches in any culture.' Davidia smiled. They certainly were. 'I remembered a group of tents outside the oasis the guard warned me against. They could be worth a visit. It's in that direction. I don't see anything else happening.'

Davidia pointed, but no one could see her directional finger in the dark. She grabbed Slirander's sleeve and led the way.

Fumbling along in the dark was slow progress. They neared the warned-about tents, supposedly full of thieves and danger. At least grandma won't have visited this lot. The inhabitants wore turbans. Many of them had beards. Each wore a swathe of clothing and a pungent distinct aroma swirled around the nostrils. It wasn't the aroma of camel shit, human shit or food, it was the hygienic element. The girls decided not to enter the camp and fall under the aerating pong.

Suddenly, from behind them, a few metres away, a series of grunts could be heard. They turned to observe many camels all rested on their knees making settling noises.

'Should we steal two of them and make our escape?' suggested Davidia.

Slirander wasn't into felonious pursuits, yet had to consider the risk and reward element of their action. They couldn't risk capture or be someone's reward. There was only a brick wall of thought to get over. She finally succumbed to the idea of becoming a thief.

'Quiet. We'll sneak up away from the guard, steal two and release the others. I don't feel brave or well.'

'Me either. Have you ridden a camel before?'

'No.'

'Me either. Let's sneak up to them.'

The girls did their best imitation of a desert serpent crawling along on their stomachs. The camels made so much noise that nothing else could be heard. They farted, belched, grunted and snorted. They noticed that the guard was snoring soundly in the realms of the sandman. His defences were down. This was their chance. Neither had ridden a camel before, so how hard was it? They both jumped into the saddles that had been left on and kicked the camel from both sides. A belligerent grunt and resistance arose. Davidia tugged at its nose rope and surprisingly it stood tall. Slirander did the same. They cut the rope and immediately headed into the dark. The guard awoke in shock to see two of his favourite backsides disappear into the distance. The warning wail was given.

'I've been attacked by subversives. They overpowered me. It was that rival tribe from the oasis. We must retrieve them.'

Soon, a posse of grunting, complaining quadrupeds bounded into the dark after the thieves. Davidia was sitting uncomfortably, being bounced like a rubber ball hurting most of her body from the waist down. Slirander was ill-at-ease, straining to hang on. They couldn't see the chasing pack, but it sounded close. Noise was exacerbated in the dark. The group was almost upon them. Suddenly, a sand storm began to blow hard. It impeded any vision. The camels knew where to go. The girls were lost. The wind howled in pain, the sand grains took revenge with repeated stinging attacks and it was impossible to know what was occurring. The girls yelled into the darkness. No one could be heard.

In an instant, the girls were parted from their steeds and floated through the air like they were in a mini tornado. Was this the doom that the forest had foreboded upon them? Oh, why didn't they listen? A huge, scraping blanket rubbed itself against them. Hadn't they felt that weird fabric before? Just as they felt there was no end to their trauma or their troubles, they were bundled onto a stone floor in a familiar room. They looked back to see the retreating hessian wall.

They had landed safely back at grandma's special room and in one piece.

What a relief for them both. Hopefully they retained the details of grandma's memories to extol to Slirander's parents and what about that award-winning thesis?

Had life returned to normal?

'I don't believe it. Safely back without a scratch. It's unbelievable and what about those other two walls?'

'Let's not press our luck.'

The girls took a moment to ponder the adventures that they just had in grandma's memories. It had certainly turned into a mixture of thoughts that a grandma had such an exciting early life.

What would become of theirs?

Would it become that interesting?

11   WHAT TO DO? WHAT TO DO?

The girls stood in the centre of grandma's space. They took a breather from almost being demised with their grandma adventures. Each had a different thought set to the other. No two minds are clones.

Davidia pondered whether she was prepared to risk another memory adventure whilst Slirander was now on a mental quest for grandma knowledge even though it may imperil her existence. Once the memory genie had been released from the memory records, in this case grandma's special space, it was difficult to stem the flow of interest. Which wall was it to be, stone or slate?

A couple of chairs placed near a small table in the corner between the stone and slate walls hadn't been noticed earlier when they had entered grandma's special space. They were keener on the walls and what they represented than being seated. Both were now exhausted after their triple run-ins and escapes from the hessian wall.

'I'll rest here for a while,' said Davidia. 'Being a memory hunter certainly is tiring.'

She sat down. The weight of her torso felt ten kilos lighter with relief.

'This needs thinking about,' said Slirander. 'I still would like to pursue one more memory wall and I don't know which one to select.'

'You can do it on your own. I've experienced enough of your grandma for quite some time. Besides, we now have enough information to plan and write our thesis. Any more might be overkill.'

'I'll give it some thought.'

Slirander also sat down. Her body relished the effort of not competing against gravity. Both girls were experiencing their contemplative period and each researched their own minds on their grandma experiences. No conclusions were drawn because their thoughts were rudely interrupted. The small table top made of one solid piece of Huon pine at least a third of a metre thick and a third of a metre square – a chubby piece of timber more like a tree trunk portion – opened at the top and the girls peered down on a scene of darkness. There was no light and nothing visible to see. They sat there patiently waiting for an event, any event. Nothing occurred. How strange was that? They were seated around an empty space.

'What is this?' said Davidia. 'It must mean something. It's not a sinkhole, is it? It's rather minute if it is. It's impossible to be a mini volcanic crater. Nothing escaped.'

'I have no idea either,' said Slirander, but she did puzzle over grandma's behaviour and whatever strange occurrences materialised, which to her, weren't that strange. 'It seems to be a square hole not large enough for either of us to squeeze through. We are petite, but not that petite. You can lie to yourself, but not to your mirror.'

'Can we shrink ourselves in?'

'I'm not sure that this is one entrance we should avoid. I don't understand what it is. It is an abyss of some sort. The table legs are still there and so is the exact size of the table. I'm not sure if there is such a thing as a table genie. It all looks normal except for that square hole. No one damages a piece of expensive Huon pine furniture. My Tasmanian relatives would be livid if they ever found out.'

The table slowly began to rise. The girls each grabbed a side to prevent it from rising. What a relief! The table resettled onto the floor.

'How odd was that?' said Davidia.

'Odd indeed,' replied Slirander.

The girls tried to remove their hands from the table edges and found to their disbelief, shock and anger, that they were stuck fast to the table edge. They tried to stand – not possible. They tried to wriggle out of their seats – impossible. It felt like they were glued fast to buttock heaven. They were physically immobilised and sat stunned, seated as if playing the piano at any concert, yet nothing moved. Their minds and voices were still free and operative.

'Now what? I suppose a marathon is out of the question. Any idea how to become unstuck?'

Davidia wasn't too happy to be adhered to a piece of furniture, no matter how valuable.

'What to do? What to do?' mumbled Slirander. 'What to do? What to do?'

It wasn't an incantation of religious proportions, a question without an answer, or a veiled instruction, it was a repeated rambling of someone else's thoughts that had been regurgitated from her subconscious. Slirander wondered what it all meant. The girls had disturbed grandma's memories by actually passing through them and it was thought that none would be altered. Was this a thought-correction editing process that had to be righted before they could depart from grandma's special space?

'How would I know? What to do? what to do?' said Davidia. 'Why not stick our heads into the space and see if that does anything? Nothing else on our bodies can move anywhere else. We're stuck like pigs on a skewer.'

'I don't see any benefit sticking my face into a dark place where I can't see anything,' replied Slirander.

She didn't have a solution to their predicament and she wasn't as adventurous as Davidia.

'Do you have any better suggestions? Maybe a spell or super glue remover might help, neither of which we have? I don't want my delicate hands damaged being stuck to a wooden furniture item for life.'

Exaggeration assisted in making a tense situation more intense.

'Grandma wouldn't leave us hanging like this. I believe there must be a reason why this has happened. We have to work out what that is.'

'Fabulous, the great guessing-game quiz has begun. Who wants to go first?'

Davidia was losing her patience. Slirander was trying to think her way through. Sound logic seemed a more plausible rationale than emotionally charged anger. Whilst the girls were pondering their mode of attack, the square table began to alter shape into an oval shaped table. It seemed as if the edges were slipping through their fingers as rope through a runner holder. Other than that, nothing else occurred. Once again, the oddity of it had them both confused. There must be a build-up to something else, but what?

'Does it feel any different to you, I mean this room?' questioned Davidia.

She felt that an electric current had visited her without an invitation.

'I felt a surge of some sort,' said Slirander.

They both inspected their anatomy to find it all located correctly. Davidia had enough of the suspense of the black hole and thrust her face into it. Slirander screamed. It was as if her head had disappeared. Without hesitation, she did exactly the same thing. Two headless girls sat at an oval table staring into the darkness. It was the girlfriend motto of one in, all in. For a moment, they both blinked in disbelief at what they had done. Both had taken a risk at plunging two perfectly good heads with attractive faces into a dark space without thinking of the consequences; however, fortunately grandma wasn't a retributive individual, so their actions were done with a modicum of safety.

'What in the hell is this place?' yelled Davidia.

She just felt like yelling at something.

'There must be a visual clue somewhere. What do you see?'

Davidia scanned the landscape of shapes because that's all she could see. The scene consisted of small multi-coloured hills, not unlike the balls of Pollital, except that here they were much larger and flatter. There wasn't another structure in sight that interrupted the smooth domes. The one striking difference was that there were separate areas of like-coloured hills and not interspersed amongst each other.

Their faces appeared on the heavenly sky landscape as cloud gods looking over the ground flock of domes. Each time they spoke, a huge cloud of mist moved toward the ground frightening the domes into flatter positions. Were they being punished for their roundness, their colour, or that they grouped with like-coloured domes? None of them fortunately burst. The girls were only chatting to each other.

'This must be grandma's strange memories. There are thousands maybe millions of them.'

'I wonder if Pole and the Pollitons inhabit here as well. Those coloured domes could be the forerunner of the balls in Pollital that Pole and others consumed. I wonder if this is a nursery memory where all memories originally arrive and are dispensed to other sections of the brain for proper recording. It is possible, isn't it?'

'That makes sense,' said Davidia, 'but where are the movers

of this mass of domes? There must be a method of transport somewhere. There's nothing we can do from here except observe.'

The girls tried to extract their faces from the dark space, but found that impossible. Their struggle was in vain. How would it be possible to extricate themselves and return to normal again?

'Who dares trap me like this?' said an agitated Davidia. 'If I could free my arms, I'd certainly give the perpetrator a double fist of pleasure. I hate being useless and unable to move. At least when I was a baby I could move, but didn't know why and now I know why and can't damn well move. I think grandma can cope for herself now.'

'It is rather perplexing, isn't it?' said a passive Slirander, who was actually enjoying the intrigue of searching grandma's memories, but she wouldn't dare tell Davidia in case a disagreement erupted. 'The domes must be a sequence of some sort. I wonder how it all works.'

Suddenly, the sky began shaking. Their faces became distorted into unpleasant, in fact, ugly poses. None of their current friends would have recognised them. What's happening? The sky didn't fart, the girls hadn't sneezed and neither had shaken their tresses. Was it a memory blip? The girls couldn't speak clearly with stretched tongues. Was it a heavenly medical condition that had asserted itself upon them? No one knew whatever it was, but whatever it was, it wasn't welcome. The girls waited for the next action moment. Two stuck heads were useless and more so when dialogue was distorted to be unintelligible. Suddenly, the domes all flattened. The memory-scape was now pancake flat. Whatever each dome held had been released, but couldn't be seen. Memories are invisible, but not where Davidia and Slirander were concerned. The atmosphere was at cross purposes with itself as memories from years of storage all intertwined into a massive group full of history and arguments over whether they did actually happen that way. It was a confused space.

'Oh, great lords of Brain Function, we seek your assistance with this unruly mass. How shall I train them again to return to their domes?' said a minute voice full of humility.

The girls were stunned with the offer. Lords of what? The sky had calmed down and their faces had returned to normal. Their voices boomed when spoken. What had contacted them? A tiny figure, no larger than a pinhead, sat astride the letter M, in small, lower-case font and waved at them. What was it?

'It looks like a collection of Ms.'

'But what actually is it?'

'I'm the Memory Bug responsible for proper memory management, which has now, thanks to your arrival, upset the complete train of thought of all these memories. None of them now know which one they were. If they don't return to their coloured domes, then history will be lost for all these memories and none will be held or translated for future generations to know of. The slate of that person's history will disappear from everyone whoever knew them.'

'You mean that no one would ever remember who this grandma was?' asked an amazed Slirander.

'The memories would be wiped clean forever. All photographs of the person taken throughout their lives would not ever be known to another. It would be a tragic loss so you see, oh Lords, that your assistance is required to return the memories to their correct dome.'

'How would we know a correct memory had been correctly returned?'

'Each dome would reflate in their correct colour sequence.'

'How do we retrain the escaped memories?'

'Relate to a story, a tale, a gentle huff of wind, a kind word, a laugh, a cry, a sadness from every resource that you have, or suggestions from your own wisdom. It is a tremendous responsibility that you have been encumbered with.'

The girls blinked with astonishment. How is it possible that they are now responsible for someone else's memories created long ago and especially Davidia who shouldn't be in any of them at all? They were stunned.

What to do? What to do? once again sifted through Slirander's thoughts. It felt like a never-ending jingle destined to persecute her mind forever. She shut her eyes to escape any outside visual influences to disrupt her thinking. Now, what is it I am supposed to do that keeps banging around in my brain like symphonic cymbals?

Blue, green, black and blue,
Orange, red and yellow hue,
Purple, pink and primrose too,
Rainbow colours return to you.

The thought struck her that Pole must be telling her to use the magic resource that her family possessed. He would know of it, having been a family memory keeper for so long. Slirander often wondered how powerful her family past was within the world of magic. Now she had the opportunity for use of it in memory restoration and it would give her further recognition of some of her capabilities.

Slirander opened her eyes, took a deep breath and repeated the short colours poem that she had mentally experienced moments earlier. Her exhaled breath spread like a bushfire throughout the landscape as an unseen well-wisher. The gentle waves it made hustled and bustled the mixed memories like a pushy relative wanting to have all the say. No memory was harmed during this experiment.

The girls watched carefully as mists swirled over the landscape uncertain of where they wanted to go. The Memory Bug was in turmoil. It rode around as if on an amusement park carousel unable to ascertain when to get off or where it was going. It had no control. Streaks of colour stretched endlessly without any definition. If all the memories became faded and blended it was a catastrophe in waiting. The new mix clouded the landscape. All those millions of stored memories were now uncontrollable and on the loose. With all the agitated airwaves, there was bound to be some disruptions and interaction with each other.

'Is that all you got?' said a memory that thought that it had a higher rating than another. 'Your colour palate is rather bland, to say the least.'

'You bastard. How did you encapsulate that detail when I should have been its storage manager?' said another, with a hint of hostility.

It tried to retrieve that particular memory and somehow weave it into its colour fabric for retention when it became a solid memory colour again. Whilst there was a state of memory flux, it seemed that all memories were up for grabs. That was a dangerous situation as it would destroy grandma's memories forever as they were originated if they cross-referenced each other.

'I never did like that relative of mine. I had a list as long as both arms on bad behaviour and what trouble they caused when they were young.'

'I didn't particularly like that school friend, the one with the all-too-bothersome grin.'

The altercations began to grow. Good memories and bad memories were testing each other like something chronic.

Slirander didn't know what she had released. It was unexpected that her exhaling would create such pandemonium. She really had no idea what to expect.

'What's happening?' said Davidia. 'There seems a lot of angst down there. Maybe all our memories have that, the good, bad and the ugly. You didn't have bad breath when you breathed out, did you?'

'Certainly not!' replied an indignant Slirander.

'Well, something has upset the apple cart.'

'Wait and see what transpires. I didn't realise that grandma had so many memories. I wonder if we'll have that many.'

'Who knows how many any of us will have? In the meantime, we are face-planted without movement. Maybe that memory bug might be helpful. It should be able to tell us what to do. By the way, where is it?'

They couldn't see where it might be. The haze that blurred their vision hid it from view. Slirander spoke.

'Memory Bug, can you hear me?'

'Yes, oh, Brain Function Lord, I can hear you, but cannot see you. How can I help?'

'How do we clean up the current mess? It seems the memories are competing against each other.'

'You created the situation so you and only you have control. I can round them up once they have reformed, but until then I'm powerless. I'll hear you when you call.'

'What to do? I'm not sure. I didn't realise memories could be so troublesome. No doubt we'll encounter our fair share of them.'

'I think I've already had a few. There's that girl at school who bullies others. If you investigated my memory of her, I'd probably be found here in the field of memory conflict. Better we leave our memories alone, there's enough trouble with this lot.'

It would turn out to be a waiting game. Time was irrelevant.

The memories' excitement after their initial release would be subdued as they gradually realised that their individual purpose and important role was to keep history alive even though it would fade in the future. No one could tell if the reforming of the memories would leave any of them undamaged; however, Slirander didn't know the full strength of any power that she possessed, just that when used its effect had to be learnt. In this instance, damage was absent and there was hope for a full recovery.

Slirander and Davidia's first experience delving into the memory bank of another was a complete unknown. A range of surprises had greeted them. Who knows what any person's memories hold? Grandma's had been a great visit to date and a complete stuff-up could be their departing legacy.

'I'm sorry, Davidia, for involving you in grandma's memories. It seems I have caused a problem too many.' That was empathy.

'It's been fun so far. This current hiccup will resolve itself.'

Their words floated amongst the twisting memories when it was noticed that some of them began to form into a more solid colour. The memory bug was whipping itself into a frenzy chasing the new colour formations. Over the landscape a few flat domes had reflated. What were the chances of that happening? The girls were surprised.

Slirander coughed in surprise. More solid colours began to appear. What did the memory bug say about relating a tale? She wondered if it had to have any importance, maybe it didn't.

'A favourite grandma memory for me was treat day. Each time I met her as a small child, she always gave us a sweet. This time, however, we were in a shop where there were a range of sweets that made us colour-blind and she didn't have any money. She tempted me to take a sweet, open the difficult-to-remove wrapping and lick the lollipop as if I had entered with it. The shopkeeper was keen-eyed and spotted the sleight of lip. He waited until we got to the counter and leant over to the little girl and removed the lollipop from her mouth amidst a wail of tears. Grandma never practised magic in public unless it was essential. The crying girl was an essential. She mumbled a collection of words and the retrieved lollipop somehow was stuck into the shopkeeper's mouth much to the laughter this time of the little girl, me. It was such a funny sight. I forgot all about being upset and missing my grandma sweet.'

'That's better,' said the memory bug, as it now had some more solid colour formations to round up. It was a busy time.

More colours combined into their solid colour pods and more domes reflated.

'Slirander, it's working,' said Davidia, quite excited at the prospect of saving the memories.

'I'm a natural,' replied Slirander.

She didn't know what of, just that it fitted the outcome.

'Many of the domes are reflating from what you said. Is there more to add?'

'I'm not sure what I've done.'

She blew a puff of wind, an air kiss over the landscape, and it sounded as if many memories found it refreshing. They inhaled its strength and that was a real grandma memory restorer. Gradually, the sky full of streaky undefined colour wisps began to merge into more solid bands of colour. They retreated from the atmosphere seeking refuge in their coloured dome. It was as if a new set of memories had been born. The memory bug was delirious with its workload, recovering all memories under its management. Slirander laughed and shed a tear of happiness and sadness at the memory of grandma who lived in her mind as a memory. The landscape had been reinvigorated, but in a good way. The domed landscape reformed into its bubbly coloured shape and it seemed as if harmony had been restored. There was only one tiny colour band left that the memory bug sat astride. It was a black dot. It flew near the faces of the Brain Function Lords.

'Oh, great Lords, thank you for restoring all the wonderful memories kept in these fields. It is time to go. Once they have now been fully restored, they need to retain their permanence without any form of interference. Happy memories.'

Before the girls could entertain a response, the memory bug had alighted from the small black dot and kicked it towards them. It began to enlarge the nearer it became. Once again, the whole area became as black as the first time they saw the table space. Their faces felt pressure, like air bubbles ready to burst from a champagne bottle by removing the cork. Suddenly, the pressure became too much and their faces popped out of the table, much to their surprise.

As their faces left grandma's memories, the last thing that they saw etched across the black space were the words, Remember Me.

'Phew! Free at last,' said Davidia. 'We're no longer attached.'

The girls relished their full body movement once again and where was that table? They stood in grandma's special place as joint occupiers. All four walls were the same. The shaking hands, the hessian, the stone and the slate stood there as pristine as they had first discovered them. Grandma's special place will always remain that, a very special place.

'I don't think that I will ever forget my grandma,' said Slirander now that she knew more about her.

'Maybe that's what she wanted,' said Davidia.

She remembers her grandma because she still exists and can create new memories with her.

'It's time to leave. Grandma can rest unhindered now.'

'She certainly led an exciting life. I hope we also live ours to the fullest.'

'I'm pleased we visited her.'

Slirander was about to leave with a heavy heart. She only wished that she had known her grandma for many years and not only the few she knew as a little girl. Suddenly, the room shook as a final gesture to their visit. All they had to do now was to find the exit.

'How do we leave here?' asked Davidia.

There was no exit presenting itself that she could see.

'The same way that we came in, except that we have to walk backwards retracing our steps. We must leave grandma's special place exactly as we found it.'

'I still don't see any exit.'

'Shut your eyes and begin to walk backwards. Feel your way. Remember it is dark in here and the special skill given upon entry will fade as we leave. Your mind will guide you; however, it's me first.'

Slirander took the first few tentative steps. Walking backwards is a lot harder than at first imagined. They were again seeing with their mind's eye. The water pipe entry enlarged as they proceeded along it. The slight breeze that blew upon entry re-emerged blowing past Slirander's hair. Did it whisper something? It was hard to tell.

'Your grandma certainly has her special place well-hidden. Will you come back here again?' asked Davidia.

'Sadly, no,' replied Slirander. 'Our visit is the last. Once we have left here, it will be sealed. That is the consequence of our visit.'

'Did your parents ever visit here?'

'No. Only one family member visitor is allowed per family and that was me. You were a bonus visitor. My new memories of grandma are now special to me. I've collected my own set to add to those I already had. Mum and dad can add more, if they wish.'

'Your grandma was certainly an entertaining lady.'

'Yes, she was; however, memories are forever.'

They neared the entrance to the water pipe. It enlarged sufficiently for them to walk through and they both fell backwards onto the ground. Girlish squeals followed by laughter greeted the outside world again where natural light and familiarity existed. Slirander had one final task to say goodbye to grandma's special place.

'Granny, nanny, it's Slirry ppoo, goodbye to you.'

A moment passed and the protruding water pipe protruded no more. It sealed shut and retreated into the hillside never to be reopened. The walk back to Slirander's home this time was not impeded by any obstacles. It was just a normal backyard again.

As the girls walked back, their memories of grandma began to settle. Age certainly had an interesting pastime when other years were explored about someone else. Grandma was once younger than them, their age, and then considerably older. It was upon which page of life throughout time that age in its many variations exists. The pages of life aren't numbered chronologically in a calendar for each person to read. It's just time and often the expiration of it is a surprise.

The answer to the question, 'How long will I live?' is an unknown for most.

All living individuals have age from the page the day that they are born to the expiration page sometime later.

The girls' next step was to prepare their thesis on age as part of their curriculum.

Had grandma's experiences influenced their understanding of age?

12   THEME

The girls made it back to Slirander's home where her parents, Rolet and Rotan, were waiting. They were pleased to see their daughter again and, of course, Davidia.

'How was your visit to grandma's special place?' asked Rolet, the more inquisitive parent.

'Different to anything I ever expected,' replied Slirander. 'There was so much that I didn't know about her. I feel I now know her better than I did before. She was such an adventurer.'

The comment half-expected a parental response, but a nodding head and knowing smile greeted it instead.

'My grandma hasn't done that many things that I know of,' said Davidia. 'When I see her next, I'll pay far more attention to what she says and ask her about her past life so that I can remember her better.'

It seemed that the visit to grandma's special place had mentally affected the girls whereby more thought was given to an older age person and the realisation that grandma was an early version of them. In time, they too may be grandmas, but not today. There was a lot more youthful life to enjoy before time took care of that.

'See you at school tomorrow,' said Davidia.

'Bye,' said Slirander.

The two friends parted.

That evening two young girls thought of their grandmas and what they meant.

*

Miss Green stood in front of the class, fully expectant that her class had all prepared the data to be used for each student's thesis after a weekend of research. A few blank looks around the classroom might have indicated a lack of effort from some. Davidia and Slirander sat quietly as Miss Green addressed the room.

'Welcome back from your weekend. In the next hour I trust that you will all attend to the outline of your thesis and if any discussions are required, please let me know.'

Miss Green was an assistive teacher who preferred that all her students excel or at least try to do well in any given task. The next hour of focus would attest to those who try. Davidia and Slirander hadn't prepared any written work. Their approach was to verbalise and record their detailed discussions. They thought that the shared approach was the easiest.

'You can record the written word,' said Slirander to Davidia.

She felt that she was the lead in the thesis recording due to her direct relationship with grandma.

'Why can't you share the recording? We both experienced the same memories,' replied Davidia, who felt that it should be a shared task. 'You should go first seeing that it's your grandma.'

Slirander was about to debate the first step to take when a sudden feeling like a pinched nerve, wound its way along the length of her writing arm. It left her arm feeling twitchy, itchy and painfully sore. Her hair also stood out in a spiked design as if she had either a great emotional shock or an electricity volt had flashed through her system frying her hair on the way through.

'I just had the strangest feeling that grandma had visited me. Isn't that uncanny. I can't explain it, but I know it was her.'

'Did she say anything?'

'Not really. I suppose I have to speak on her behalf through the thesis. There's no starting this with, Once Upon a Time.'

The table desks where they sat were next to each other.

Davidia moved her table next to Slirander's. When the edges touched, the tables did the one-foot hop. Davidia's table was shunted back to where it belonged. There was no explanation. Next, she placed her chair next to Slirander's and as soon as she sat down, it was bumped sideways with an occupant floor-kissing. The chair didn't return to its upright position. Next, she put her hand onto Slirander's table and received a stinging rebuke, somewhat like a spider's bite. She instinctively withdrew her hand in fright.

'What's going on? Does someone want you alone for some purpose? You don't think that it's grandma trying to keep her secrets, do you? I can't think of another explanation. It's all spooky. None of the other students have experienced any strange events. They probably think we're having a spat. I do like your new hairstyle, though.'

'I haven't done a thing. I'm sitting here quietly thinking. Grandma must be here somewhere because we are going to write about her.'

Slirander tried to stand up to stretch her legs with the seat adhered to her buttocks. It wasn't thought to be a student prank. She quickly sat down in case she became the butt of any jokes. There seemed to be an issue occurring. She observed that all the other class students were intensely engaged in note preparation and ignorant of her predicament, whatever it was.

'Do you think that you are being told something because we have to write about grandma?'

'There's nothing written on my mental blackboard to reproduce on paper.'

'Maybe that's it. Grandma wants you to write about her. It seems plausible. The reason we are here is to write about her. Try and think only of her.'

Slirander shut her eyes and relaxed. Her mind was experiencing a torrent of information about grandma, current and previous. The pen on the desk rose and nestled into Slirander's hand. She now had a six-fingered hand, albeit one digit was false. A trance-like feeling took over her body, which she had no control over. Her arm began writing automatically. The written word was a mirror image of the thought that she had just experienced. There seemed to be a self-editing text when words were illustrated in alphabetic form on paper. Davidia felt rather useless standing by without contributing. So much for the shared experience.

Slirander sat still as if in a robotic trance with her eyes shut. Her writing hand began scripting her thoughts of grandma, or so she thought she was. Davidia watched over her shoulder quite amazed at the silent scene. At first, she took no notice of what the written word on the paper said. After a few minutes and page one of the notes had been completed, she checked the content. It read like a family history; however, she didn't recognise the handwriting. It was in the flowing cursive style that hadn't been in common use for decades. The shape and symmetry of the alphabet was almost perfect.

'Slirander,' Davidia interrupted, 'that's not your handwriting.'

'Who cares? Leave me alone to finish my thesis.'

'Your thesis! What about the joint effort we're supposed to share?'

'Stop interrupting. In fact, do your own thesis. This is mine.'

Slirander hadn't opened her eyes or moved. Her voice was tinged with a nasty unfamiliarity for her, but not for her grandma. Perhaps she was influenced by past life factors that they had recently experienced in that wacky world of grandma's memories and these had taken control of her mind. Her unusual family history and magical qualities might be at play here also. Davidia snatched the page of notes and walked off in a huff, upset at her friend's unfriendly dismissal of her. How dare she? She seethed with anger as she went to her own table and sat down with a thump, causing grief for the floorboards underneath. Slirander simply ignored the antics of her friend, or was it to be ex-friend? It is hard to tell how disagreements sometimes end up.

Davidia noticed that Slirander didn't flinch with the page loss or her storming off. It appeared that she continued by rote and another page of script was appearing. Davidia decided to ignore her friend and prepare a thesis of her own. Miss Green noticed the dispute between the two friends and promptly came over. She wasn't having any female angst in her classroom. Leave that in the schoolyard quadrangle.

'Is everything okay here, girls?' quizzed Miss Green.

Slirander was as responsive as a stone.

Davidia had seen her approach and had an excuse for both of them. She didn't want Slirander to be in trouble because her mind had momentarily been infected by displacement thoughts.

'We are both concentrating very hard on our thesis. We decided to individualise our thoughts and then combine them afterwards into one work. We felt that it was an easier approach than cross-commenting every thought we had and avoid any public display of disagreement. Slirander gets into a trance-like mode and doesn't like to be disturbed.' Davidia had explained that well.

'As long as you are both happy with your approach.'

Miss Green returned to her normal duties of overseer. Slirander still didn't flinch. Davidia began to read the snatched page of notes.

What did it reveal?

*

The first page title read, TOP SECRET. This wasn't anything

to do with grandma's age. Davidia read closely. It soon became evident that Slirander was reproducing a highly classified document during the time that grandma had been The Blue Rat in the Second World War. Whose handwriting was it? It definitely wasn't grandma's. Had she access to highly confidential material that no one knew about? Davidia pretended to pen her thoughts on age. What did it mean? Who had it? What can be done with it and so on? Her heart wasn't in it because the secrets that were revealed on page one by Slirander had intrigued her more.

She walked past Slirander again, who by this time, had penned quite a few pages more. MOLE was expressed atop of page two and other pages had interesting headings and so on. Davidia stood quietly behind her and observed more of the content. She took aside the completed written pages, sat down and read them. It was more of the same. Treason stood out like dog's balls for someone in the current Government. Davidia became quite agitated with the reveal and wondered about her and Slirander's safety if this information was disclosed to anyone. In summary, it suggested a direct link from the past to a traitor in the current British Government. Davidia knew the name of the person mentioned. It had recently been in the press discussing overseas operations. Was it true? The past often packs an unknown punch.

Slirander stopped writing. Davidia had completed reading the information.

'Slirander, do you know what you have written about grandma?'

'I don't remember. Where exactly am I?'

'In school, in Miss Green's class.'

'I thought that I fell asleep for a moment.'

'You weren't asleep and you have been busily writing a few pages on an interesting subject, but it wasn't about age or our thesis.'

'What was it about?'

'Here, read for yourself.'

'Did I write this? It isn't in my handwriting. What is this stuff?'

After Slirander had read the information, she wondered how she knew to write the detail. Grandma's last words before they left her special place were, 'Remember Me'.

Maybe this is what she meant. The girls didn't want anyone knowing about grandma today. Davidia had a brainwave.

'Let's research the library computer system and see if anything written is actually true. I know we met her first-hand in her Blue Rat role memory, but we need to confirm whether this information has any legs. There's nothing worse than publishing unproven suspicions and then be sued for the privilege. Look, Miss Green is coming over. Here, take my few scratchy notes and exaggerate how much we have already done.'

'Show me your progress,' said Miss Green.

Slirander handed her the few lines of effort by Davidia.

'We have had a few discussions and found it difficult to agree; however, we have made a start,' said Slirander.

No one wanted ownership of the poor note preparation. Miss Green perused the offering, but knew their abilities and so overlooked any reprimand.

'I expect better tomorrow.'

'That was close.'

Class finished for the morning break. The girls headed straight to the library. Lunch could wait.

*

The librarian was surprised to see two students prepared to forego their lunch break and use the library facilities instead.

'How can I help you?' she asked.

'We need access to a computer for research for our age thesis that we are preparing for Miss Green,' said Davidia.

'That would impress her that you are using your lunch break for academic purposes. Please come this way.'

The girls knew exactly where they were, but needed an escort to be allowed entrance to the library.

'Please don't make any noise.'

The librarian left them alone. Slirander sat at the computer desk. She turned it on. The small screen lit up, eager to supply any information requested.

'Is there a password amongst the pages?' asked Davidia.

If there was, access would be simplified.

'I can't locate any,' whispered Slirander, as she too scanned the document.

'How will we gain access if we don't know the access code?'

'With great difficulty. There must be a clue somewhere.'

'Wherever it is, it doesn't want to be found, much like the contents of the document. There must be a military website. Let's see if we can find it.'

'I'm not sure that this is such a good idea. What if we access any strategic and sealed information and get caught doing so? Their website would be monitored and have a firewall to prevent hacking. It's a crime if we do. I don't want to be educated behind bars. Imagine, wearing that drab uniform and eating generic mass-produced vitamin deficient food. It doesn't bear thinking about.'

'Snap out of it,' said Davidia tersely.

She wanted to discover if there was any truth to the document pages that had been written. There was an edge of excitement to the exercise. Slirander checked the document and fortunately for them a website address had been included with the written document scribbled on the bottom of the last page with a warning note, which read, Access Of This Site Is A Death Wish.

It was unusual for evidence traces to be left behind on an official document if the information wasn't to be disclosed. Maybe an official had placed it there due to the sensitivity of the document. Whatever it meant, the truth of its meaning was not speculation. Had anyone tried to open the document? No one knew. It could have been buried in historic archives never to be retrieved until now. Will someone be unmasked? It was a delicious thought.

'That note on the bottom of the page has a site reference. I'll type it in. It must have some meaning by whoever inscribed it there. It looks like an afterthought reference. Perhaps someone was researching the case,' said Slirander.

She cautiously entered the site reference and waited for a few moments. Both girls sat wondering what intrigue was behind a few key strokes prompted by a written report. Davidia pondered over the possibility that it could be fake news and that the report would amount to nothing but wartime speculation involving foreign countries. Many reports on matters of national importance were probably penned every day. Why would this modest report be any different, if it was? The food trough of thoughts was full today.

'This is so bloody slow. The school should upgrade to a higher access speed. My internet at home would eat this dinosaur for speed.' Davidia wasn't always the most patient person when her keenness was on full alert. 'Hurry up. Lunch break is almost over.'

She began to show signs of agitation. Before any volatile personality misbehaviour erupted, the computer said, Hi, with a military logo screensaver. The site looked ever so official.

'Now what?' said Slirander. 'A site does actually exist with high definition graphics.'

'It does look official, doesn't it?' replied Davidia.

'There's no chance of accessing it. It requires a security code, password and probably other layers of security which we don't have. It's impossible to break in without any of that detail. This is a wild goose chase, if ever there was one. Let's write our thesis and forget about grandma's Blue Rat memory notes.'

Slirander felt that their case to learn anything further was hopeless. Davidia was still uptight about it all. Reluctantly, she had to agree to defeat and wasn't too happy about it. Incensed at failure, she pushed Slirander off the stool and sat down heavily almost causing furniture fatigue. She stared at the computer screen for a while whilst her own mental computer whirred with ideas. None were presently well-constructed. She passed a few key strokes and nothing startlingly different evolved. The screen altered each of its screensavers as she clicked onto the individual headings on the tool bar of information. Finally, the last screen saver was the Home one where contact details are found if someone wants to get in contact for any reason. She located the email address and sent an angry email. It read, Remember Me. Click and it was gone, sent into the stratosphere of digital impulses within the universe. They collected the document, closed off the computer and headed toward class. Their lunch break was over.

'That really didn't tell us anything,' said Davidia. She had half hoped it would.

'I thought we might have learnt something,' said Slirander. 'I suppose we'll just have to complete the age thesis now. Grandma was interesting, wasn't she?'

The girls headed to class oblivious of the chaos that they had just caused without knowing it.

*

'Sir,' said a high-ranking military official. 'Read this email. It has just surfaced a few moments ago. It was received by the general office and it has been passed on according to protocol if trigger points of secrecy are activated.'

The General read the email consisting of its paucity of words; however, the content was virtual dynamite.

'What does this mean?' queried the General. 'Is it an emotional goodbye from someone?'

He was young, recently promoted and wasn't fully across all historical aspects of his department.

'Sir, it's a secret password used in World War Two for clandestine acts by one particular individual only. Any reports concerning that individual are top secret, never to be opened. We believe that operative is now deceased; however, this secret password has resurfaced after all these years. It requires immediate investigation. If any information is exposed about those exploits, it could create a national embarrassment to the Government. These are a set of files that should never be sighted by anyone outside of the military. I hope that this isn't from a whistleblower.'

'It could also be an innocent prank. We need to know.'

'Where did it originate from?'

'That's the curious component from the email. It is an overseas school library. I'm certain we don't have any ex-members working overseas as librarians.'

'Send a team of two of our best operatives including you, immediately. Dress in civilian clothes. We don't want to be in the national news creating international headlines that the British Military raids a local high school. By the way, which school is it and where is it?'

'It's Vlad College in Australia, sir.'

'Where?'

'Australia, sir. That operative with the secret password originated from there.'

'There goes the budget bottom line into stress mode. Leave

when ready. The sooner that this is bedded, the more secure we will feel. I must stress tact and diplomacy; be discreet and do not draw any attention to yourselves. The country is relying on your expertise to put out this small flame or burning secrecy ember. Be expeditious. We must maintain good international relations. The less anyone knows, the better.'

The following day two suits dressed as shadows embarked on a flight. They were members of the military special task force. Their departure was a hoped-for brief overseas holiday.

Where will the sun shine?

13   Flow On

A few days had passed. The girls and every living creature had also aged by exactly the same amount of time. Everyone was on the same life cycle path. Where it would lead to was often an unknown. The girl's recent research on grandma had certainly left an impression.

'Those younger photos of her were fabulous to remember when she was young. These other photos show her in later years where the same strong eyes had a worn covering with other sagging components instead of a taut body holding it altogether. You know skin is the body's largest organ outstripping the male dream of what their version is. Look at the smoothness of youth and the well-lived senior years. Age had been kind to grandma even after all her adventures.'

Slirander was reminiscing about grandma. She had been a strong influence in her short lifespan to date. She was still a young girl vulnerable to impressions; however, grandma had formulated conversations which added years of understanding into such a youthful mind.

*

Davidia was standing in front of her mirror, the good-looking one, stretching her face like a contortionist. Had she read the latest book on facial exercise to keep eternally youthful looking? She studied her wrinkle movements as she pushed them out of place and they sprung back into their previous position. She noted a few permanent lines around the edges of her mouth as if the beginning of a trench was being formed. Her face was pulled, pushed, squeezed and slapped as her skin stretched and returned to its correct place. She thought that she was at a nice stage in the age cycle. Tomorrow, she and Slirander would have to present their thesis progress.

'Mum, what do you think age is?' asked Davidia.

Her mother had more of it than her, so the question needed to be asked.

'It's the length of time a person has lived or a thing has existed,' replied mum.

'Is that it? I thought that there was more to it.'

'We all have it. It's just in different phases. You look younger than me. I have more years of wear on the clock and parts don't react as well as they once did. It varies with all of us from babies to centenarians. There is no time control on it. No one usually knows how much of it they will have when they start. Life determines the balance. All I can say is enjoy your time and appreciate it every day.'

Davidia thought that her mum was wise. Perhaps age gives that to you too – wisdom.

*

'What is the purpose of this intrusion?' asked Principal Jones, having been verbally accosted on the telephone by a foreign accent berating him in the same manner that a bully attempts to best their perceived foe.

Principal Jones had received an urgent telephone call earlier in the morning at his home. His crumbed toast-and-egg arrangement were almost at the consumption stage when the damn thing rang.

'What's so urgent at this time of the morning that it can't wait?' he mumbled, as he picked up the receiver at the risk of having a cold and soggy breakfast. Fortunately, he hadn't taken a mouthful to splutter and spit over the receiver in annoyance. 'Principal Jones here,' he said. 'How can I be of assistance?'

'We need to see you urgently, sir,' said an English accented voice.

'Are you wishing to enrol your child by skipping the queue with your living requirements?'

'It's far more important than that. We need an appointment immediately.' The voice became rather forceful. 'Don't mess us about. It's important.'

'What's more important than school enrolment and getting in? Most parents are relieved once a school placement has been secured.'

'National security. We cannot discuss matters over a live line. It needs to be face-to-face. When are you available?'

Principal Jones was used to parental harassment, which put him in good stead to bat any intrusion into his manner. To breakfast or not to breakfast, that is the immediate question.

'Meet me in my office at 11 am. We'll discuss matters then. Now, if you don't mind, I have a date with a two-oval-and-one-rectangular item.'

The telephone line went dead. It was hoped that that wasn't a precursor to his early morning meeting. Breakfast was contemplatively consumed with an additional chewing motion as if eating an actual thought. The call played on his mind. There wasn't any reason available to concern him about national security. Perhaps he misheard the comment due to the heavy accent. Maybe it was Nat's insecurity. Kids at school often suffered from emotional problems and had he another cantankerous parent, who knew better – they always think they do – to deal with? Harmony was the calling of the day.

Principal Jones arrived at school, met the teachers in the staff room and asked innocently whether there were any national security concerns or was there a kid called Nat at school? The teachers were one in response. No national concerns and no kid called Nat. That cleared the anxious desk. Principal Jones was relieved he didn't have to experience another morning crisis. His day might just be in harmony with him. It was 11 am. A loud knock on his door with the frosted glass window shook with the intensity of an earth tremor. He imagined the fists of a cage fighter bursting through and threatening him. The knock was repeated. There wasn't a charge for deafness door knocking. He arose from his seat and opened the door. There stood two large, well-groomed men with smiles a model would emulate. Two huge hands were proffered forward, but both were not from the same body. The grips were firm, vice-like and short.

'What is the purpose of this intrusion?' asked Principal Jones.

'This is Commander Droig and I'm Commander Digby of Her Majesty's Military Forces. We have received information that there may be clandestine activities operating from within your school. We cannot divulge how we chanced upon this secret cell. It's top secret so we are not be able to reveal any information, other than to say it's vital that we discover the sender, otherwise lives may be put at risk.'

'This is a secondary college. There aren't any cells of anything here except the art of learning knowledge. I doubt if you'll find anything incriminating.'

'We know there is a cell here. It needs to be discovered and eliminated.'

'Where is it then? What emanated from here that you would travel halfway around the world to visit our school. You don't have a relative here who wants entrance, do you?'

'Definitely not. Don't waste our time. We understand that the signal was sent from an end building from an in-house computer. State-of-the-art encryption may be being used to blind their cover. Our information points us there.'

Commander Digby pointed in the direction of the school library.

'The only building over there is the school library. It does have a bank of computers for school usage. I don't believe for a minisecond that any of our students are spies. Sure, they may overdo game time but real spying, I doubt it; however, I suppose there could be a practising hacker amongst them.'

The trio walked briskly across the schoolyard. Eyes were watching everywhere. Perhaps they were visiting teachers. That seemed plausible to the students. The pace of their strides stressed urgency. The librarian was surprised to see three grown men enter the library, as it was usually only students. Principal Jones stepped forward and did the introductions whilst toning down the oral pleasantries.

'Gentlemen, step into my office,' said the librarian. 'That way, the Do Not Disturb protocol doesn't need to be implemented in front of the students. It avoids embarrassment. Please sit down. How can I be of help? You did say national security, didn't you? Has someone stolen a flag or joined an overseas terrorist site?'

'No madam. We have reason to believe a secret coded message was sent to the United Kingdom from this very site.'

'It wasn't a prank, was it?'

'The message sent was no prank. Whoever has hold of what was sent can threaten our Government. We need to know quickly who sent it.'

'This is a school and not a training ground for subversives. Secret coded messages and spies do not fit our education mantra.'

'Has anyone suspicious passed your notice? Do you have a record of computer usage? We need to see those records, now! Where are your computers?'

The librarian gave them the usage records, showed them where the "spying" took place and left them alone.

'Principal Jones, what's it all about?'

'I'm at a loss as you are. Electronic records could have been crossed somewhere in the Cloud. There must be something in it to send out two high profile military staff to sort it out. It will become clearer once they have completed their investigation. Fancy our school being paid attention to by overseas high-ranking military personnel. I'll be in my office if needed.'

Principal Jones exited, leaving the librarian as the only other school adult within the library. The two officers were so focused on their task that they missed lunch, usually the highlight for many others. The librarian watched carefully. She noticed furrowed brows, scratchy chins, reassembly of small body parts created by the anxious itch, wiping hands, nasal intrusions, head scratches and the head-on-the-hand stand. Singing fingers danced over the computer console, but there wasn't a song of pleasure to be found. After a few hours of toil, the two men sat back in their chairs with frustration written across their faces. Had it been written on their behinds, no one would have noticed. Suddenly, they twirled in their chairs, not as a measure of success, but to leave the scene of abject failure. There wasn't any record of a clandestine cell, international menaces or a secretly coded website for military actions. They approached the librarian, not for a date, but for confirmation that the library seemed clear of suspicion.

'Can you remember who last had access to any of your computers or anything strange and out of the ordinary recently that you may have noticed?'

The librarian thought for a moment.

'Well, I did think it strange that two female students gave up their lunchtime to be in here. It was a few days ago. They were researching a topic for their age thesis. They weren't here long.'

The men thought that was also odd. Libraries for lunchtime wasn't their understanding of high school educational entertainment. Was there more to an innocent visit? Often, it's the not noticed, shy and quiet persons who are the perpetrators of mass evil. Death can never be sugar-coated, whatever the cause.

'What a fantastic cover posing as a student. I mean it's almost perfect. No one would give credit for youth to be involved so young. We better tread carefully. I don't want to upset Susie.'

'Who's Susie? Your daughter?' asked the librarian. She was a parent as well.

'She's a metallic friend with a family of ten small missiles.'

He patted his pocket. It wasn't a pristine 'kerchief', but his signature defence weapon, his gun. The other man patted his pocket, but on the left side.

'Mine's called Mummy for no particular reason. It is also metallic. We could be the Metallica Brothers,' he said, with a wry smile.

The pudginess of their fingers was well-worn in spots where pressure points had often been exerted in their duties of delivering messages, usually successfully.

'Who were the students? We may need to speak to them and quickly. We aren't here to waste time and resources. We need results.' Commander Digby was showing signs of agitation. At home he was used to bossing his colleagues for instant results; however, a school full of students weren't that accommodating. 'Who are they?'

'It was definitely those two female students.' The librarian ran an educated finger down the list of attendees and spied the two names she was searching for. 'There they are, Slirander and Davidia, two of the smartest girls at school. I'm sure it was them.'

'Where are they?'

'They'll be in class. Miss Green is their teacher. You can find her room along that corridor over there. Remember me to Miss Green.'

Commander Digby upon hearing two particular words spun

around weapon drawn and had the librarian splayed on all fours on the floor. She began to sob.

'That's enough of the waterworks. Repeat what you said.'

'I said, "Remember me to Miss Green". I don't see her too often due to the heavy workload we all bear. She's a friend, that's all.'

'Does it have any other meaning to you?'

'Does what have another meaning? You can lower your weapon. This is a school and you might upset the students.'

'Those words, Remember Me. What did you mean by them? You weren't signalling to another member of your cell, were you?'

Commander Digby turned to Commander Droig and indicated that maybe they had discovered the leader of that clandestine cell they were searching for.

'She doesn't look like a spy.'

'They never do.'

'May I stand?' said the librarian. She didn't want to inhale dust mites in case the school cleaners hadn't vacuumed that day. 'It's tiresome lying on the floor. Perhaps I should seek a book on good behaviour for you both to read. It seems you both need anger management lessons. By the way, Remember Me is a pleasant greeting we all use here at school as a means to signify that someone isn't completely forgotten. I'll definitely remember you two though.'

Commander Digby re-holstered Susie and Commander Droig did likewise with Mummy. Had they got their focus all wrong? There was nothing to suggest in any equipment or personnel that they had studied that an active spy ring was in operation. No lead should ever be ignored; however, youthful women, computers and a desire to change the world might be the very thing that turns "normal" into "abnormal". Where were those girls?

'Sorry, ma'am, we need to visit those girls. Our apologies for the heavy-handedness. We deal with harm in some form every day. You're clear to go.'

Both men left the library. The librarian was still flustered at her treatment. At least she had some male attention, unwanted or otherwise. The male students were too young to occupy that emotional space.

*

'Please present your draft thesis at the end of the lesson.'

It was late in the afternoon and Miss Green's class was the last for the day. She wanted to collect the theses to examine if all students were on the right track with their written knowledge. Slirander and Davidia had, fortunately, compiled a working document for perusal; however, they didn't reference amongst the details the handwritten notes that Slirander had produced under trance-like conditions with references to Top Secret and so on. They had each made a copy so they could independently study the memory of grandma's life and whether it had any effect on preparing their age thesis. Little did they know the powerful impact of what they had, would cause.

In the meantime, Davidia had questioned her parents about the Second World War and whether they knew of a person named The Blue Rat. Surprisingly, they had. Her father explained about the secret French Resistance and an operative with that name. No one knew of her identity. Was she a myth, a mirage, a figment of French folklore, or was there truth in the rumours? All that was publicly known and as far as he knew, she was female and of Australian stock. Wartime operations were often hidden from the general public. Davidia now had some authenticity about Slirander's grandma. She had filed her copy of that report in her bedroom behind a stand-alone dress cupboard where it could join all the dust a historical document could wish for. It gave her a tingling sensation now that she knew what was in the report.

It was dynamite, but in written form. She consciously filed it at the back of her subconscious, but like a permanent bubbling mud pool, it kept rising into her conscious. Pop! Pop! Pop! It worried her that she knew something never intended for public reporting.

*

The lesson was almost over when two serious-looking men stood outside the classroom door. They knocked politely. The door retained its form without a hint of decimation. Miss Green looked up. Her glasses balanced on the tip of her nose, which gave her cuteness to a pleasing eye. She came over.

'Remember me,' said Commander Digby as if he was a past dalliance which could have easily been forgotten.

'I don't remember you at all. Have we met before? With your accent, I wouldn't have thought so,' said Miss Green.

Commander Digby scanned for any recognition of the phrase. There were no tell-tale blinks, gasps, fidgety body movements, clasped hands or facial expressions of shock. Miss Green had age as the two men, but she was in the good-looking phase. Nothing too important had deteriorated for good relations, especially her mind. Commander Digby realised her innocence and discounted her as an adversary.

'I'm Commander Digby and this is Commander Droig of Her Majesty's Military Forces.'

'I'm Miss Green, class teacher. To what pleasure do I owe your visit? You are a long way from home.'

'We understand that you have two students called Slirander and Davidia in your class. Could you kindly point them out to us?'

'For what purpose?'

'We need to speak to them on an urgent matter.'

'They haven't got an English aunt who has left them a fortune, have they?'

'Can you please point them out so we won't waste any more of your time?'

'And if I don't?'

Suddenly, the two Commanders forcibly brushed past Miss Green. The doorway wasn't sufficiently wide enough for all three at once. Commander Digby put out one arm in front as a shield to push Miss Green to one side for access; however, his arm encountered two small, soft marshmallow mounds that reacted with sultana buttons. Miss Green's face flushed. The cause of what happened was left for her to enjoy. The Commanders stood like two well-dressed sumo wrestlers, albeit smaller, with one hand patting their family member, their guns, in case they were needed. The students reacted with surprise. There was almost a stampede for the exit. Commander Digby raised his hand, palm forward like an apostle appeasing the masses with a hand palm.

In a firm, direct and authoritarian voice, Commander Digby spoke.

'We're sorry for the sudden intrusion. We need to speak to Slirander and Davidia. Please present yourselves.'

'You aren't a relative, are you?' asked a student.

'No. We need to speak to them. It's urgent. No one is to leave this room until we are introduced.'

Slirander and Davidia, just like the rest of the class, had no idea who these men were or what they wanted. A crowd murmur grew. Slirander stood up.

'Why do you want to know those two girls in particular? You sound British. I'm pretty sure that they don't know any British people. Who are you? Why don't you tell us who you are and the two girls will reveal themselves?'

It was time for show and tell.

A moment passed. The Commanders eyed each other and a head nod signified agreement.

'We are two commanders of Her Majesty's Military Forces who have arrived today on a special visit to your school at the request of your Government. Our brief is to advise students on cyber safety from a military perspective in a modern world.'

Commander Digby had taken licence with the truth. He was really searching for spies who had access to top secret wartime documents and the danger that knowledge may pose if publicly released. Now that an explanation had been presented, the girls stood up.

'I'm Davidia,' said Davidia.

'I'm Slirander,' said Slirander.

The Commanders saw two youthful women who made a school uniform impressive.

'Why do you want to meet us? We're too young to date.'

Davidia's humour was her constant companion.

'We need to talk privately,' said Commander Digby.

'The girls will need a chaperone,' chimed in Miss Green. She wasn't having two middle-aged men left alone with two young schoolgirls. It wasn't school policy. 'I'm responsible for their safety.'

'Clear your classroom. You may stay but do not interfere.'

The students were pleased to leave early; however, they were all intrigued with the cloak-and-dagger exercise. Were the girls being interrogated first then arrested? If so, what was it about? Had they breached a forbidden emotional site? Were they being groomed for an unpleasant exercise on a British website and were discovered? Were the two visitors really cyber cops? The rumour mill flourished as word spread around the school about the two British foreigners. It was a delicious time for jumping to wrong conclusions but what a feast of impure, unpleasant and totally incorrect thoughts it created. Where is the fictional author amongst the students? It could be a salacious read. Anything more innocent wasn't imagined. The room was soon clear except for the two Brits, the two schoolgirls and the chaperone. It had the beginnings of a deadly novel.

'Remember me,' said Commander Digby.

He waited for any response. He'd tried that tack on Miss Green, which became a bubble of useless comment.

'I've never met you,' replied Davidia. 'How can I remember something I've never known?'

'I don't know who you are either,' replied Slirander. 'You aren't known to my dad, are you? He's got friends I've only heard him speak of. You could be one of those.'

'You're positive you haven't heard that phrase before?'

'Not that I can immediately recall. Many people say that to others, especially the elderly.' Slirander wondered what this meeting was about. She was astute, a student of humanity. A thought flashed through her mind. It was fortunate it didn't escape otherwise desecration to good manners would have erupted. She settled for a more measured comment. 'Before we get to the thousand-word quiz, why are you really here and what is it you want?' Slirander thought that she knew, but did she?

Commander Digby was startled by the directness. He wished he had staff as succinct with their thought processes. He took a deep breath. His chest cavity developed momentary mini breasts, it was so deep. What could he actually reveal? He had to operate under a Secret Service Act otherwise treasonable information could be disclosed and that was the possible end of a career and life. His mood became less tense and conciliatory. He gave the impression of relaxation. Slirander wasn't buying the store produce today.

'You girls were in the school library a few days ago. What were you researching? I'm told it was on an age thesis. Is that correct?'

'Yes.'

'What did you discover?'

'That we all have it.'

'Have what?'

'Age.'

'Anything else?'

'Some of us have it more than others. That's all.'

'You didn't accidentally stray onto any official websites, did you?'

'None by accident, no.'

Davidia leant over and whispered that they did try to trace that military website. Maybe that's what he's trying to establish. Slirander nodded that maybe that's his interest. Then she realised that strange hand-written report that she had reproduced whilst in another dimension was sitting neatly folded in her bag of mystery items, her schoolbag. It was next to her. Was it evidence of some sort and if it was, was it real? She thought that the secret report should remain so. She had no intentions of alerting the world to her grandma's memories. This might be the most dangerous of them all. She didn't realise at that moment the importance of that particular document, but understood that it had some importance. Commander Digby might just reveal how important. The game of cat and mouse continued. Davidia wanted her four-penny worth of conversation. It was a question about the cheese.

'Mr Digby, sir, do you have any pets?' she asked.

He thought that was a strange and quite frankly, a stupid question. He didn't have, but what has that got to do with websites?

'None at all.'

'My family once kept rats. Do you like rats?'

'They're revolting creatures.'

'We dyed them a particular colour. Most were brown and grey when purchased. Can you guess what colour we dyed them?'

Where was this going? Definitely not to the shopping centre. He began to tense. This was very unusual dialogue being presented.

'Why would anyone dye a rat when their natural colour is their best?'

'We wanted to pretend that the rats were really large mice. We liked the dyed colour better. It was blue. Imagine that. Blue rats. We were the talk of the neighbourhood. They were kept on a leash when we visited the park. No one knew their secret of being rats. We told everyone they were monster mice, a throwback of a bad breeding program. Imagine calling them something they weren't. They have all perished through age; however, we can remember them whilst we still exist with our own age.'

Davidia stared directly at the two Commanders waiting for any flicker of recognition of any of what she had said. She felt a movement in the atmosphere and it wasn't that old, stale favourite of wind. The hair on the nape of her neck imitated an echidna or porcupine at best. Slirander suddenly realised that Davidia was clueing them in on what they had found without directly referring to the document. It was her grandma that was the topic of conversation.

'Is there something you want to tell us?' asked Commander Digby.

He usually did all the talking.

'Not particularly,' replied Davidia. 'Oh, there is the reason why you are questioning us about whatever it is that we are supposed to know and yet we can't answer because the question hasn't been asked. All you've said so far is the two words, Remember Me, and that's it. It seems to be hardly worth an overseas visit. Talk about a time waster. Slirander, do you have anything to add?'

'I don't know how to answer the unasked question. Do we have to guess? We'd be here for years without resolving the question guesser. Why don't you tell us exactly what it is you want and we can tell you the answer. The teachers at school are always asking questions and we do our best to be truthful, but we don't reveal every detail, especially about relationships, because they are private. This is like a merry-go-round where no one knows how to get off. Cut the power source and you have the result.'

Commander Digby was certainly up against two savvy schoolgirls with deep and insightful questions and some obscure explanations. So far, his penetrating, experienced and fearful questioning tackles had left the squad still in the centre of the pitch as if they hadn't made a solitary play. Was it time to kick the ball?

'Excuse me a moment. I have to talk to someone.'

Commander Digby left the room. No one spoke. Miss Green wondered what exactly had her two students been up to. Never before had any military personnel visited the school. It was a quandary. Commander Droig sat still like an adder ready to strike. It was tense. The girls stared at the ceiling thinking they were still in class being attentive. Commander Digby returned.

Permission had been granted.

I apologise for my evasiveness to date. We are restricted in what we can reveal to any layman where British National Security has been breached. Permission has been granted to discuss this sensitive issue and the reason for our visit. We have it on expert authority that a secret coded reference was forwarded from your school library and it blipped on the British International War Records Department email address site. It was a secret code used during the Second World War, never to be revealed to protect the identity and any documents associated with one particular individual. We are the case managers assigned for all matters concerning that individual. No one else has access to those classified documents. Do you know anything about sending that message?' There was a razor-sharp edge to that last question.

'You mean that those two words, Remember Me, are a secret code word?' said Slirander. 'I have no idea how it was forwarded to your office. Davidia and I were in the library and we did look up the military website, but couldn't gain access. We were researching information on my grandma for our age thesis. You are sure that it was sent from there?' It seemed it was confession time.

'Absolutely positive.'

'The only other person in the library with me was Davidia.' Slirander glanced at her friend who began to fidget. 'You didn't do anything in there either, did you?'

Davidia seemed agitated and uncomfortable. The room suddenly seemed small, real small.

'Well, I may have sent something.'

'Out with it. What did you do?'

'I was so pissed off at being unable to access the website, I sent in those words, Remember Me, in spite because those were the last words grandma had said. I didn't think anything of it. I was just annoyed, really. There you have it, Davidia the spy. Arrest me if you must. I had no idea that they would cause any interest.'

The Commanders were stunned, not with the words, Remember Me confession, but the word grandma. What did it have to do with anything? It had never been mentioned in any conversation before.

'Whose grandma and how would she know those last two words?'

Slirander grasped the situation. They were here about grandma and her time as The Blue Rat in the Second World War. What did she really do? In the memory where they had visited her, she saved some people. Is this what this is all about? She pondered carefully her next comment. She felt the icy edge of the questioning and wondered whether she should reveal the report in her schoolbag. The truth had a way of alleviating any tension.

'My grandma was in the Second World War. She was simply known as The Blue Rat. I'm not sure of what she really did except that it was secret and terribly important. Neither my parents nor grandma ever mentioned any detail about the war. I had no idea about that section of her past when she was young. She was mostly a mystery to me as a young child.'

'Then how did you know the secret coded words?'

'They were the last words she told me when I visited her memory.'

'You did what?'

'Davidia and I visited some of her memories and that was one of them. It wasn't that exciting. I was the Blue Scarf in it and Davidia was a victim saved from being ravaged and killed. We walked through the shaking hands wall first and then through the moving hessian wall. It was tricky, but we did it.'

Slirander watched their faces react to her comments. Suddenly, the age they possessed moved around their faces and she's sure she saw the formation of a new set of wrinkles. Age was evident in body growth. The Commanders began to doubt the sanity and truth of the explanation. It sounded like bullshit from an overactive imagination. They were about to discount what they heard as rubbish and it seemed that these two young girls weren't any threat to National Security. Their trip might be that waste of resources often spoken about.

'We don't think that we need to bother you any further. We will report that there was nothing serious amongst the email and that no terrorist cell exists. As a word of caution, never send that email detail to anyone. Serious consequences may ensue and lives may be put at risk.' It was said as a dire warning. 'Remember, to no one. Forget this episode ever occurred. Get on and enjoy your life.'

Miss Green was mesmerised by the events. She nodded constantly. Whilst Slirander held court, Davidia had moved near Slirander's schoolbag and had extracted the first page of the hand-written report reproduced in class. No one noticed her access the report. Had a magician been born? She had sleight of hand to match her sleight of word.

'Excuse me, sir, I noticed that you had dropped a sheet of paper. It was found on the floor near where you are sitting,' said Davidia calmly, as she handed it to Commander Digby.

Of course, it was a lie. He read the report page. His surprise couldn't be masked. He had seen the report once only before and being the custodian, filed it under "Never To Be Revealed". He had recognised what it meant. How in the hell did these girls get hold of it when he fully well knew that he had brought no such documents with him on this trip? He knew instantly, that the girls had provided it. There was no other explanation.

'Where in the hell did you get this? I can have you arrested for access to secret documents unavailable to the public. You could be up for treason. This is serious.'

Davidia wasn't flustered with threats. She had played netball where the other girls were verbally officious and nasty. That didn't bother her either.

'Is it real?' asked Davidia, 'I mean, is it a real secret report?'

The document page he held had never been released publicly. It was a closely guarded secret. He recognised the handwriting and confirmed that it was part of a secret report.

'Yes, it is real. Danger threatens any person in possession of such material. Are there any more pages?'

'Do we get immunity from any prosecution? We don't want to find our futures short-lived. We have an education to complete. We don't fully understand the ramifications of the report,' another mistruth, 'and came across it by mistake. If we give you what we have, will our futures be safe? There is only one copy,' another mistruth.

Davidia was pleased that she didn't have to take a lie-detector test. It would have been her only school fail. She waited, in fact everyone waited. Thank goodness Miss Green was present as an adult witness. It was difficult enough to believe the insanity of the conversation; however, with an adult present it supports the truth of what has been said.

'Show me the complete report. I assume it's complete. Then I will give you my answer.'

'Guarantee first.' Davidia switched on her smart phone to recording. Slirander and Miss Green did the same. 'Guarantee first,' she repeated as three delicate hands all held the interminable device to interruption of living and pressed the Record button.

'I Commander Digby of the British Military guarantee the future safety of Davidia, Slirander and Miss Green in exchange for a secret report that has accidentally come into their possession.'

'Thank you, sir,' said Davidia.

She then texted the recording to her father for security in case matters became messy or her phone was confiscated. Fortunately, she was quick enough, sight unseen. Dancing fingers relayed the message. Whew!

She delved into Slirander's schoolbag and retrieved the balance of the hand-written report and handed it over. He perused the report. It was the real deal. He thrust it into his pocket next to Susie who was itching for some exercise. Commander Digby felt the cool steel of his weapon, which he would use without hesitation if it was necessary. Davidia had outsmarted him, but he wasn't aware that she had. He had no intention of leaving those recordings behind. He withdrew Susie and pointed it at the ceiling.

'Now ladies, kindly pass me your phones. I'll only ask once. Susie doesn't mind a visit.'

The girls went weak at the knees. They all handed over their phones. They didn't want their bodies to have breathing holes other than the one in the centre of their faces. It was a tense moment.

'Who's going to pay for my new smart phone? Don't you contact my friends for a date. They're all too young for you.'

Davidia began to rant with the shock at having a dearly loved asset stolen under duress.

'This is the only copy of this report, isn't it?'

He waved Susie around his head. It was an intimidation sequence.

'That is the only copy. Slirander wrote it from a grandma memory that has now been lost. We don't know where her grandma is now. Do you know if she's visiting this weekend?

Perhaps we could visit her. Does she live in England? Do you know where she's buried? Was her hair really blue? Was she an actual rat dressed as a human? Biological warfare can give rise to permutations turning rats into horses, why not humans. Is Slirander related to a real rat? The only rat in my family was Uncle Bob who's now compost. We don't mention him anymore. He was a human rodent.'

Slirander stood up and slapped her face. It abruptly halted her rambling. Shock had delivered an array of nonsense that covered the reality that there was another copy and this was a cover-up to avoid any further questioning. Davidia's idiocy certainly had a proper place this time. It was the perfect verbal camouflage.

Commander Digby reeled from the onslaught and was certain that there wasn't another copy of the report, why would there be? He was only dealing with two schoolgirls who he dismissed as amateurs and weren't a spy's arsehole. Susie went home to daddy. Commander Digby and Commander Droig left the building satisfied that the secret of The Blue Rat files was safe again. They didn't even say goodbye to Principal Jones. How bad are those manners? They returned to England. Before they did so, they burnt the report and destroyed the three phones. Evidence often disappears, but why would that report be evidence? Grandma was a wartime operative and surely the report was one of many reporting on actions undertaken. Was there a mystery to this report? It didn't seem so.

'You bitch. That hurt,' said Davidia, as a red welt grew on one cheek to blemish her smooth skin.

The other girls will think that she's forgotten how to apply rouge consistently.

'It was necessary. Now, what? I'm glad that's over. I'm going home.'

Slirander was exhausted with the afternoon. She had no

further interest in that report. Grandma may have been an interesting topic for their thesis, but it was almost at an awful cost of their lives.

Miss Green was stunned with the events that had unfolded in her very classroom. She needed a stiff drink to settle her nerves. That night she had more than one sedative. She self-diagnosed her anxiety disorder.

'See you tomorrow at school. We can finish the thesis.'

As Davidia headed home, she thought that the report she had hidden may need further analysis. She hadn't trusted those two Commanders. Threats never did it for her. A sixth sense had warned her, but was it misplaced? Were her feelings an overreaction to the unfolded events?

It was hard to know.

*

Slirander explained to her parents what had occurred at school, about how grandma was an important Second World War operative and how the British Commanders had treated them. They had nothing further to add. They suggested that grandma's memories were better left where they were and not regurgitated into a modern-day witch hunt of the past. Many unpleasant events may arise which the public didn't know about and could cause Governments embarrassment. That old saying of, Let Sleeping Dogs Lie, would be an apt phrase in this circumstance.

'Did you know about grandma?' asked Slirander.

Rolet put a parental hand on young shoulders as a comfort cushion and explained that they were aware of some details of her past; however, the war experience was rarely mentioned. History has a way of leaving things alone.

'By the sounds of it, it has been a huge day. Sleep well.'

Slirander shrugged her weary shoulders as she climbed into bed.

'Yes, grandma, I do remember you.'

*

Davidia made a beeline straight to the rear of her bedroom wardrobe to retrieve copy two of that secret report. She didn't explain any of the day's events to her parents. It was safer that way. Her bedroom was dimly lit as she huddled under the bedclothes believing that she was reading a horror short story. She was. The content wasn't suitable for young eyes or a young mind, yet it sat well with her understanding of injustice. She couldn't help but see the word "treason", not reason misspelt, but "treason", mentioned a few times about another British person who it was thought was a double spy and operated for the enemy. That particular name was a current British Government Minister that she had read about recently in the overseas news occasionally reported on in local papers. The name just stuck. Was it true? Should she alert anyone? The Commanders knew that she and Slirander were the only two other persons who knew what was in the report. Miss Green was never shown the copy. Would she and Slirander be at risk if it became known that a traitor was a British Government Minister? What should she do? Life is about taking risks and was this that moment for Davidia?

That night, a restless young schoolgirl wrestled with her thoughts of right, wrong and risk, or should they be ignored? The darkness was not an escape from her subconscious, but a welcome delay from reality.

'Yes, grandma, I remember you. Nice to have met you,' she said, as her eyelids closed.

Would tomorrow bring closure?

The following day the girls met to finalise their age thesis. They had a salad bowl full of grandma ingredients as well as fellow family members from which to draw upon; however, it was the visit of the British Commanders that occupied their brain spaces.

'Did you discuss it with your parents?' asked Davidia.

'They said to leave the past alone. Any resurrection of it could be painful for someone.'

'I read the copy of the report I had hidden. There's a traitor in there who has recently been reported in the world press doing good things for his country. I wondered if I should alert someone, but thought better of it. I didn't want to visit a cemetery accompanying a wooden box as its contents. That would be the end of age for me.'

'Did you destroy the copy?'

Davidia had her fingers crossed behind her back. She wasn't signalling her doubles partner into a corner to serve, but superstition had grasped them and telling a lie seemed to have less responsibility.

'I sort of did. It's gone. No one will ever know it existed.'

That was her best effort.

'I'm glad we can relax and complete this thesis.' Slirander began to write.

The girls could now turn their attention to what started the chain of events. Age is what exists with all of us once we are born. It's a journey for the amount of time each person is allotted without explanation. It is of different lengths and indeterminate as to what each is allowed to enjoy. Both were now humming with meaningful written dialogue without the stress of threats.

'I wonder what your grandma would think about what's happened,' said Davidia.

'She would be proud, I would have thought,' replied Slirander.

Davidia glanced over Slirander's shoulder at her written notes and noted that it was in the same font as that secret report. No, it couldn't be. Slirander's not grandma, surely. Apparently, family genetics can pass down familiar unexplainable traits.

'How are your notes coming along? Mine are virtually swimming with details.'

The girls both sat quietly and contemplated those wonderful adventures with grandma.

They both finished their notes with the words, Remember Me.

*

A few days later, the local press ran the headlines about The Grey Mole, an undercover double agent in World War Two who had recently been unmasked.

Headlines emblazoned around the World, "Grey Mole Digs Last Hole".

The British Government had sacked and imprisoned a traitor who had been hidden for years. Apparently, the paper reported, a recent report resurfaced identifying The Grey Mole for what he was, disloyal to Britain. The girls read the contents with delight. They now knew that the two Commanders who visited them won't be returning and the doubts they may have had about them vanished. They could now experience more of that life thing called age.

'Slirander, did you see this morning's paper? It must be because of that report you recreated. Isn't it exciting, catching spies?' Davidia was elated.

Slirander read the report and as pleased as she was, it was her grandma that uncovered The Grey Mole. At last someone had taken real notice of that report. It was rumoured through the press that ongoing investigations from a secret source were being undertaken.

As Slirander closed the newspaper, those two haunting words, Remember Me, flashed before her eyes. She thought that she saw a smile accompany them.

It must have been grandma.

She will always be remembered.